THE PHANTOM'S BLADE

The Sword of the Dragon

Book 4

SCOTT APPLETON

For Joseph,
because in you I see the same spark
of creativity that brought me to where
I am today. Live courageously and
keep the faith. 1 Timothy 6:11-12

Other books by Scott Appleton:

The Sword of the Dragon series
Swords of the Six
Dragon Offspring
Key of Living Fire
The Phantom's Blade

The Neverqueen Saga
Neverqueen
Neverqueen 2: The Suffering Chalice

Anthology
By Sword By Right

For more info visit: www.AuthorAppleton.com

THE PHANTOM'S BLADE

Special Edition

FLAMING PEN PRESS

DESPAIR BEYOND
THE SEA

Caritha gazed out over the inlet's deep blue water to the sea beyond, and she sank to her knees on the sand. Despite the clear sky on this cool afternoon, the sea boiled around the splintered hull of the Maiden Voyage. Sea serpents raised their heads out of the waves as the coils of their slimy dark bodies squeezed the ship and foamed the water. Somewhere beneath the waves sank the bodies of the captain and the crew. They had fought bravely to ensure that the last Warrioress made it to dry ground.

Sweat had dripped from the captain's thick nose as cold salt water had sprayed his face. He had driven a pike into one serpent's body, drawing its attention away from her. "Get to land, lass! The ship is lost," he had said.

"No! My sisters and I can fight with you." She had aimed her sword at another of the creatures as it twisted its length around the ship's bow. The sword had responded to her. Its blade had glowed dull orange, but no matter how hard she had tried she could not get it to throw any energy at the serpents.

"No!" She knew then, knew all too well that her gift to Ombre had cost her more than she had imagined it would.

The deck had buckled, throwing her against the rail. Water had rushed beneath decks and the captain had braced himself, his large feet set wide apart. "Fight? You cannot fight in the water. This ship is going down. You have only minutes to make up your mind."

Another serpent had leaped out of the sea, smashing its length over the prow of the Maiden Voyage, and Caritha had glanced at the monster. But the captain had somehow moved across the splintering deck and grabbed her in his thick arms.

"When this ship goes down the serpents will make short work of all of us, my lady. With God as my witness I'll not let you die when I could have saved your life." He had heaved her over the ship's side. When she had floundered from under the frigid water and her head had broken the surface, a serpent had swum under her kicking feet. But it had ignored her and rammed the wooden ship. "Get to shore while there's time," the captain had yelled at her.

She had felt tears stinging her eyes as she, with difficulty, sheathed her sword and swam toward an inlet that was surrounded by mountains of ice. Her last glimpse of the captain, was of him and a member of his crew desperately clubbing a serpent's body as it coiled around the main mast and snapped it.

Now, standing on that unknown shore with her sisters, she felt hope sink with the Maiden Voyage. Not only had they failed to find a land suitable for relocation, but until now they had found no land at all. This mountainous place on which they had landed appeared desolate, and the cold wind whispered down the slopes of the sharp peaks that glistened like diamonds in Yimshi's light. They were cut off from civilization, far from home without a means of returning. It had been a long sea voyage. She couldn't even guess how far they were from home.

Laura stepped up beside her and laid a hand on her shoulder. Rozel trailed Levena and Evela as they too joined her.

Rozel growled as she grabbed fistfuls of her dress and wrung water out of its material. Her eyes narrowed as she glanced over her shoulder at the frozen world of white. "I don't care what's in that sea. I am going to swim back across, find a little house in the Hemmed Land, force a nice gentleman to marry me, and then settle down until I am old and very, very gray."

"Be serious for once, Rozel." Caritha turned toward the ice mountain that rose a couple hundred feet away from the water. She studied its jagged form, the smooth polish of its surface, and she dropped to the ground and punched the sand. The mountain blocked her view to the east, its peak slicing a thin white cloud that hovered there against the sky.

Laura knelt beside her and lightly rubbed her back. "It will be all right, Caritha. Do not fear. Remember what Father said to Evela when we started our mission to find Kesla?"

Caritha remembered. She recollected the powerful white dragon turning his pink eyes on her and her sisters as they faced the portal to the Eiderveis River. She had been merely seventeen years old at the time. "I will be watching over you even when you cannot see me," he had said.

She shook Laura off and rose. "Don't you see? Things are different now."

"No they are not!" Laura said.

"Look around, my sister. Better yet, take a look at the sea and tell me if you see anyone alive. Where are the captain and the crew of the Maiden Voyage? Do their lives matter to you? And what of Ilfedo, Oganna, and Ombre? They are waiting for our return before they set out to find the dragon Venom-fier. We have failed and they have no way of knowing."

Laura and Evela hung their heads. Levena sniffed.

"Feel glad that we are alive," Caritha said and covered her face with her hands. "But weep that so many have died on our account."

Suddenly a realization came over her, and she withdrew her hands from her face. Why hadn't she noticed before that the shore on which she stood and the mountains of ice . . . they were familiar somehow? White clouds rose over the ice mountains, sailing over the peaks and filling the sky. A frigid wind caressed her arms, threatening to freeze her soaked dress.

The sandy ground trembled and the mountains of ice crackled, sounding like miniature releases of thunder. Something living warbled in the distance. Before them and between the mountains, a long-necked creature slid into view. As it drew closer, Caritha caught her breath, for the creature was enormous with four flippers for limbs. It was as white as Albino, with a bulbous blubbery body.

Water shot forth from the creature's nostrils and struck her. Her sisters fell back and rolled into the inlet. But she drew her sword and closed her eyes, with all her might focusing on deflecting the water. The sword fed off of her dragon blood, splitting the water to either side of her. The creature kept up its deluge until Rozel and Levena stumbled to Caritha's side and joined their blades with hers. Blue energy blasted from the united blades, knifed through the water, and struck the creature's head.

The creature warbled as the water ceased to flow from its nostrils. It lumbered back a hundred feet and warbled toward the mountains. Suddenly the mountains filled with innumerable warbles and another of the creature's kind slid into view. Only, when it approached, it loomed even larger than its companion.

Its head rose far above them and it smiled down upon them. Needle-like teeth ringed its enormous mouth. It dwarfed even the great albino himself. In his presence the Warrioresses trembled.

"Daughters of the great white dragon, how foolish of you to come to my lands. Do you not know that all who come here are never heard from again? Not even your dragon father could save you from the fate you have brought upon yourselves, for he dares not touch me. I am Cromlin, king of the water skeels, and today your lives are at an end."

His nostrils cast water upon them and, as they threw their swords up to block the deluge, beams of light shot from his eyes. The beams cut through their defenses, and struck them to the ground.

They ran toward him, swords aimed for his thick body. They reached him and stabbed. The blades sank up to their hilts, yet drew no blood. Cromlin gazed down upon them and warbled, while his companion did the same. The sound rang into the mountains, into their ears, and built its intensity.

Pressure built in her ears. Caritha saw first Evela and then Rozel drop to the ground, putting their hands to the sides of their heads. Soon she, too, succumbed.

Cromlin lumbered toward the inlet and smashed his foreflippers together. A soundwave struck Caritha's chest, forcing air out of her lungs.

Addressing them in a voice that rang around them and into the ice mountains, Cromlin said, "You have fought worthy of a water skeel." He lowered his neck, bringing his head within ten feet of their heads. "But you are no match for me!"

Caritha felt exhausted. She tried to summon her dragon blood. It warmed, then cooled inside her. She glanced at her sisters, but their faces froze in terror and tears formed in their eyes. Cromlin pulled back his head and a stream of water from his nostrils slammed into Caritha's chest. The impact threw her backward and her body was crushed against a boulder. The water continued to storm upon her, unending and unyielding. Every bone in her body conformed to the stone against which she was pressed, painfully stretching and bruising her body.

Beside her, Rozel was pressed into the sand beside Levena, unable to move from under the water's force. On Caritha's other side Laura and Evela raised their swords into Cromlin's onslaught.

Painfully raising her own sword, Caritha touched

her sword tip to theirs. "Join with me, my sisters!" A wall of energy formed between the swords, a wall that surged against the water and turned it away.

Cromlin laughed and bore down upon her. His gargantuan body slammed into the beach. He slapped a flipper atop Rozel and Levena, and struck Caritha, Laura, and Evela with the other. She might as well have attacked a fortress wall as defend against so large a flipper. It rammed her against the boulder, and then withdrew.

"Your puny powers cannot compare to the might I wield!" Cromlin slid to the inlet and dug his flippers into the water. Five cubes of ice formed between his flippers, each one larger than her, and he effortlessly plucked them out of the water and chucked them at Caritha and her sisters.

Caritha glanced to either side, but her sisters had been separated too far from her to intercede. As a cube shot toward her, time seemed to slow. She watched it somersault through the air and she felt, as it were, ice darts precede the object. Stabbing pain peppered the front of her body. She could barely move.

Tears that she longed to cry refused to come as she struggled with her sword. At last she managed to sheath it. She reached with a trembling hand into her pocket and untied the precious ring that Ombre had given her, slipping it onto her finger. Her body temperature dropped and icicles formed on her hair, hanging in front of her face. She was freezing alive!

But with her last moment of consciousness, as the end embraced her, she laid her hand against her chest and looked down at the engagement ring. The diamond glistened as ice covered it. She should have said yes to Ombre a long time ago. Now it was too late. "But

I do love you," she whispered. "And if God had allowed me to see you again, I would have been fully yours."

WHEN SERVANTS SHALL BE LORDS

It was early morning when Ilfedo awoke. But he did not awake from a dream. He sat on the edge of the bed and pulled the bearskin blanket around his broad shoulders. The winterish chill had seeped through the walls of his forest home. He had built this home with his own hands. Built it, brought his bride here, and seen her die to give birth to his precious daughter. Her sisters had remained with him, all five of them. Without their help he never would have been able to raise his daughter, of that he felt sure.

But he had let them leave the Hemmed Land. Leave his protection. In his mind he imagined the sisters marooned on an unnamed island in the Sea of Serpents, yet in his heart he feared he had sent them to their deaths in some storm. He hoped that no worse fate had befallen them, yet his soul felt that they had already joined his wife in the eternal Creator's arms.

In the rafters above his head the nuvitors, his trusted bird companions, slept soundly. Ever since returning from his harrowing quest through the underground realms with the nuvitor, Seivar, the bird had been content to take it easy. Perhaps too much time had passed. Seivar and Hasselpatch were showing their age, in little ways that drew a tear from his eye even now. Just the other day Hasselpatch had stumbled into a lamp instead of landing on the tabletop beside it. Her silvery eyes did not see as keenly as they once had. Ilfedo listened for a moment to the gentle wheeze of their breathing. He had become accustomed to them sleeping in his bed with him, snuggled under his arms, but they rarely did so anymore.

He hung his head. Time had changed many things, but nothing had changed the bond he had with them.

Downstairs in one of the bedrooms he knew that Escentra was asleep. The poor girl seemed a bit lost in the Hemmed Land ever since he had brought her out of the Hidden Realm. He remembered the distrust with which Vectra the megatrath had regarded the girl. Yet to him Escentra was a lost soul, and she must be allowed heal.

Oh for a return to the simplicity of his life as a hunter, back when Dantress had filled this home with her smile. As he sat on the edge of the bed he turned to look over his shoulder at the other side of the bed. He kept a second pillow there. He never used it but left it there as a token of the wonder of love that he had found when Dantress had slept there.

His thoughts turned to Caritha, the eldest of

Dantress's sisters. He remembered how she and Ombre had grown so close. He felt that, given more time, their love would prove as deep as his had been with Dantress. He longed for that to happen, for he could not think of two people he wished it upon more than them. If he had indeed sent Caritha and her sisters to their deaths, even though the journey had been by partly by their request, he would never outlive his guilt.

He should never have allowed it.

On their day of departure from the Hemmed Land, as she had set forth across the Sea of Serpents, Caritha had given him a sealed envelope. Ilfedo reached to the little nightstand by his bed. He had kept the envelope that she had given him safe in this drawer. He had hope that it would always remain there. Opening the drawer he pulled out the envelope and held it delicately in his fingers.

In small, flowing script Caritha had written: *For Ombre, my only love, in the event of my death.*

Ilfedo understood what the words meant. By giving him the letter she had ensured that Ombre would not receive it unless Ilfedo felt certain of her fate. When first Ilfedo had looked at the envelope he had been standing on the shore of the Sea of Serpents, watching the Maiden Voyage set sail to the distant horizon. A deep dread had held his heart from that moment and with haste he had slipped the envelope out of sight into his trouser pocket.

A few months had passed since that day. Still no word had been heard from the sisters, his Warrioresses.

He slowly turned over the envelope and studied again the seal that Caritha had placed there. It was emblazoned with an emblem unfamiliar to him, but of one thing he was nearly certain. The crimson color of the seal glistened in the light of his lamp. He had surmised that Caritha had applied fresh blood to the wax seal. To what end he could not imagine. He had seen strange things in his life and when it came to the Warrioresses, their veins flowed with dragon blood. Its power was unpredictable and could mean a number of things.

He hoped to never know. It was his fullest intention to leave the envelope hidden in the drawer until Caritha returned to give it to Ombre herself.

Ilfedo returned the envelope into the drawer, and slid the drawer closed. If, and only if he was forced to leave the Hemmed Land before the sisters returned would he give up hope. But then he must give the envelope to Ombre.

He laid back in the bed and closed his eyes. He needed rest, for the dawn would bring a necessary ride to Gwensin City and he intended to bring Escentra along. The girl needed to acclimate to her new surroundings. She had remained behind in his home when he had seen the Warrioresses off on their journey.

His daughter Oganna had promised to return home to get acquainted with the girl as soon as she was able. But for now she was preoccupied overseeing the construction of Fort Gabel and he did not want to push her into dropping the task. Unlike his, her bond to the people reached deep into men and women of all walks of life. He had led them in war, yet they looked to her in matters of state. Him they respected. But her they *loved*.

His weary mind finally faded into sleep, and soon he would awaken to the new day. When he had slept a few hours longer he awoke refreshed in his spirit and his body to greet the new day.

* * *

Snow. Beneath the moon a blanket of it had been thrown over the fields beyond the forest. As Ilfedo rode out of the woods, his stallion snorted into the frosty air. A band of mud showed through the snow. It led from the forest's edge, through the fields, and to the edge of the City of Gwensin.

The buildings in the city had been built of wood and stone, some blue, others gray, and some cream white. In the moonlight the city took on an ethereal glow, making Ilfedo feel almost as if he were gazing at a city from some distant and strange land. But this was not a strange place, this was his city, for Ilfedo ruled over all of the Hemmed Land. He was Lord among these men, not so much by choice as by the destiny God's prophets had set for him.

Hauling back on the reigns, Ilfedo turned in his saddle to glance at the tall young woman who rode behind him. Escentra was her name. Her blue eyes responded to his as she emerged from the shadow of the trees, the moon washing over her long blond hair. Not long ago she had been an agent for a distant wizard, indeed she had been a witch in her own right. But no longer.

Ilfedo thought back to an evening back at his home. It was shortly after the five Warrioresses had set sail across the Sea of Serpents to seek out possible territories where Ilfedo could resettle his people. That evening Escentra had told him and Oganna a dreadful story of a distant place where she had been born. While she was a young girl, a strange army had appeared from the northwest, conquering peoples and subduing or annihilating them. Escentra and her father had been taken to an underground fortress. A wizard had told Escentra that she would become a witch in the service of the most powerful of all sorcerers. If she had resisted, her father would have been slain and her mother would have been tortured.

At this point in the story, Escentra had fallen to the floor in convulsions. Blood ran from her nose and her eyes turned beet red. Through her mouth a man's voice had spoken, and by her lips a vile laugh sounded forth. "Who is this that intrudes upon my dear Escentra? Is this why you never returned to me? I had thought you dead in Hidden Realm! Poor child, your mother and your father will suffer greatly for this betrayal. Ah, but you, my dear Escentra, your suffering must be greater."

Only by laying the sword of the dragon against Escentra's thrashing body had Ilfedo been able to ward off the evil that was attaching itself to her. Beside him Oganna had drawn her crimson-bladed sword, the Avenger. As the glowing silver dress covered her body she had laid it beside the sword of the dragon, willing its power to join his in expelling the evil presence. He had knelt and prayed over Escentra and fed the healing power of the sword into her body. In his hand the sword had thrummed and living fire had spread over her until, with a great cry, she had fainted. Her breathing deepened and slowed and she fell into a deep sleep.

Since that day, Escentra's memories prior to meeting Ilfedo in the Hidden Realm had been wiped from her mind.

"Is this the place?" Escentra's voice carried softly to his ears.

Ilfedo nodded and looked again at the city. "The mayor here is named Vortain. A powerful man and sometimes, I think, he considers himself a rival to my position in the Hemmed Land."

"You have mentioned him before," she said.

"Yes. He is the one I spoke to you of." Ilfedo shook his head, then hastily guided his horse forward. As they approached the city, Escentra's horse pulled up alongside of his. Ilfedo reached out and touched Escentra's shoulder. "Vortain is a forceful man and he was not pleased that I spared you. Do not be surprised if he or those around him seem withdrawn or even hostile toward you. Your presence will confuse them. If they ask you questions about your past, ignore them or defer to me. I do not want to risk a repeat of your last attempt at that."

Escentra started to reign in her horse. She swallowed hard. "Perhaps," she said with eyes lowered, "you should proceed alone then. I can return to your house and wait for you there."

"Nonsense!" Ilfedo grasped her horse's bridle and led it again toward the city. "I did not mention those things to frighten you. In fact, I daresay Vortain has fewer friends in his own city than I do, for the people place a great deal of trust in me. You, my dear Escentra, will be treated as a distinguished guest." He smiled. "Much to Vortain's displeasure, to be sure, but it matters not."

"Then I will follow you into the city. For though I do not relish meeting the man, I do not fear him." Escentra urged her horse ahead and soon the padding of hooves on the cold ground was all that could be heard in the still night.

They rode through the fields, following the path through the snow, until the horses' hooves clip-clopped onto the cobblestone streets of Gwensin City. Escentra slowed her horse as they passed under the stone arch that marked the city's edge, then she circled the blue marble statue of a horse that rose from the midst of the broad highway beyond.

Ilfedo called for her to follow him and rode down the highway. The squat buildings and the tall ones rose on either side of him. Due to the lateness of the hour most of the windows were dark, yet warm lantern and fire light still spilled out of a few of them.

They followed the cobbled road into the heart of the city, and rode up to the iron gates of the mayor's residence. Ilfedo nodded to the four men who were standing guard. "Lord Vortain is at home I trust?"

With deep bows, the guards stood aside. "He is, my lord," one of them said as he turned a large skeleton key in the gate's lock. "We will inform him of your arrival. And may I say, welcome again Lord Warrior to the State House! It is an honor, as always, to see you here." The man stood aside as the others pulled open the gate, but he cupped his hand to his mouth and called toward the mansion beyond. "Hail! The Lord Warrior has arrived."

The guards stood at attention as Ilfedo rode through the gate with Escentra immediately following. With the hour being late, Ilfedo expected to find the manicured gardens covered in snow. They were, but delicate flowers still rose through it, their white petals glistening in the moonlight. Ice covered the fountains and the park benches that were scattered throughout the gardens. Stone pathways crossed one another on their way around the mansion.

As the main door to the mansion swung open, Ilfedo reigned in his horse and dismounted. His boots impacted the ground with a note of finality as he helped Escentra down as well. The horses' silvery manes and tails shone in the moonlight and their silvery hooves sent sparks into the air as they pawed at the ground. Ilfedo patted his stallion's neck and spoke to it under his breath. The horse whinnied, then stilled as a young man ran from around the corner of the mansion.

"My lord," the lad said, catching his breath, and his eyes shifted to Escentra for a moment.

"Are you here for the horses?" Ilfedo asked.

The young man bowed, then cleared his throat as he glanced at Escentra, then back to Ilfedo. "I am, sir. May I take them to the stable?"

Ilfedo chuckled a bit at the lad's flushed cheeks. The young man was having difficulty keeping his eyes on the horse because he kept glancing at Escentra. But she did not even seem to notice and the lad swallowed hard. Ilfedo handed him the horses' reigns, then turned to the mansion and strode up the steps.

A butler greeted them at the front door. Escentra's eyes went first to the man's white shoes and then to his bright yellow pants and dress jacket with its long tails. Ilfedo grinned down at her as the butler led them up a broad stairs to the guest rooms.

Escentra spoke to Ilfedo in a whisper. "Your people are very strange to me. Some dress moderately, others dress—" She glanced up and down again at the butler.

The butler directed them to take two rooms at the end of a long hallway, then he excused himself and returned downstairs. As Escentra opened the door to her room she gasped, for inside were bed sheets, gowns, and furnishings worthy of royalty.

Ilfedo sighed as he gazed passed her to the lavish accommodations. "Many of my people place great value on living simply. However, Lord Vortain does not, and neither do many of those who serve him." He patted her on the shoulder. His gaze passed over the panels that covered the walls in her room. He had not expected Vortain to direct his servants to put Escentra in a room as stately as this, yet he was pleased the mayor had made the effort. He turned to face the door to his room. When he opened it he found a large albeit modest poster bed with three changes of clothing laid out for him. A large window fronted the room, offering a view of the front of the mansion.

As Escentra closed her door, Ilfedo called back to her and she hesitated with her hand on the door knob. "I will be speaking with Vortain in a few minutes," he said. "You are welcome to join me, if you wish. He usually provides refreshments for his honored guests."

The girl shook her head. "I have heard enough of the man and I don't want to stir the pot of troubles that you already have. I will say goodnight for now."

As Escentra's door shut, Ilfedo entered his bedroom. He was pleased at the modest way in which Vortain's servants had handled his accommodations. Perhaps the mayor was trying to demonstrate a deeper understanding of Ilfedo's preference for simplicity.

Ilfedo walked to the window, placed one hand on its frame, and leaned against it. The city was so quiet. So peaceful. He sighed inwardly. The Hemmed Land was finally at peace. It had been for some time now. Yet, this peace could not last. He knew it to be true. Sandstorms still assaulted the southern part of the Hemmed Land. The farmers along the southern border had lost hundreds of acres, for the wind-swept sand had eaten through the vegetation as if it were an enormous beast.

The Hemmed Land was dying. Ilfedo could well imagine that a dozen years from now the people would be crowded into cities like Gwensin. But they would be starving for lack of farming land and freezing during the winter for lack of firewood. The forests were being hewn down for homes, businesses, and many other uses. The people were prospering and multiplying, but too much so for the Hemmed Land. They needed to move, relocate to a territory vast and visionary.

That is why he had sent the Warrioresses across the Sea of Serpents. To discover other lands. But they had not yet returned. He closed his eyes and slowly exhaled. "Come back to me," he said. "Oh how I need you all by my side in the days ahead."

Ilfedo unbelted the sword of the dragon from his waist and laid it on the bed, then he changed out of his woodsman clothing into something more formal. He almost left the sword on the bed, then thought better of it and girt it around his waist before heading out into the hallway. Wearing it seemed unnecessary to others, yet the sword had become a part of him and he acknowledged that sometimes it seemed more like a close friend than a mere tool.

At the hallway's end he descended the carpeted stairs and made his way through the mansion. He stopped at a tall doorway. The form of a tree hung with apples had been carved into the door's surface. Carved beneath the tree's branches were three children, hands held out in anticipation of the fruit.

Putting his hand to the door, Ilfedo pushed it open. Warm firelight flowed through the room beyond.

Tall shelves lined with scrolls and oversized antique books filled three walls, while a desk rested against the other one. A man with long blond hair was hunched in a leather wingback chair, his hand busily scratching with a quill on a long sheet of paper. The man was the mayor of Gwensin, Lord Vortain the careful and patient with a subtle lust for power. Ilfedo gently closed the door behind him and then waited as Vortain continued to write.

As Vortain finished a sentence he returned the quill to the inkwell and dusted the page he'd been working on with sand. Vortain stood, turned to face his Lord Warrior, and bowed. "My lord, welcome again to my humble city. I trust that my servants have seen to your every need?"

"Indeed they have," Ilfedo said.

"Then we can sit down to the business at hand." Vortain pulled a smaller chair out from under a shadow between the bookshelves. He indicated for Ilfedo to sit in the larger one as he himself took the small one.

For half an hour they chatted about nothing of importance. Vortain asked if any word had been received from the Warrioresses, then remarked on what a fine queen Oganna would become one day in the Hemmed Land.

At last the idle conversation died and both men looked upon each other solemnly. "Something troubles you," Vortain said at last.

"Sadly, yes." Ilfedo let his simple response foster questions in Vortain's mind. "Rumors are spreading, a vile gossip really, and yet it persists and I believe it has originated with you."

Vortain drew back a few inches and his eyebrows rose. "The truth, my Lord Warrior! You have spoken what you mean with a greater candor than anyone else I know." He chuckled, some of the tension leaving his pale face. "Even my wife struggles to speak to me with such forthrightness."

Ilfedo folded his hands and leaned forward in his chair. "Are you confessing that your hand was in these rumors?"

Vortain's eyes narrowed and his mouth formed a hard line. "There are many rumors circulating in this city, my lord. To which ones are your referring?"

"To the rumors that Escentra's heart still belongs to the practitioners of sorcery," Ilfedo said. "That she returned with me only as a means to deceive us and undermine our culture." Ilfedo rose to his feet but lingered his gaze upon the man. "You have often been the voice of dissent in matters that require the Lord Warrior's authorization—"

"It was not I," Vortain assured him. "However, I will not say that I have discouraged the rumors. My personal belief is that the girl is a great threat, not only to the nation but to you personally."

Ilfedo felt as if fire raged into his heart upon hearing the mayor's words, but he held back his response and let the man speak.

"Escentra was only a short time ago, by your own confession, a sorceress skilled in deception and wizardry. I cannot in good conscience support her attachment to you or your apparent adoption of her into your household." Vortain reached to the back of his neck and scratched it. "You have brought the enemy into your home and she has attached herself to your side. Who is to say what her purpose is in doing this? She may be waiting for the right moment to slip a knife into your heart while you sleep."

Ilfedo let his anger simmer for a moment. His first reaction was to punch Vortain's jaw, and drop him hard to the floor. Instead he laughed. "You are showing yourself to be a fool in this matter, Vortain."

Vortain's face reddened and he struggled to keep the anger out of his eyes.

Ilfedo grasped the man's shoulder and stared into his eyes. "You do not know war, as I do. You have not bathed in the blood of men and of beasts, so you have no understanding of what happens when I sleep. Conflict has honed my senses, and evil awakens me with its presence. The cold edge of a knife will not take me in the night, and no assassin will reach my bedchamber and find me helpless."

Vortain's jaw twitched. "I fear that your arrogance will be your undoing, my lord."

"And I fear that your lack of faith in me will be yours." Ilfedo released the man's shoulder and half-closed his eyes as he took a step back. "Don't you see Vortain? I know that my time will come. I know that I will die, and something deep in my soul tells me that I will welcome death long before old age claims me. I will die on a battlefield, not by an assassin. I will face my enemy and he will slay me. My blood will mingle with that of my warriors and my allies will weep over my corpse, but I will look my killer in his face."

Ilfedo chuckled and pulled Vortain to his feet. "But as for you, I have little doubt that you will live to a very old age."

Vortain's anger seemed to vanish as Ilfedo spoke to him. "My lord, do not speak in such a manner, I beg of you," he said. "May God see that you outlive me."

"No, I do not believe that." Ilfedo smiled as he and the mayor walked out of the library. He put his arm around the man's shoulders and looked ahead, feeling all the while the fear in Vortain's eyes as they stared up at him. The mayor walked with his face toward the floor, and now and again he swallowed hard. "Take courage, Vortain," Ilfedo said. "Don't you want to live to an old age?"

"Indeed, but you speak as if my path is so very different from yours," Vortain replied. "You speak as if you know that when we leave this Hemmed Land to resettle our people, that the journey will cost you your life."

A maid emerged from a door along the hallway and smiled at the men as she bustled past them with a heap of clean shirts. Ilfedo glanced over his shoulder and waited until she could not hear what he had to say. "Your wife is precious to you, Vortain?"

"You know that she is," Vortain said.

A lump rose in Ilfedo's throat. "Then imagine that death takes her away from you."

Vortain stood still and listened.

Ilfedo dropped his voice to barely above a whisper. "What would death seem like to you if you knew that she was waiting on the other side?"

The mayor's shoulders slumped. "I would welcome it," he said.

"Ah!" Ilfedo exclaimed. "Then you do understand, at least to some degree. That is why I go fearless into battle. That is why, when the moment comes, I will welcome my enemy's blade through my heart! I will leave this brutal, lonely existence and be reunited with the one I love. I will be whole again. But until that time

I am half the man I used to be."

Vortain nodded and guided Ilfedo farther down the hallway. "I cannot fully follow your reasoning, for it seems to me that you still have much to live for, including family and friends." As he opened the door to the large dining room, he dropped to one knee and lowered his gaze to the floor. "You have never opened up to me in such a way, and I am grateful. What you have shared with me will remain with me. I give you my word that no one shall hear these things that you have spoken to me."

Ilfedo touched the man's shoulder. "You are a good man, Vortain. If birth had placed you in the forests instead of in the coastal towns I think we could have grown up friends."

"It pleases me to hear you say so," Vortain said.

"I said that I 'think' we would have, not that we 'could' have," Ilfedo said with another chuckle. Then Vortain stood and together they sat at the table as a maid brought in a plate of sautéed mushrooms.

* * *

That night the moon lit the way for a lone rider and his horse. Ombre arrived from the east and pulled his stallion to a stop at the city's edge. The stallion's hooves sparked on the cobblestones and its silvery mane flung across its eyes. The horse snorted as its rider patted its neck.

"We are here, Midnight," Ombre said to the stallion as he gazed up at the city. "And we will both soon be at the humble abode of his majesty, Lord Vortain." The man slapped himself on the cheek and clenched his fists. Humor mixed with sarcasm did not suite a man of his station. The people of the Hemmed Land needed leaders with a positive outlook on their future. But the negativity arose from an empty place in his soul, and he knew it.

"Stop thinking about her! You can do nothing about it." He closed his eyes and filled his mind with thoughts of good friends and of princess Oganna. She was like a niece to him and she had brought him such joy.

When Ombre opened his eyes and saw again the City of Gwensin, another face filled his mind. It was Caritha and she was smiling at him, as she had on the day that he had escorted her to the mayor's banquet. Oh she had been beautiful that day. He remembered fondly how she had walked with him in the dark gardens surrounding Vortain's mansion.

A tear rolled down his cheek. He could remember the day that Ilfedo sent Caritha and her sisters across the Sea of Serpents. They had gone willingly, believing that they could help Ilfedo discover a land in which to resettle the people of the Hemmed Land. Ombre had seen the pain in Caritha's eyes as she'd set sail on the Maiden Voyage. The sea had taken her into its embrace and he had vowed that when she returned he would take her into his arms and never let her go.

The stallion snorted its concern and twisted its neck to nuzzle his knee. Ombre patted the stallion's neck again. "Ignore me, Midnight. I am turning into a lonesome fool. Before long that ship will return over the sea, Caritha will be standing at the prow, and then I will make her my bride!"

Forcing a smile, Ombre urged his horse into the City of Gwensin. He navigated the broad streets and soon drew up to the mansion's gate.

"Do you have an appointment with his lordship?" the guard asked.

"No one is expecting me, but I need no invitation." Ombre turned his horse in a quick circle.

The guard took a step closer and a smile lit his countenance. "Lord Ombre? Well! I did not recognize you at first." He gestured to the other men and they began to open the gate. "Have a pleasant visit, my lord!"

As he rode down the driveway Ombre grinned. Vortain and he did not agree on many things, and sometimes it felt as though they despised each other, yet he knew that in his heart Vortain was another loyal son of the Hemmed Land. Ombre looked around at the snow-covered gardens and the high fence that divided them from the city outside. Vortain was a man of strength, an ally in whom Ilfedo would need to rely when his crazy scheme for relocation to a new land was put into effect. Yet in this matter Ombre doubted that Vortain could be counted on. Vortain's roots were here in Gwensin, his legacy was here, and above these things his pride was rooted here. He would not easily give up the Hemmed Land.

A young man, one of the mayor's stable hands, shuffled through the snow and accepted the stallion's reins from Ombre. "I will take good care of him, sir."

"You had better!" Ombre laughed and patted the lad on his curly head. "Now be off to the stables with you. Midnight has had a long trip. Dry his coat and warm some oats to feed him."

The stable hand furrowed his brow. "Warm the oats, sir?"

"Yes, warm them." Ombre glanced over the lad's confused face, then he slapped him on the shoulder, glanced at the butler who waited in the mansion's open door, and walked toward the stable. "Come along, lad. Would you want to eat cold oats on a cold day? I will show you how to do it."

The stable hand's face blanched. "Forgive me, my lord, I did not mean to ask you to work with me." He looked at the mansion and back at Ombre. "Lord Vortain would be most displeased if I allowed you to work in the stable. You are his guest and a lord, after all, and I am but a servant."

Ombre threw his head back and laughed to the moon.

"Do you find my words amusing, my lord?" the lad asked.

"Oh yes, I do." Ombre walked briskly toward the stable, throwing his arm around the lad's shoulders and guiding him along. "Your lord Vortain is a fine man, my lad, but he has little concept of the things that are in store for all of us. Suffice it to say that soon every servant will be his own master, and every master will feel as a servant, for even lords like Vortain will be homeless wanderers in search of a strange land."

"You mean," the lad gasped as he spoke the words, "the impending exodus of our people? The one that Lord Ilfedo has spoken of, it is real?"

"As real as the snow on this ground." Ombre rounded the corner of the mansion and found the stable a short distance beyond. As he opened the stable door, he patted the young man's head. "When we find a new homeland, even young men such as yourself will set up homes in the wilderness and begin to establish your own legacy in our society, a new station in life. Servitude will be outdated and men such as Vortain will find themselves in a new situation that may not be entirely to their liking. For lords shall be equal with their servants and some servants, I daresay, will rise above their masters."

Having said this, Ombre began to demonstrate how to prepare the oats for his horse. The lad watched him warm the oats in a pan over a bed of glowing coals and then, when Ombre dumped the oats in a sack and gave it to Midnight, the lad said, "If ever I become the master of other men, Lord Ombre, then I would strive to be like you."

Ombre smiled. "Who knows? Someday you may have the opportunity."

SHADOWS
UNDER HEAVEN

Ilfedo ran his finger along the edge of the wine glass set on the table before him and listened to the ringing sound his action caused. "Winter is ending and our path to Resgeria will soon be clear," he said.

Across from him, Vortain stared down at his own glass. "Then you are still intent on forming an expedition into the desert, even though the sandstorm persists?"

"Completely set on it." Ilfedo raised the glass to his lips and sipped at its contents. He set it back on the table. "Ahh! That is a fine wine."

Vortain brightened a bit. "I'm glad that you are enjoying it. My grandfather prided himself on the finest grapes in all of the Hemmed Land. This particular glass is sixty years old."

The door at the far end of the room swung open

on its brass hinges and a maid blushed as she hurried in. "Forgive me, my lords, but Lord Ombre is waiting in the hall."

"Waiting? Why would I wait?" The voice was loud and cheery. A man of average height stepped around her and into the dining room. He strode over to Ilfedo's chair and clapped him on the back. "So you have once again emerged from your forest hideout, eh brother?"

Ilfedo stood to embrace his friend, a smile stretching his own face. It felt good to see Ombre again. After all, they had grown up together in the forests of the Hemmed Land. Ombre's father had cared for Ilfedo and raised him after a bear had killed his parents. There was no one more loyal than Ombre, and among those he knew, Ilfedo had no greater friend.

Ombre's hazel eyes shifted to Vortain and he recognized him with a nod. "My lord Vortain."

"My lord Ombre," the other man acknowledged, rising from his seat.

The room seemed suddenly cool and Ilfedo spared the men a longer greeting. He thanked Ombre for coming, then asked him to take the seat next to him.

"I have asked my other counselors to join us here in one week's time, gentlemen." He smiled apologetically at Vortain. "I'm afraid I will be imposing heavily on your hospitality, but it could not be helped."

"Think nothing of it, my lord. Only ask and I will see to your guests' accommodations." Vortain sipped his wine and then set it again on the table. He raised his hand and the maid who had ushered Ombre into the room departed, then returned with a glass that she set in front of Ombre.

Ombre thanked her, then asked her for a mug of grape juice instead. "Thank you," he called after her as she hurried back into the hall.

Vortain directed his attention back to Ilfedo. "May I know what matters you will be addressing with the council tomorrow?"

"It is no secret, and I think you have already guessed." Ilfedo rested both of his hands on the table and looked into the man's eyes. "The people that live beneath the Resgerian desert must be found and liberated from the ancient spirit of Brunster Thadius Oldwell."

Vortain leaned forward and folded his hands. "Consider what you are doing, my lord. You will ask fathers and sons of the Hemmed Land to risk their lives on a venture that could very easily lead to their deaths. You will have them risk that on the hope that the people who you encountered can not only be found again, but that you will find them alive. What if this demon spirit has slain them? Your mission of mercy will have been in vain."

"You cannot understand what happened down there," Ilfedo said. "And even if you did, you were not there." He stood from the table and gently held up his hand to stop the man from saying anything further. "The decision has been made. The people of that sad city are as much your kinfolk as they are mine. However distantly we are related, they come from the same ancestral roots, our very bloodlines, and their hopes of salvation from that dark underworld are real and warrant the compassion of us all. I will not permit you to undermine my decision on this, so do not attempt to sway other counselors to your position. This is a time when my decision as the Lord Warrior may not be brought into further question."

Vortain stood and solemnly bowed. "It will be as you say, my lord."

Ilfedo took a last sip from the wineglass. "Thank you for the drink. Now I must retire for the night. Tomorrow we begin preparations for an expedition into Resgeria." He walked to the door, then paused and looked back, chuckling as he did so. "No one will die on this expedition, Vortain. I will enter the underworld with a powerful force and not even the spirits of the dead will be able to drive me away."

* * *

That same evening Ombre barreled out of a side chamber and jabbed Ilfedo in the ribs. "It is about time I caught up to you! Why the long face, brother? Dinner was served, our bellies are full, and a long night's sleep is ahead of us. Besides which, I will sleep well after watching you silence Vortain the way you did."

Ilfedo patted his friend on the back and started to turn up the stairs to the bedrooms. "How goes the construction on Fort Gabel?"

Ombre laughed. "Oganna sends you her love. Oh, Ilfedo, you should see her. She is at the height of her glory, learning from the architects and making judgment calls on how the fortifications should look. She is looking forward to seeing you though."

"Ah, and I cannot wait. But I will be unable to join her for some time. This expedition into Resgeria must take precedence." Ilfedo sighed. "Home is too quiet without my daughter or the sisters." He paused, considering something in his mind, then he voiced it. "I miss Rozel's snide remarks, and Caritha's steady judgement. Perhaps I miss Evela the most, her smile and tenderness."

Ombre hesitated at the top of the stairs, his hand clasping the rail and his gaze fixed ahead. "We should have heard from them by now," he said. "It has been too long."

"It is not as long as it feels," Ilfedo said. He put his arm around Ombre's shoulders. "Fear not. They are in the hands of God. If he blesses their journey, they will return to us soon."

Thus encouraging each other, the two men walked down the hallway. Ilfedo wished his friend a good night, then he entered his chamber and soon fell asleep, knowing that Escentra was in the next room.

Ombre, too, did not wait long before he retired to a room, for he harbored little love for the mayor's house. He carried with him a bottle of red wine and a glass which he filled. It fell to him that the room which Vortain's staff gave him that night overlooked the snow-dusted gardens through which, not that long ago, he had walked with the beautiful Caritha. Her soft voice filled his mind and he closed his eyes. Lifting the glass of wine he toasted the memories of sweet moments with his beloved lady.

* * *

As lords Ilfedo and Ombre lay in their beds, Escentra slept in hers, unaware that a tall man with long blond hair stood in a hidden stairwell beside her room.

One of the wall panels slid open, revealing a narrow doorway. Vortain and two of his guards slipped into Escentra's chamber, the former man towering behind the others. They covered her mouth as she awoke with an attempted scream, and Vortain, with a harsh gesture of his arm, silently instructed the guards to carry her out of the room via the secret stairway.

She struggled only a few moments for their arms were strong. Too strong. One man held her by the legs and the other by her torso. The stairway was dark but shafts of yellow light edged through slits in the walls. She wondered whether other guests were sleeping in those rooms, unaware of the crime their host was committing mere inches from their beds.

The men pushed open another wall panel and carried her into a dim room. As Vortain closed the wall panel, the guards gently stood her on the floor.

Escentra did not know how she should react, but her mind flashed a memory back to her. It was a memory that she had suppressed and, gratefully, had not recollected since Ilfedo first rescued her out of the Hidden Realm.

She remembered a little man rocking in a chair beside the fireplace in the late evening hours. His expression toward her was warm enough to reach into the depths of her heart, and she knew him to be her father. She ran to him, leaped into his lap and he wrapped her in his arms. She felt so little. She was little, for this memory was many years ago. The house in which they had lived was wooden with plastered interior walls. Some walls painted hues of green, and others painted blue.

A sound of thunder shook the house, and she looked through the darkened windows. Stars shone in the sky outside with an occasional cloud floating between them and the green fields of her family's property. There were many fields in front of their house.

Fifty paces away lay the dirt road. She and her father watched in growing anxiety as a shadowy column marched down the road. Her father doused the lantern and carried her to the window. From here she fully saw the dark army passing by, a thousand hooded figures resting their long scythe blades over their shoulders as if they were all brethren of the Grim Reaper. The blades swung back and forth over their heads as they marched and Escentra began to whimper.

But the memory faded and she realized that she had been staring blankly at Lord Vortain. The man frowned at her and as she glanced up at his eyes she felt she would freeze beneath his stare.

Vortain folded his arms across his chest and circled in front of her, but he kept his distance. Apparently he did not wish to frighten her, which was surprising considering he had stooped to abducting her in the middle of the night. "You will not be harmed," he said softly. Then he rested his hands at his sides and nodded to the guards. The men released her and bowed to her in apology.

It was the dead of night. A gold-faced grandfather clock chimed one o'clock in the morning. Deep shelves lined the walls and the ceiling was at least twelve feet high. Escentra noted a musty odor in the air, a pleasant odor like that of old paper. A small brick fireplace threw both light and heat into the room. This was not the atmosphere she'd expected. The fireplace flared for a moment, revealing rows of scrolls stacked on the shelves.

"My lord," she said softly to Vortain. "I do not know why you have brought me here, but I do know that Lord Ilfedo will be angry about it. Let me return to my room. You cannot imagine the painful memories you are awakening in my mind."

"You are not what you seem. Are you, Escentra?"

Vortain did not wait for her to answer the question. "To the world you appear to be just another beautiful young woman. But to me—" He made a sweeping gesture of his hand across his face. "I see a fallen foe, more specifically a witch who deceived Lord Ilfedo and sought to kill him. Now I am bewildered, and so are many of Ilfedo's people, for you follow my lord like a stray kitten. You are in his shadow at all times, under his protection. Many men have desired to have the Lord Warrior's ear and yet they have not received such an honor, yet somehow you have." He leaned toward her. "What should I make of this? What should I make of you? Have you had a genuine change of heart, or are you a wizard's spy clever enough to work yourself into our ranks?"

Escentra felt a familiar venomous edge creep into her voice as she stared at the floor. "I am under your lord's protection and you have treated me in a despicable manner." She raised her eyes to his. She felt cold, as with the cold of hatred that had long ago spread through her soul. She did not want to remember that feeling. It made her helpless, made her want to lash out by any means possible and free herself.

Vortain gestured to his guards and they sprinted to her side, forcing her arms against the sides of the chair. "You will cooperate with me, witch!"

Vortain's words meant nothing to her. In Escentra's mind she had already drifted back to the day that the armies of the wizard had invaded her homeland. She had been an innocent child, safe in her father's care, until he came. A being more beast than man, a servant of the wizard Letrias. His legions had taken her father and then her. They had forced them onto their knees before the terrifying figure known as the Death Knight. The blades of his swords were as black as night, equaling the gloom of his presence. She remembered her father's screams as the torture began with his arms strapped to his sides and a blade run down his chest.

She snapped back to the present situation. She would not allow herself to be handled in this way. Letrias had shown her how to do it. She did not need to suffer at the hands of men as her father had.

But she hesitated. Much was required in order to free herself, even a return to her old ways. "Embrace the spirits of the accursed," she remembered a wizard saying. Voices dark and weary had come out of the shadows and she had connected to them, drawn upon their strength, the latent energy of corrupted creations. Her soul had torn to do so. She had felt the hand of God recoil as the spirits covered her in their pain.

A familiar figure walked by her in her memory. It was him, the master of the Valley of Death. Letrias himself. Letrias paused and faced her. "My child," he said with a smile, and Escentra caught her breath. "Ah! At last you have revealed yourself." Letrias's high leather boots stepped into a pool of blood. He stood there analyzing her. "How miserably you failed me, Escentra. And that after all that I had done for you. A pity that you did not return, at least a pity for those you are now living among. For I have used your memories to re-establish my connection to you, and now you and those around you will die."

"No!" Escentra gasped as the wizard's hand touched her. Heat rose in her chest, exploded up her throat, and rammed open her mouth.

Letrias laughed mercilessly. "Now I will see through your eyes."

She felt her old master's power take total control of her body. Her eyes took in her surroundings as if for the first time, resting on Vortain, and her mouth spoke, but not with her own voice. Out of her mouth the wizard said, "Now I will take this girl's life and you will never even know my name. Is that not a wondrous thing?" She laughed, but it was Letrias's laugh and not her own.

Black tendrils of energy lashed out of Escentra's skin, and she tried to scream for mercy, but Letrias laughed through her lungs instead. Faintly she saw Vortain's guards collapse to the floor on either side of her, their bodies convulsing.

She rose from the chair and the effort of it sent shivers of pain down her spine. Her hand grasped at Vortain's throat, but he pinned her to the floor. She felt Letrias's rage over being thwarted as he sent fresh waves of dark power through her body. But Lord Vortain's gloves would not allow the current to pass through them.

Letrias spat from Escentra's mouth, covering Vortain's face in saliva.

Vortain did not shift his position. He kept Escentra pinned to the floor, his eyes hard. "Escentra, come back to us. Break this connection with whoever is holding you under his power."

Escentra saw in Vortain's eyes a hint of something she did not expect. For this lord in the Hemmed Land bit his lip in remorse. "What have I done in bringing you here? Forgive me, child."

"Ha!" Letrias scoffed. "The powers with which you now deal are beyond your control, for she is now under mine. You thought to learn things of me, but instead I learned of thee!" The wizard paused long enough for Vortain's eyes to widen. "Escentra, my pitiable child, death is visited upon you."

* * *

Ilfedo awoke late in the night and he did not know why. All was peaceful and his sleep had greatly refreshed him. But there was a soft knock on the bedroom door, then a more insistent knock followed.

"Of all that is good in this world, who is it?" Ilfedo shouted. But there was no answer. He forced himself to get up, a bit dizzy as he felt his way to the door. "Who is it?" he repeated.

Again, no one answered. His patience fled from him as he tore open the door and peered down the hallway. The lamps on the walls burned low. Nothing moved and no one was in sight. Ilfedo closed the door and shook his head. "I need more sleep."

He walked back to his bed, pulled back the covers, and lay down again. He stared at the ceiling. What had roused him at this hour? He had heard a distinct knock at the door. Surely no one in Vortain's mansion would play a prank on the Lord Warror, not knowingly anyway. He shook his head again and closed his eyes, settling deep into the comfort of the goose down pillows.

Suddenly a door in the hallway thudded shut. Hurried footfalls followed, nearing Ilfedo's door, and a hand pounded upon it. "Ilfedo." It was Ombre's voice. "Wake your lazy bones and get out here. So help me, I will break this door with my sword if you do not open it."

Ilfedo was at the door and thrusting it open before Ombre could draw another breath. "At this hour of the night?" He let his shoulders sag and glanced down at his friend. "Ombre, please, I need my sleep."

Ombre drew his belt around his hips and growled as he slapped his sword's sheath. "One of the house maids tried to wake you, but you drove her away. She decided to try reaching me instead, and I responded as you should have. As a gentleman."

"Responded to what?" Ilfedo was fast losing patience again. Every problem in the Hemmed Land and beyond seemed to come to him for a solution. He needed a reprieve.

Ombre clapped his hands in front of Ilfedo's face. "Get your sword, brother. Vortain has proved himself a foolish man. A very foolish man indeed. I think you will have need of the sword of the dragon."

As Ombre related what the maid had told him, Ilfedo belted on his sword. Apparently Vortain had not accepted Ilfedo's warning, for he had ferreted Escentra out of her bed to a room where he might interrogate her privately. The reality of it sent Ilfedo's fingers scratching along the hilt of his sword and the living fire played over his hand, wanting to be released.

Together the men walked the long hallway until they came to the stairs. One of the servant girls stood there, her eyes looking at the floor and her fingers wringing the ballister.

"Where can we find the mayor?" Ombre spoke as if fearful she would run, but she did not answer. Just stood there trembling.

Ilfedo gently lifted her chin with his fingers until she returned his gaze. "Show me," he said.

The girl's face relaxed into a resolved expression. She lifted her pink skirts and flitted down the stairs. On the mansion's ground floor she guided them down hallways that Ilfedo had not seen before. Here the walls were paneled in dark wood and only a handful of lamps lighted the way. The doors were spaced farther apart as well. He noted that the wood stains had thinned, worn by age.

"This part of the mansion predates the upper floor and much of the first," the girl whispered in response to his query. "My lord Vortain does not entertain guests in these chambers but keeps them for himself and his family." She pointed her wavering finger at a door ten paces ahead. "He is in there . . . with the girl."

Ombre ran to the door and grasped its handle. Ilfedo was about to follow when he noticed the door on the opposite side of the hallway opening. A woman peeked out and he recognized her instantly, for she was Vortain's wife.

"Glenda, why are you here at this hour?" Vortain's wife said to the maid. Then the woman's eyes found Ilfedo and they widened. "Forgive me, my lord, I did not see you at first." She glanced at the sword. Flames continued to play along its pommel. "Is something wrong? I have never seen you come to this part of the house."

She stuttered a little on her last words and Ilfedo could not help but feel sympathetic toward her. Her husband had committed a serious offense and he would suffer the consequences as dictated by the Lord Warrior.

Ilfedo purposefully turned away from her. His anger began to boil in his heart as he shoved Ombre aside. His friend grunted with displeasure at being thus dismissed, though he did not otherwise object as Ilfedo let the raw strength of the living fire surge through his arms. Ilfedo shoved the door with his free hand. The thick hardwood splintered under the impact and fell into the room beyond.

Behind Ilfedo, Vortain's wife screamed, and Ilfedo imagined that she did not cry out because of him but because of her husband. For Vortain had wrestled Escentra to the floor and held her down, his face grimacing with the effort. The girl had spit in his face for his trouble.

Ilfedo raised the sword of the dragon in both hands and prepared to lop off Vortain's head. But what Ilfedo heard coming from Escentra's lips stopped him from killing the man.

Vortain did not shift his position from off of the girl as a masculine voice spoke from her beautiful lips. "Ha! The powers with which you now deal are beyond your control, for she is now under mine. You thought to learn things of me, but instead I learned of thee! Escentra, my pitiful child, death is visited upon you."

Escentra's body convulsed, her back arching in a most painful manner. Vortain released his hold on her, standing to his feet and crying out over and over again, "Forgive me for what I have done!"

Facing Ilfedo, Vortain's eyes widened. Then he dropped to his knees and bowed his head. "End my life now. I have done an awful thing and this girl is suffering for it. End my life now, I am asking you to do it."

Those who stood by backed silently away from the two men and from the girl. No one took their eyes off of them. Ilfedo felt their stares as if they were needles stabbing into his head.

Vortain's willingness to accept his punishment drained away Ilfedo's desire to execute him. He raised the sword's blade in front of his eyes and looked into its glassy surface. The flames played inside of the blade as if they belonged to a separate world self-contained in the sword. It was a world uncorrupted and able to discern the right from the wrong.

"Kill me! I am begging this of you, my lord," Vortain repeated.

Ilfedo stepped away from him with a grim shake of his head. He looked upon the girl instead and knelt beside her, setting his sword over the length of her chest. The living fire latched onto her body, fed her its healing energy, yet still she thrashed about.

"You cannot stop me from killing her," the man's voice said from her mouth. "She is mine!" Then he laughed horribly through her lips. "She is dying now! The pain which I am inflicting is terrible, too terrible to stop. Living fire may prolong her agony, yet in the end its power will be drained and the victory will still be mine." Again he laughed from her lips.

Vortain stood and his wife looked up at him with tears flowing down her face. "I am sorry," he mouthed.

Flashing with white light the sword of the dragon hovered over the girl's body. Ribbons of fire swam through the air toward Vortain. The man did not move until the flames lashed his face, then he screamed as blood ran down his cheeks. His wife screamed and ran out of the room.

Ilfedo found he could not remove his gaze as the man's skin baked and cracked. Vortain's hair began to smolder and he, trembling, collapsed to the floor. He looked like a corpse. At the sight of him, the maid who had guided Ilfedo to the room fainted in the doorway.

As Ilfedo picked up Vortain's limp wrist, the sword of the dragon stabbed itself into the floor. The man's pulse beat, albeit faintly. Ilfedo exhaled with relief, then his attention turned to Ombre.

Ombre walked to Escentra's side and helped her sit up on the floor. The girl held one hand to her forehead, then she glanced at Ilfedo and Vortain. Not a trace of her ordeal could be seen on her body. Her skin had regained its youthful vitality and her bosom rose as she took a deep breath.

Marveling, Ilfedo pulled his sword out of the floor and slid it back into its sheath. Somehow the ancient weapon had transferred the sorcerer's attack to a new victim: Vortain.

"Well," Ilfedo whispered in Vortain's bleeding ear, "it appears that death was not a suitable payment for your crime."

With that, he summoned Vortain's wife. "Your husband is in need of help. Shall we bring him to your bedroom?"

"I will go with him, if I may," Escentra interrupted. "I think I owe him my life."

Ombre could not hide the shock on his face. "Owe him? He owes you! This should have killed you. It was the power of that mysterious sword that pulled you from the brink of death."

The girl looked up at him and her gentle expression silenced him. "The sword offered him a choice. I could hear it speak with a voice in my mind, even as my former master sought to destroy me. It offered to pass my pain into Vortain's body if such a deed would save my life, and he accepted its offer." She turned to Vortain's wife. "Will you please let me tend to him?" The woman was taken aback, yet she nodded.

Ilfedo and Ombre carried Vortain into the room

across the hall and laid him in the bed, then they left Escentra and Vortain's wife to care for him. It felt like a strange twist in circumstance to Ilfedo, and by the expression in Ombre's eyes Ilfedo knew that he was not alone in that thought.

THROUGH
THE SANDSTORM

Vortain's wounds stood out as thickening scars on his head, his face, his neck, his arms, and his hands. His skin had parted like the broken shell of a hardboiled egg. His recovery would prove painful, of that Ilfedo felt sure.

Ilfedo stood in Vortain's bedchamber, arms crossed over his chest. "The remaining counselors have arrived," he said as the man lay immobile in his bed. "We will be meeting in a few minutes to discuss my proposal to find the City of Dresdyn and liberate its people."

Escentra sat in a chair beside Vortain's bed, a bucket in her lap as she patted his forehead with a moist cloth. Vortain did not open his eyes. Through his bleeding lips he replied, "I would be there if I could. Please tell Brindel and Lord Northill that I hold in my convictions and I do desire that they hold to theirs." He forced a laugh from his throat. "Many sons and fathers will die in this attempt to save a nation of strangers. I will not have their blood on my hands."

"No, Vortain." Ilfedo shook his head and patted the mayor's shoulder. "As always their blood will be on my hands and in my memory, and if they die they will die for my legacy, not yours. This is my burden, the burden that I bear as your Lord Warrior."

"You speak well, my lord," Vortain said. "But remember what I have said, for the time may come when the people will resent the lives your conflicts have cost them. They may not be correct in doing so, but they will be justified in their attempt to preserve the lives of those they love."

Ilfedo let out a long sigh. "I am not here to argue with you again. Your recovery from last night's ordeal is enough to occupy you at this time. We will talk again when you are well."

Ilfedo left Vortain's bedchamber and strode down the corridor into the main house. Resolution filled his heart. He would speak to his counselors and they would listen, for the people must follow their Lord Warrior if order was to rule in the Hemmed Land.

When Ilfedo's counselors had gathered at the table before him, Lord Vortain was not among them. Without his dissenting presence the counselors bowed to Lord Ilfedo's will in the matter of seeking out the people of Dresdyn. Even those who Vortain might have counted on for dissent, voiced their strong support for Ilfedo's cause, calling him honorable and valiant. At one point Ombre glanced sidelong at Ilfedo, and nodded with relief. The mission would move forward. All that remained was to organize the expeditionary force to march into the Resgerian desert.

Ilfedo departed the City of Gwensin, leaving Escentra in the care of Vortain's wife. For the girl had truly attached herself to the mayor's household and she wished to remain behind. Ilfedo breathed a relieved sigh when he glanced back at the city. He had taken Escentra under his wing, perhaps prematurely. His time with her had been troubled and now he could plan his expedition without worrying about the girl he was leaving behind.

By his command, word was carried on horseback to towns throughout the Hemmed Land. The call to arms for the warriors who bore the swords of light, and the request for men and women who would volunteer to accompany the army as drivers, as cooks, and as nurses.

The thousand warriors of light girt on their swords, and left their homes and families to march southward. Ilfedo set up camp in a stretch of fields barely a couple of miles away from the edge of the sandstorm that still howled as it ate into the Hemmed Land. He pitched a large tent and waited for three days.

Teams of wagons pulled by horses came first. The wagon masters formed a circle around Ilfedo's tent. They had brought wood, rope, and tools. On the next day as Ilfedo left his tent, a dozen young men trooped out of the forest and lined up before him. Each of them slung an ax over his shoulder. They were woodcutters from the Western Wood and they offered their strong arms and backs.

"We can wrestle, my lord," the group's spokesman said. "But we cannot wage war. We were told that you are leading a peaceful expedition of mercy to find the poor souls that are trapped beneath the desert." The young man paused, grinning widely. "We are up for an adventure, if you think you can use us."

Ilfedo smiled back and waved them toward a place beside his tent. "I am honored to have you accompany me, lads! Pitch your tents beside my own."

As the woodcutters set up their tents Ilfedo turned his gaze to the east, for there appeared over a hundred women carrying baskets. They were all in colorful dresses. He marched out to meet them and, in unison, all of them bowed their heads—with the exception of one.

Oganna stepped out of the women's midst and strode forward to meet him. He stopped to study her. She had grown into a woman now. His child she still was, but the child in her had been replaced by a wise spirit. She had grown her hair even longer than it had been when last he'd seen her leaving for Fort Gabel. Her blue eyes swallowed the sunlight and glinted back with golden hues. Belted to her waist was her sword, the Avenger, its crystalline handle deceptively transparent. Avenger was more than a match for any sword in the Hemmed Land, save with the exception of his own.

Her pet viper was wrapped around her arm, its tongue slicking in and out of its venomous mouth. Neneila, the serpent was called, and a valuable guardian Neneila had proven to be. She seemed to despise all humans and other creatures except for Oganna, and her affection for her mistress was eclipsed by nothing.

Oganna smiled at him and dipped a curtsy. She was wearing a plain brown blouse, riding pants, and long leather boots. "I was told," Oganna said with a light laugh, "that my father is undertaking a quest into Resgeria to seek out the city beneath the sand." She approached and kissed his cheek.

Ilfedo embraced her, then held her shoulders at

arm's length. "What of Fort Gabel?"

"The artisans are nearing completion on the project." She glanced past him, her gaze taking in the busy scene of men, horses, and tents. "Please, Father, in all your expeditions we have been separated. Let us do this one together." She turned out of his grasp and swept her hand toward the women behind her. "They have requested to accompany me as well."

Ilfedo nodded to the group and bade them stand. "I have no objections, my daughter. After all, these are their fathers and brothers who will accompany me. Who better to tend to their needs than these?"

"Sssooo wise, Lord Ilfedo," the serpent said but its quip was lost as Oganna turned away and shushed the creature.

The women dispersed into the camp to find their relatives while Ilfedo led Oganna to his tent. They sat in the tent door and watched the camp organize in impressive fashion. Cooking fires glowed into existence as evening arrived. All around them warriors pulled out their swords and were instantly garbed in glowing white armor. Ilfedo built a small fire in front of his tent. He sat down with his daughter, enjoying the warmth as the night air dampened.

Ombre strode up to the tent as Ilfedo and Oganna sat there. With a wink at Oganna, Ombre smote the flat of his sword against his chest and looked at Ilfedo. "The expeditionary force waits only the command of their Lord Warrior to move into the desert," he said.

Another man barreled toward them out of the darkness. He was broad, but not overweight. He stood a little shorter than Ombre. He wore a long coat of chain mail that glittered in the light of the fire, and his smile shone almost as brightly as his mail.

Ilfedo beckoned the man to sit by the fire and he could not help but smile back at the man. "Commander Veil, forgive me for saying so, but your physique has changed somewhat."

"Ah, I had plenty of extra chub for a while," Veil replied. "But my duties have required nearly-constant and heavy work. The chub, as I like to say it, has turned into muscles of iron."

Ombre grunted and sat down, too. "Do not forget, Veil. You still owe me another go at arm wrestling."

Commander Veil waved his thick arm to dismiss the challenge. "Yes, yes, whatever you wish, my lord." He held his hands toward the fire, then solemnly regarded Ilfedo. "My lord, the officers are wondering how you plan to find this lost city. If it lies beneath the sand and you stumbled upon its entrance only by accident the last time, it is entirely conceivable that this endeavor will be for nothing."

"They are worried about the sandstorm," Ilfedo stated as he rested his hands on his knees.

"Well, yes," Veil continued. "They think that any holes in the desert floor will be indistinguishable as visibility in that mess of wind-swept sand will be little better than a couple paces ahead of us. And they are correct by my estimation. We will be more than hard-pressed to locate the cavern's entrance, much less direct everyone in this expedition to its location if and when we do locate it. Not to mention this raises concern for our safety. We do not want men and women falling into hidden holes in the desert floor. Forgive me if I am speaking out of order, but your men deserve an answer to assuage any doubts."

As Veil finished, Ombre pulled off his boots.

"Give them this answer," Ilfedo said, "and I do believe this will be sufficient for now: The sandstorm persists and it is enormous, however it has moved north since my last visit. It does not extend over the entire desert, rather it cuts like a scythe blade along the border of the Hemmed Land. We know that there are no cavern entrances hidden along the border. All we need do is push our expedition through the storm. Once on the other side we need only deal with the heat and the search for the cavern."

"Really?" Veil chuckled. "That makes it sound easy, my lord. I was all set to march for days in the desert storm."

"The cavern entrance was relatively close to home," Ilfedo replied, and he let the revelation settle in Veil's mind. "Our greatest task will be the underground journey and, hopefully, the rescue of the city's inhabitants."

Veil stood, bowed to Ilfedo, and barreled off into the darkness.

Oganna read the creasing lines on his forehead as he thought about the task ahead of him. "Everything is in place, Father. Let tomorrow do the worrying while you rest here tonight."

Ilfedo let himself smile. "I think your mother, if she were alive, would have said something very similar."

* * *

The sun sent a warm glow across the cloudless sky. Ilfedo gazed skyward for a few moments, then he turned to the young man standing beside him with a pail of water upheld in his hands. Ilfedo smiled at him, then glanced at the line of trees to the south. Behind him he knew the camp had been broken. Tents had been packed away and the people were awaiting his command.

He about-faced, raising his arm for silence as a hum of conversation rose from the vast throng which stood in the fields. The Elite thousand had split into groups of a hundred men. Their swords were sheathed at their sides.

Ilfedo waved his hand in two slow gestures and the group to his far left marched forward. Their swords clanged against their sides in unison, ringing through the air, and they pushed south into the tree line. Ilfedo pointed to his right and waved the next group forward. A hundred men marched out, paralleling the direction the first group had taken.

Then came the other eight hundred, their divisions led by Ombre at their head. Line upon line of warriors who had proven themselves in battle against the giants in the city of Netroth. They were a magnificent sight. Armor polished to a sheen. They passed by him on either side, line upon line, and on many a proud breast he saw a lady's scarf whipping in the wind that came from the south. The women of the Hemmed Land had urged these men on for a cause of mercy, to save a people whom they did not know.

"God be with us this day," Ilfedo shouted as he drew his sword out of its sheath. The living fire wreathed his body and armor grew like scales over it.

The thousand men returned with a shout of their own. "God be with us!" Their call reverberated across the far-reaching fields and into the patches of forest in the Hemmed Land.

At the distant rear of these magnificent men he made out a flash of silver and he knew that Oganna had drawn out her own sword, the Avenger, as she led the women and the woodsmen with the carts and the supplies.

Ilfedo turned again and slid the sword of the dragon back into its sheath. The fire retreated from his body, returning into the sword, and he strode purposefully into the forest. Around and behind him the multitude of men filed through the forest. Birds cried out and fled before them, and trembling rabbits ran into the underbrush. Nature seemed ready to be tamed . . . until they reached the edge of the storm.

The first taste of salt nestled on Ilfedo's tongue and in the distance the wind screamed through the trees. Ilfedo called a halt and the young man with the water pail ran up beside him. Ilfedo handed him a long cloth and the youth bathed it in water, then handed it back. Ilfedo wrapped the wet cloth around his face so that only his eyes showed. The moist cloth now covered his nose and his mouth.

To his left he discerned three other youths carrying water pails to his men. The warriors followed suit, dipping cloths into the pails then lashing them around their faces. Someone to his right sneezed and Ilfedo glanced in that direction. Tall and handsome, and a bit thin, the man looked familiar. Ilfedo smiled as he recognized the warrior as James McCormick, once stationed in Fort North during their fight against desert vipers. The man had been a good cook, too, and his courage on the battlefield in Netroth had earned him recognition from a trusted officer.

James dipped a blue cloth into the pail, politely thanked the youth carrying it, then dutifully tied the cloth around his face so that only a slit remained for his eyes. He returned Ilfedo's gaze with a polite nod, then fixed his eyes ahead of him.

Ilfedo raised his arm and pointed forward. The tramp tramp of boots filled the forest. Like a human wave he and his men shoved into the sandstorm. Quickly it engulfed them in a partial darkness. Thanks to the wet cloths over their faces the sand did not get into their nostrils or mouths, but it rubbed like sandpaper over their bodies, slipping between the joints of their armor and coursing down their backs.

It took over an hour to push through the storm. An hour in which they felt their half-blind way past the Hemmed Land's trees that had been stripped of their bark by the storm. The sand had thoroughly destroyed the forest floor, leaving only the naked trees to indicate that this used to be a lush habitat.

When Ilfedo broke through the storm he felt instant relief. The wind died and sunlight revealed the flat desert stretching to the horizon east, west, and south. The sandstorm formed a shifting wall a couple hundred feet high behind him. It was in stark contrast to the calm desert ahead him.

Out of the undulating wall of windswept sand emerged a line of fifty men. A few of them took off their boots and turned them upside down, draining them of sand. Soon the other men did the same. All of them stepped back into their boots and marched forward a hundred yards as another line of men emerged from the storm.

Far down the undulating wall of storm another group broke through, then another, and another. To both sides of Ilfedo his army formed up. Then they all waited in silence until a dozen horses pulling wagons lumbered out of the sandstorm. These were closely followed by princess Oganna and the women of her company. Ilfedo folded his hands across his chest, waiting as another wave of men, horses, and wagons emerged a few hundred yards down the line.

Ready. At last he was ready to return to Dresdyn and confront the spirit of Brunster Thadius Oldwell. He gazed out over the desert. First step, to find the entrance to the cavern. Then a camp must be set up around it as he and his men journeyed into the underground world.

TO WRESTLE A HAIRY BEAST

Lifting the sword of the dragon like a torch in his hand, Ilfedo let the light of the flames wreathing its blade illuminate the tunnel before him. The place was just as he remembered it. The mound of sand beneath his feet. The stone walls of the small cavern rising around him like a cathedral ceiling with a hole at its pinnacle. Ahead of him lay the tunnel.

But this time he was not alone and instead of falling in by happenstance he had climbed puposefully down a ladder. Ombre leaned into view over the hole above his head. "So, is this the place you were looking for?"

Taking out a compass, Ilfedo waited for the needle to settle, then he aligned it north. The tunnel pointed south, a true, direct line. He laughed aloud and grinned up at Ombre. "Let the Elite warriors climb down this ladder and unsheathe their swords. It is time to bring light to a dark world and free a people that were long lost. Is there any cause more noble than that?"

As Ombre ducked out of sight, Ilfedo saw commander Veil swing himself onto the ladder to begin the descent. Ilfedo slid down the pile of sand, planting himself squarely in the tunnel's entrance. Last time he had traveled this way his destination had been the home of the mighty megratraths. Instead he had followed this tunnel to the hidden city of Dresdyn and when he had left that place it had not been by his choice. "But I am now here by my own choice," he whispered into the tunnel.

"All right!" Commander Veil shuffled to his side, staring into the tunnel as well. "I must admit, my lord, ever since I heard that you wanted to undertake this expedition I have been looking forward to it. I learned a great deal on our journey into Burloi and the ensuing battle for Netroth. It was like walking alongside our ancient ancestors and participating in the battles only legend and lore relate. Today, I am honored to march with you again and explore new territories."

They clasped each other by the forearms.

"This will not be an easy task," Ilfedo said. "But I pray that we have success in it, and in so doing bring our lost family to the home our forefathers gave us."

"Indeed," Veil replied as he glanced back at the mound of sand. A dozen warriors had now descended and were standing on the mound. In unison they drew their swords.

They were clothed in nothing more than trousers and shirts. The ring of their metal echoed down the tunnel. Light flashed from their swords and their bodies glowed brilliantly, then the light faded to reveal a white armor covering their bodies. White helms adorned their heads, their breastplates appeared metallic and they had also been given greaves and white-leather garments underneath. The swords did not cease to glow with white light.

Commander Veil glanced once again at the tunnel lying before them. "Strange that this has been down here, undiscovered for so long," he muttered under his breath.

Ilfedo turned away from the sight of his assembling warriors, and took his first steps into the tunnel. His heart yearned with a very deep longing to reach his destination. He desired to see again the strange underground city that was lighted by a million bee-sized, pink, glowing birds. Somewhere at the end of this tunnel the city lay, but when he had last seen it, the terrifying spirit of Brunster Thadius Oldwell had possessed the body of the captain of the city guard. "Oh, Bromstead," Ilfedo whispered, "May the Creator have mercy and shine his light in your heart so that the demon may be cast out."

"What did you say, my lord?" Veil said from behind him.

Ilfedo glanced at the man but continued to walk down the tunnel. He had proceeded a hundred yards. Behind him the line of glowing swords grew as the Elite warriors filed into the tunnel.

He considered telling Veil of the conflict that was likely awaiting him in the heart of the underground city, then thought differently. Bromstead had been a strong man. Perhaps he could be redeemed, but the last time Ilfedo had seen him his body had still been possessed and fully controlled by the spirit of the dead Lord Warrior, Brunster Thadius Oldwell. Ilfedo took comfort in the memory of the people of the city stealing the wicked green sword from Oldwell, and in their newfound alliance with the young black megatrath. Perhaps Ilfedo had not left them as helpless as he had thought at first.

Instead, Ilfedo said to Veil, "I am working out a few things that have been on my heart since I left this place. It was not an easy thing, being forcibly rushed away from those people. I fear for them in that dark city. Yet I have great hope in the light that we are bringing to them now."

"What was it like, to be carried by a dragon made completely of metal?" Veil lowered his glowing sword as he asked the question.

Ilfedo merely shook his head. He did not know how to describe the experience. He had been wearing the gold dragon ring given to him by the mighty dragon prophet, Albino. Unexpectedly the ring had swelled, growing off of his finger, and had loomed over him as a gold beast impossibly strong. It had held him against his will and . . . Oh, it was senseless to re-examine those events now.

The here and now! That is what mattered. The journey to Dresdyn lay before him. The quest to find the key of living fire lay behind him.

Veil must have sensed Ilfedo's mood. "There is no need to sate my curiosity, my lord," Veil said.

Ilfedo knew that the man spoke those words with conviction. Veil was not the sort to pry for details. It was not his way, and Ilfedo did not owe him a discourse on the subject. At this time his mind was on the path ahead and that is where he wanted his thoughts to remain.

They proceeded down the long tunnel with Ilfedo gradually edging farther ahead of Commander Veil and their men. The once-dark walls of stone revealed their crevices, cracks, and sedimentary layers. The tunnel proceeded for as far ahead as the light of his sword revealed, stretching a straight path ahead of him.

There were no caverns through which it passed and no other tunnels that branched into it. For a moment Ilfedo imagined what would happen if the entrance behind them were to collapse, for they would be trapped with nowhere to proceed except ahead into the dark underground world.

Long hours passed as he led his men through the tunnel. Despite the multitude that followed him, the tunnel was remarkably quiet, at least for a long while. He lost track of time as they proceeded and the murmurs of soft conversation grew in volume behind him. One of his men laughed in response to another's jest, and a deeper laugh joined in.

Ilfedo felt tension ease from his face, a tension that he had not even realized was there. Perhaps the laughter of his soldiers was all that he had needed to remind him that this time he would come into Dresdyn with irresistable power at his command, enough strength to turn the tide of a war if the need arose.

When at last he called the column to a halt, he turned about. The men's faces were brilliant in the white glow of their upheld swords. Ilfedo ordered them to rest for a short while, then he sat on the tunnel floor and leaned his back against the cool wall of stone. With a clatter of arms the Elite warriors set themselves down in the tunnel behind him. Half of their number leaned against one side and the remainder against the other. Their glowing boots stretched in parallel lines for as far as he could see, leaving a narrow path between them. Someone in the column's rear must have received word that a rest period had been initiated, for before long jam sandwiches were being passed from man to man. The warrior beside Ilfedo handed him a sandwich and Ilfedo bit into it heartily.

"A short break. That is all," Ilfedo said to Veil as the man sat against the opposite wall of the tunnel.

Veil, in turn, nodded to the warrior sitting beside him.

That man passed the order to the man beside him. "A short break," he repeated in monotone. And so the order passed from man to man down the long column of glowing warriors.

Ilfedo wondered in those moments if Oganna had remained with the women at the rear. Or, had she started to work her way forward through his men, for he knew that she desired to be among the first to look upon the lost underground city. He threw the thought down the tunnel with the remaining bit of crust from his sandwich, then he stood to his feet. It was time to resume the march.

* * *

The columns of glowing swordsmen split down the middle, sitting down to rest their backs against the tunnel wall. Ombre smiled warmly at Oganna and she returned it with a smile of her own. Though he did not wield one of the magnificent swords of light, Oganna thought that Ombre looked more dignified than any of the elite soldiery as he marched between their feet to proceed deeper into the tunnel. Somewhere up ahead she could join her father. Ombre was cheerfully ordering the men to pull back their glowing legs to widen the narrow path she must walk to advance from the column's rear.

Oganna let her sword, Avenger, hang in its scabbard. She had no need of it at this moment. Plenty of light revealed the path already and she did not want to draw the stares of every man huddled in this tight space by unsheathing her distinctive weapon. Her sword clothed her in a dress made of silver light whenever she drew it, for it connected somehow to the energy generated by the dragon blood that flowed through her veins.

She walked behind Uncle Ombre, taking care not to step on any man's feet. Around her shoulders the faithful viper snoozed. Oganna stroked the creature's head with her fingers.

"Your father is probably a good ways ahead of us," Ombre said as he tapped the boots of a man in his path with the broadside of his sword. The man drew his knees higher to his chest, huddling closer to the wall so as to make space. Ombre pranced over another pair of feet then glanced over his shoulder. "You sure you want to do this now?"

She chuckled softly. "I have not been able to see him much lately. Any time I can spend with him is needed, for both of us."

"Of course you're right," Ombre said with a deep chuckle. He hesitated so that she caught up to him, then whispered in her ear. "He is getting rather old. Make the most of the time you have left."

She laughed, shaking her head at him as she darted ahead of him down the tunnel. But she proceeded only a short distance before the echoes of a command filled the tunnel, each warrior standing to his feet and starting to march again.

THE SWORD OF THE DRAGON

* * *

Several hours after giving his men a break from their journey through the tunnel, Ilfedo and Veil found themselves engaged in a sober conversation. The affairs of the Hemmed Land were a mutual concern to them, in particular the persistent sandstorm that was eating into the southern border. They bemoaned the homes and farms that had been lost, the pastureland and forests that had been shriveled and drowned in sand.

"Our hope lies in leaving the confines of the Hemmed Land," Ilfedo offered. "But the difficulty is in the journey and the vagueness of the dragon prophet's instructions. We will find a new home, and I will lead our people there. We cannot continue as we are for thirty more years. Each time I travel to our towns and cities the forests are thinned farther and the wild game is harder to find. Even the Western Wood is being utilized for its timber, which we need, but our numbers are growing. We need a new frontier to conquer. A land with vast resources."

"Many will object to leaving, my lord," Veil said, clenching his fists. "And not only from Vortain's camp. There are others. Dissenters, some of whom would rather die than leave the homeland. A foolish quest, they will say."

Ilfedo was about to respond, but at that moment the tunnel wall behind him crumbled away. Thinking that he and his men had been trapped by a cave-in he spun around. "Get clear!" But his shout was lost in the cloud of dust that filled the tunnel where the breach had occurred.

He waited as the dust settled and the light of his men's swords revealed a large hole in the tunnel wall.

His men were not alone, for a hairy beast hulked into the breach. It swiveled its flat, leathery face to gaze upon the men, its round dark eyes opening wide. It looked like an ape, as described in one of The Count's many tales that Ilfedo had read as a child, yet this beast was different. On its head grew a set of horns that were as thick as sapling trees. The horns curled like those of a mountain ram.

Ilfedo's men froze as they looked up at the creature. The ape, however, opened its fang-ridden mouth in a howl that sent a few warriors stumbling back against the tunnel wall. The beast swept out its hairy arm, flattening several warriors against the floor. It tore into the men, flailing with its arms and howling again.

Some raised their swords and stabbed at the creature, but their weapons appeared not to penetrate its hide. The ape lowered its head and rammed half-a-dozen men against the wall.

As his men dropped lifeless to the floor, Ilfedo struggled to reach them. He raised the sword of the dragon and shouted for the soldiers to stand aside so that he could pass them and reach the beast. But his men were packed tightly in the tunnel and he made slow progress.

Amid the chaos a sword flashed brazenly as a lone warrior ran against the beast, a deep cry of anger loosing from his lungs. He slashed the blade against the beast's chest and arms. The creature lowered its head and rammed its horns against him. The man grabbed hold of one horn and clambered onto its head, wedging himself between the horns.

The man's armor of light glowed like a poker pulled from a furnace. His sword rose in his hands as he held it with both fists and stabbed it down into the creature's nostrils.

Ilfedo shouldered ten paces closer to the conflict and glanced up at the lone warrior atop the beast. In a moment he recognized the man. It was James McCormick. James's face furrowed in a deep scowl as he held tightly to his sword, the blade piercing the beast's nose. The beast smashed its horns against the ceiling and tried to pluck the man off its head. Drawing a dagger from his belt, James drove it into the beast's finger.

With another howl the creature lowered its head. Two other warriors ran toward the beast, each taking stabs at its head. But the beast swept them aside, crushing them against the tunnel wall.

The nearby warriors retreated several paces and their armored bodies blockaded Ilfedo. He could no more reach James than he could call his slain warriors to their feet. Helplessly he watched.

James drew his sword up and out of the creature's nose and, for a moment, the ape hesitated. James gripped his sword's handle with both hands and raised the blade as if to stab down into the ape's brain.

With a twisting, thrashing motion, the ape threw James against the tunnel ceiling. As the man fell to the floor, lying stunned, the beast turned and loped back into the dark cavern through which it had come.

Ilfedo realized that his men must have been shouting during the fight, for the tunnel now quieted. James sat up, shook his head, and coughed on the dust left in the creature's wake. "Stand aside!" Ilfedo commanded. "Allow me to pass." His men divided before him with slight bows as if apologizing for being in his path.

Then something happened that made Ilfedo hesitate, for the brave James stood unsteadily on his feet, raised his glowing sword in his hand, and with a crazed laugh he ran into the adjoining dark cavern. "You're not getting away from me that easily, you big dumb monkey!"

Running onto the scene of the fight, Ilfedo stared openmouthed into the dark cavern that now adjoined the tunnel. The warrior of light, James, held his sword ahead of him like a torch and raced into the deep darkness. He ran over broad paths of stone that appeared to rise out of the black depths, narrowly avoiding falling into dark chasms that opened at many points along his run. His tall form stumbled over a bridge-like path, then dipped out of sight beyond it.

Though Ilfedo called out for the man to stop his foolish pursuit, he heard no response. Behind him the Elite warriors formed a half-circle as they too gazed into the cavern.

A throaty roar was heard and shortly thereafter the distant whoop of a man. Ilfedo sent his warriors out in groups of six as they attempted to locate their missing brother in arms. However, they found no evidence of James's trail and at last Ilfedo ordered his men to return to the tunnel. "I cannot risk losing any of you in this endeavor. There are too many unknowns and I know from experience that the subterranean world is far from hospitable. Wrap the bodies of our dead and send them to the rear. We must march onward."

As Ilfedo strode back in the direction he had been leading his army, toward the city of Dresdyn, Commander Veil blocked his way. "Respectfully, my lord, might we leave a contingent behind to guard this place until we return? If it should happen that the warrior survived, I would like him to find friends waiting for him. And, if the beast should return, I believe it would be of great benefit to ensure that it does not come upon our troops from the rear."

"Make it so, commander," Ilfedo said. He marched down the tunnel as Veil issued orders. A dozen warriors stood in the gap in the tunnel wall, their resolute faces turned to the darkness of the cavern beyond.

Above the tramping of his warrior's feet Ilfedo heard Oganna's voice calling to him. He raised his fist and the column halted and parted to make way as his daughter came to him. She glanced at the opening into the cavern where James had disappeared. Sidling close to him she lowered her voice to a whisper. "I heard what happened, but should you really leave that man in the underworld without hope of rescue? Should we not send a full contingent in there?"

Ilfedo almost laughed, though not because he found the idea amusing but rather absurd and impossible. "My dear child, an army cannot effectively scour the intricacies of this subterranean world." He shook his head, a steady resolution in his voice. "That man first proved himself brave by coming to the defense of his comrades. Then he acted the part of a fool by pursuing the beast."

Oganna looked back at the cavern opening. "Then he is a fool, for I thought the beast had taken him."

"No," Ilfedo said, "he followed it after it fled. We cannot risk more lives following a vendetta." Raising his flaming sword above his head, Ilfedo waved it ahead of him and the march resumed.

When Ilfedo reached the column's head he strode a short distance ahead of his men and maintained that gap as he led them deeper into the underground. Oganna kept a couple of steps behind him and soon Ombre joined them.

"The bodies of those killed by the ape have been sent back to our camp where they will be prepared for burial." Ombre shook his head as he said it and his shoulders sagged. "Ilfedo, we have not even reached the city and already there are casualties. You know how Vortain will twist this for his purposes."

Ilfedo laced his words with fire. "Perhaps Vortain will consider good sense and not prey upon the sorrows and fears of the widows and the orphans. If he does not, perhaps he will demonstrate the courage to resign his position."

Ombre let out a guffaw. "Right! And to what do you attribute that fantasy? Vortain is a man elected by the popular vote of his city."

"You are not brightening my mood, Ombre," Ilfedo said.

"Someone has to advise you, my brother, on the situation that you will likely face when you return from this mission," Ombre replied.

"Let the matter rest for now," Ilfedo said, calming his voice. "I have no interest in what Vortain may or may not do as a result of those men's deaths. They were my men. Not his. It is I who will grieve for them and it will be my task to inform their families." He fixed his gaze ahead and let his anger feed the furious flames on his sword. He pointed the blade ahead and released a small ball of fire, sending it down the long tunnel. The flaming ball rolled along the stone floor, bouncing each time it hit a rough surface, until it faded out of existence.

If Ombre had more on his mind he did not voice it.

When the first day's march had ended and the army had fallen asleep in the long tunnel, Ilfedo began to pace back and forth. The sword of the dragon still burned in his hand and the armor of light and living fire still covered his body. He was eager for the final march. Eager to see Dresdyn. He hoped that everyone there was still alive. Every time he tried to imagine how events might have played out after he was abducted by the metal dragon, he saw Bromstead recovering the green sword and slaying the city's inhabitants.

Oganna read his anxiety and began to tell him about her projects on the shore of the Sea of Serpents. She was particularly pleased with the artisans sent by Vortain to assist her in the building of Fort Gabel, though she glossed over Vortain's input, instead emphasizing the artisans themselves.

At last Ilfedo sat down and listened to the sound of her voice. He could hear a part of his wife in his daughter's voice. Ah, it was a wonderful thing. Soothing and reassuring. Nothing eased his mind as greatly as knowing that she was a steady soul, holding unwavering faith in her future.

He closed his eyes and remembered when she was a toddler laughing and squealing with delight as she ran around the living room. There had been logs steadily burning in the fireplace and there had been five women, the sisters of his deceased wife, all of them glowing in the warmth of the fire. Their cheeks reddened by the heat, their smiles filling their faces. Even Rozel, the grumpiest of the group, had tickled the little girl and sent her running across the room to another aunt who would take a turn tickling and send her to another. Those had been good days. It saddened him, looking back, that his wife's death had made him retreat into himself for a time. She would not have wanted him to do that. She would have wanted him to play carefree with their little girl.

Ilfedo checked himself mentally. He had raised her well. Oganna had grown into a daughter of whom he was deeply proud. The only regret he need allow himself was that her mother had not had the privilege of watching her grow.

The tunnel felt damp and nearly all of the warriors of light had sheathed their swords in order to sleep in darkness. Ilfedo opened his eyes and gazed at his sword. He positioned it so that the tip rested on the floor, balanced by his fingers entwined around its handle. The blade was a marvel, its multi-faceted surface seeming transparent, like a window into another world that burned forever with fire and swam with pure white light.

Across from him, Oganna had slumped against a hiking pack with the viper coiled in her lap. Oganna's chest rose and fell in deep sleep and her mouth was slightly open. Beside her lay Ombre, flat on his back with his arms folded behind his head. There was no mistaking the furrow on his brow. His dreams were taking him to a place he did not want to be, or reminding him of something he would rather not think about. Commander Veil slept behind Ombre, though he had propped himself against the tunnel wall and his breathing came out in gentle snores.

For as far as back down the tunnel as Ilfedo

could see, his men lay asleep. A few warriors had kept their swords drawn and where their hands still held their swords the weapons glowed.

Ilfedo looked at his own sword and drowned his gaze in the blade, focusing his mind to draw out its energy. Like a warm wind its power washed his body and soaked into it. He smiled. He needed no sleep tonight.

He stood and sheathed his blade, still grasping its handle. The armor of living fire continued to burn on his body, lighting the path before him. He strode a short distance down the tunnel, then he picked up his pace. His legs soaked in the sword's renewing energy as he ran toward the City of Dresdyn.

IN SEARCH OF
THE LIVING

As Ilfedo emerged from the tunnel into a vast cavern, he slowed his pace and smiled with relief as he shone his sword into the darkness. This was the place he had been seeking and it was just as he had remembered it. He knelt on the flat stone surface and pressed the tip of his blade against it. He focused the sword's energy against the stone, using it like a molten rod to etch an unmistakable arrow aimed straight across the underground chamber.

He stood and darted across the cavern. From his first trip he knew there was a sheer drop on both sides of the path, so he paused to etch a warning into the stone for those who would follow.

The path widened. Farther on, a cool fog billowed upward from either side of the path but did not cover it. The fog flanked the path with walls of white, leaving it clear for him to pass between them into the strange world that awaited his return.

On his last journey, he had walked the remaining distance. This time he etched another arrow in the stone, and ran the remaining distance to where the walls of fog bent to the left and the path curved downward.

When he reached the base of the path, Ilfedo exited the fog and stood on the broad shelf of silky smooth stone that he remembered so well. He lifted his sword, shining its light on the giant pillars of chiseled stone that supported the pathway he had just descended. Indeed, the pillars not only supported the path but continued downward past the edge of the stone shelf on which he stood, their thick columns hinting at the depth and vastness of the cavern that surrounded him.

He walked twenty paces to the edge of the shelf. The last time he had entered this realm he had touched his sword to the stone and it had seemingly awakened the millions of tiny pink birds that inhabited the cavern. The dewobin creatures had glowed with a steady, unblinking light, revealing to him the city that now lay hidden in the darkness far below and in front of him.

Retreating a couple of steps, he tapped the tip of the sword of the dragon against the silky stone. As before, the stone shimmered, a ripple of blue forming where the sword's point touched it. But instead of expanding to the stone shelf's edge, the ripple faded a few paces ahead and darkness remained in the cavern.

Ilfedo stared into the darkness ahead. By the sword's light he could see only a limited distance.

Where were the dewobins? Those glowing birds had provided not only the light to the people of Dresdyn. They had also spun a silk that the city's inhabitants harvested for use in making clothes and other necessities.

Ilfedo internalized his frustration, sending his will into the sword and calling upon the living fire. Like the torch of a god the sword erupted, fire spiraling upward. The light lasted briefly, yet it showed him a portion of the cavern's stone ceiling. Gray stone was all that he could see. He could not even discern a hint of pink from the feathers of the dewobins.

Below him lay the city of Dresdyn, strangely quiet. Even from this height he should have seen indications of life by now. Perhaps even a single lantern in a house window. Surely the church would have a light. Unless the spirit of Brunster Thadius Oldwell had succeeded in destroying them all.

He paced along the shelf's edge, fire seething along his sword's blade. He dragged its point along the stone and watched the sparks fly. Why did the stone not glow at the sword's touch?

Something had happened down there. In his absence something had changed for the worse.

He raised the sword in both hands and ignited his entire body with the living fire. Perhaps someone in Dresdyn would notice.

Into the darkness he shouted, "Ho! My brothers of Dresdyn, awake. It is I the Lord Warrior." Though the living fire raged around his body a while longer, he heard no answer. He lowered the sword, allowing his anger to cool. The sword's fire abated but its glow persisted.

A deep fear nudged at his heart, for he knew the truth. He had waited too long. He dropped to his knees and bowed his head, closing his eyes. Only the Almighty could help those people now, and he begged that God would grant that he and his sword might be the tools by which the people could be saved.

Letting himself over the edge of the cliff, he hung by one hand and stabbed the burning blade up to its hilt in the rock face. Grasping the handle with both hands he summoned the fire from the sword. As the blade burned through the stone, Ilfedo descended into the darkness. Sparks showered his armor as he slid down the cliff and the living fire blazed from the sword, leaving a thin line of molten rock up the towering wall of stone. The sword screeched against the stone, plunging him toward the outskirts of the city of Dresdyn.

Denser segments of stone jarred the sword, threatening to shake him free. He clung to it with all his strength and felt the living fire spread, renewing his body with energy, albeit at a slower rate. His feet thudded to the floor of the cavern and he drew the sword out of the rock.

For a moment he stared at his sword. Was it possible that the weapon was weakening? Was his intense use of it draining its power? He shook off the thought. The Hold of living fire still burned in the Hidden Realm and it was the source of the sword's strength.

Dropping to one knee, Ilfedo rested his forehead against his fists as he held the crystalline pommel of the sword of the dragon. An aura of light grew from his armor and the sword, so that when he stood again he could see a little distance in each direction.

He pointed the sword ahead and blasted fire from the sword's tip. It did not take long before he found one of the outlying houses. First he saw the short picket fence, then the rotting walls and collapsed timbers of the house's roof. He picked his way around the building and found the next in a similar condition. He suspected he was very near the haunted house yet could not determine its position until his light revealed a broad road.

Stepping onto the road, he kept his back to the cliff and also to the remnants of the haunted house. He did not wish to revisit that place. He knew it was there, as well as the condemned church across the way.

Ahead of him, the highway led into the heart of the city. Like the spoke of an enormous wagon wheel it pointed straight ahead to where it would converge with the city's other highways.

All was quiet. If this had been an abandoned city above ground perhaps a breeze might have stirred the air, but those were rare in this place and seemed only to come from the depths of adjoining caverns in the underworld.

He strode down the highway, wondering if any unfriendly eyes were watching him. The city was unchanged from his previous visit. Some of the houses were dilapidated, porches rotted and roofs caved in. Other homes were solid structures, well maintained by their residents. Children's toys lay abandoned on the moss lawns in front of several homes.

He paused beside a two-story home with blue siding and white trim. There was an unlit lantern resting in the window on the second floor. He pushed open the gate and crossed the front yard. The porch boards did not even creak as he ascended the steps and walked to the door. He knocked three times and waited for several minutes. But there was no response. "It is I, Lord Ilfedo," he called. "Is anyone in there?" Still no one answered.

Turning the door handle, he pushed it open and

let himself inside, holding the sword of the dragon before him. The darkness receded before the radiant weapon, revealing the room and its contents. Beside the living room fireplace sat a wooden rocking chair with a small pile of yarn on its seat. He crouched beside the fireplace and held his hands over the coals. They were cold on the surface so he dug his fingers into them. Not even a hint of warmth.

Wiping his hand on his breastplate, he proceeded into the dining room. The table was clean, the dishes had been stacked in the cupboards. Even the silverware was in its proper place in the drawers. He ran his hand along the slick countertop. There was just the slightest trace of dust.

He directed his attention back into the living room, then climbed the stairwell. There were small paintings on the wall. Paintings of two young girls and their parents. The top of the stairs placed him in the midst of a short hallway with pink carpet on the floor and three closed doors.

Cautiously he opened the door at the far end of the hall. The rather large bed had been left tidy with sheets and pillows in their proper place and a large dresser against the wall did not have a single drawer open. He closed the door to that room and opened the next, a small bedroom with twin beds. On one pillow lay a doll, hand-sewn with scraggly yarn for hair.

He closed that door, too, and walked to the other end of the hall. Opening the final door, he peered inside. This room had two windows overlooking the front yard, although the extreme darkness outside prevented him from actually seeing anything except a narrow strip of moss that his sword's light revealed. The lone lantern that he had seen from outside sat in one of the windows, its tall glass chimney glinted in his sword's light. Even the brass fittings on its base had been freshly polished, though a hint of dust lay on the windowsill.

No one had been in this house for some time and no one had returned for their possessions. "Curse you, Brunster Thadius Oldwell," he said under his breath as he left the room and shut the door behind him. He descended the stairs and opened the front door. Glancing a last time at the abandoned living room, he shuddered. At this moment he would almost prefer a ghost to show itself. At least then he would have the option of interrogating it.

He slammed the door behind him and thundered down the porch steps. "Where are you?" he screamed into the darkness. "Where are my people!"

He did not wait for the silence that he knew would follow. With purposeful steps he strode down the highway, ignoring the homes that had fallen into ruin and those that stood whole.

The frustration he felt built his pent-up rage and the sword's flames coursed over his arms and surged over his body. He knew that he must be an electrifying sight in the darkness but he found comfort in the fact that his aura spread farther than it had before and allowed him to see a good distance in all directions.

The land rose beneath him and he turned down the side road where he knew the Church of the Seekers had been built. When he arrived, he stood before the stone-fronted structure and called out, "Everett Matthaliah, if you are still in this cursed city, speak up so that I may hear you."

For a minute he waited, yet the church was as silent as the rest of the city. He could not at first make out the belfry, so he approached within a dozen paces of the structure's base and raised his sword high. As the light washed over the belfry a chill ran down his spine, for the belfry had been broken and charred wood had fallen over the bell. Worse, the bodies of three men in pink robes hung over its edge, their sandaled feet dangling.

"No." Ilfedo dropped to his knees. "What happened?" he asked the corpses. "When I left this place the people had arisen with you. Oldwell was defeated. The people were free!"

At that moment a light grew in the distance above the city. A light that appeared as a thread high on the cavern wall. It spread, growing and overflowing the cavern wall. Small points of light separated from it and began descending the wall.

Ilfedo turned away from the dead monks and faced the awesome sight of nearly a thousand warriors of light following him into the dark city of Dresdyn. "And now, Oldwell," Ilfedo said, "I will occupy this city and spread a light of redemption throughout it. Hide in the dark shadows for now and gather your strength, for you know not what wrath you have awakened in me."

Like many streams of white light the army of the Hemmed Land descended the cavern wall. Ilfedo watched them for a long while until he spotted a blaze of silver off to one side making the descent alone into the city. He smiled at that. Oganna had no doubt elected to throw her own rope over the cliff's face and had proceeded to clamber down either by herself or with Ombre in close pursuit. Ilfedo bet on the latter half of his guess, for he knew Ombre too well to think that he would willingly let the princess enter the unknown by herself.

Directing his steps deeper into the heart of the city, Ilfedo crossed between homes and over green moss lawns. He crossed a roadway and another lawn, until at last his glowing aura revealed a high pink wall ahead of him. The dewobin factory. On his first visit to the city he had entered the factory and found a multitude of women and children hard at work harvesting the silk and the meat of the tiny, glowing dewobin birds.

The city council had delegated the poor of their communities to work the factory to provide for their families, while the fathers had been conscripted into the city guard. Ilfedo remembered the little man, Everett, the kind shepherd of the Church of the Seekers. "Their fathers have been conscripted into the city guard and sent into the tunnels on the far side of our city," Everett had said of the child laborers. "They fight to safeguard us from a race of black beasts that sometimes encroach upon our territory."

Ilfedo shook the memory out of his head. Now was not the time to reminisce. He strode a short distance farther and found one of the thirteen heavy stone doors that accessed the interior of the long structure. The sword fed strength into his arms as he grasped the door and slowly pulled it open. The effort exhausted him, for the door was exceedingly heavy. But as it opened, rays of pink light shot from inside the factory.

Ilfedo stood back and held the sword above his head, poising it to stab the door. The blade glowed white-hot, fire sprinted along it, and he ran forward, burying it up to its hilt in the stone. Then he released the sword's energy and the living fire tore through the stone door, fragmenting it into a hundred pieces. The blast threw him into the air, jerking his hands from the sword.

He landed hard on the street and his breath was knocked from him. He lay in the darkness, separated from his weapon and not knowing how to find it again. Within moments, though, thousands of pink, glowing dewobins shot out of the factory. They swarmed upward, spiraling in a unified dance. A small band of them divided from the main group and circled over his head. Like waves of the sea they spread through the air, illuminating the way before him to the shattered factory door and the magnificent sword that now lay on the ground.

Ilfedo laughed as he stood and gazed up at the beautiful creatures. "I am relieved to see you, my little friends," he said, spreading his arms. The dewobins fluttered around him, many of them landing on his arms and twittering in his ears.

At last they fled after their companions, heading for the distant and dark recesses of the cavern ceiling. Ilfedo walked over to his fallen sword, pausing to watch the swarm still spilling out of the factory. When he picked up the weapon, he ran farther down the factory's length, stopping at the next door. He drove his blade into that one as well and blasted it apart.

Again he was thrown, though this time he rolled with the fall and stood immediately to his feet. Now the swarms fled from both doorways, and still they came. It was as if the factory had been stuffed to the brim with every dewobin in the cavern.

The darkness receded from the city as the glowing birds coated the cavern ceiling, and Ilfedo laughed long and loud. He sat on the street and watched the transformation.

It took a long while for the factory to empty of

its dewobin prisoners, but when it had the city was lighted as it had been before. Certainly not as bright as sunlight, but enough that his forces could explore it.

Ilfedo retrieved his sword and sheathed it. The tramp, tramp of boots on gravel alerted him to his reinforcements' impending arrival and he spun on his heel. He could now see the city hall with the stone monoliths surrounding it, as well as the giant statue of Brunster Thadius Oldwell standing behind it. That cursed thing should be brought down in a pile of rubble, then melted and used for a latrine. The face of the building still bore the marks of the flames from Oldwell's green sword, yet remarkably the flames had not spread farther. The doors were blackened but the building was intact.

He pulled his attention from the statue and walked instead to the head of the main highway. He put the communal fountain to his back and faced the long road. The warriors of light marched toward him, their armor blazing pure white light.

A thousand strong they marched toward him, the last bands of them sliding down the ropes that had been thrown over the face of the cliff far in the background. Their light excelled that of the dewobins. It was as if the sun had at last found a peephole in the desert floor and shone through the cavern ceiling.

As they approached, the man at their lead raised his sword, arresting Ilfedo's attention. It was Commander Veil. With gestures of his thick arms he shunted small groups of warriors to the sides of the highway as they advanced, leaving them in strong lines facing the abandoned buildings, guarding the army's flanks while the main body continued its advance between them.

When the column had reached a hundred paces distance from him, Ilfedo raised his arm and Veil raised his in return. The lines of white-armored warriors slowed to a stop and each man clanked his sword against his right shoulder. They stood there in silence, but in the distance the clinking of still more warriors could be heard as they let themselves onto the cavern floor and assembled at the rear.

A figure in a silver dress emerged alongside the head of the column. Oganna walked toward Ilfedo, her blond hair tied back in a thick bun with the excess hair hanging somewhat wildly. She sheathed her narrow crimson blade. On her belt she wore her deadly blade boomerang, and the viper moved in a gradual circuit of her neck.

The glowing silver dress receded from her body as she released her hold on her sword. She had long ago named her sword the Avenger, and aptly so for with it she had avenged the deaths of many innocent people and preserved the lives of many good men under his command. "Father," Oganna said, her eyes glancing at their strange surroundings, "truly this place is hard to describe. It feels lonely, hopeless. There is a dark oppression here."

Ilfedo nodded solemnly. "We have much to do." He gestured with his hand and Commander Veil stepped forward, coming close to him.

"Your orders for the men, my lord?" Veil asked.

"Have the command tents erected here, but we will establish our headquarters in the city hall," Ilfedo said.

Veil nodded.

"Follow me, commander." Ilfedo walked back in the direction of the dewobin factory, stopping when his line of sight was clear to the left. He pointed to the large building with the four stone monoliths surrounding it. "That is the city hall. Due to its centralized location it seems the ideal place to organize a search for the missing inhabitants of this city."

As Veil left Ilfedo's side, lumbering over to the waiting warriors, Oganna spoke up again. "Father, if I may, the women who have accompanied the men should be situated near you. It would give them a greater opportunity to respond immediately to any needs they can tend to."

Ilfedo smiled. "Such as food—"

She looked back at him with a sober expression. "And medical care, should it be needed."

"Of course, let it be done as you suggest, my daughter." Ilfedo watched as she darted back in the direction she had come, heading for the rear of the column where no doubt the women awaited her.

"My lord," Ombre shouted as he emerged from behind the first lines of waiting warriors. He jogged over to Ilfedo's side, clapping him on the shoulder. "I think this journey is doing me some good, Ilfedo," he said. "It has given me something to focus on. This underground city is an incredible achievement. Although—" His eyes turned to look over the abandoned homes and businesses. "You did say this place was full of people, right?"

Ilfedo shook his head. "If I had been able to stay a little while longer, every soul in this place might have been saved. As it is, I have returned to an empty city and all we are left with is a mystery." He pointed his sword toward a few different streets, indicating the houses there. "We are going to need to conduct a thorough search to determine if everyone is truly missing, or if there is another explanation. I hate to think of the possibilities."

Ombre patted Ilfedo's back and looked up at him with a gentle encouragement. "Let's not cry rain before we even feel the first drops, brother. We know that we are in God's hands and so are those missing people."

Ilfedo relaxed his shoulders and lowered his sword's point to the ground. Ombre's words were exactly what he had needed to hear at that moment, a good reminder to leave his worry behind and instead focus on what could be done.

The next hours were filled by menial, albeit important tasks. Ilfedo delegated his orders through Veil, Ombre, and Oganna. Veil dispatched groups of twenty warriors to search the nearest homes for any signs of life. Ombre oversaw the raising of the tents and instructed the officers as they organized the army to encamp around the city hall.

Oganna kept her crimson-bladed sword unsheathed and raised it above her head. Following this beacon, a small group of women trooped down the highway, smiling and nodding to the armored warriors. The warriors snapped their swords to their thighs, shifting sideways to make a path for them. The lead women conferred with Oganna in low voices as she led them over to the city hall, until they stood on its lowest step. The women kept wary eyes on the viper coiled about her neck, for the creature slicked its forked tongue in and out of its mouth so that thick beads of venom dripped to the ground.

Ilfedo, however, marched up to the building and climbed the steps ahead of them. He had no intention of allowing his daughter to enter that place first. Not until it had first been checked. He could hear a strange sound inside, as of the buzzing of many flies. If Oldwell had hidden himself in the city hall it would be better if Ilfedo discovered him, instead of Oganna stumbling into his green blade.

"Father—" Oganna said, as if to ask a question. Her voice trailed off as he grasped the high double doors fronting the hall and pulled them open.

Through the doors an enormous room could be seen. He heard Oganna let out a startled cry and one of the women with her collapsed in a faint. When Ilfedo had come here before, the room in front of him had been filled with government officials dressed in pink clothing woven from dewobin silk. This time the room smelled of rotting flesh. Heaped in the center of the floor around the blue marble pillar that stood there, were a couple hundred bodies.

As Ilfedo slowly walked over the smooth floor, the buzzing of flies deafened his ears. Most of the bodies wore the red and bronze armor of the Dresdyn city guards. He rested his hand on one of the dead men's helmets. "I am sorry, brethren," he whispered. "I should have been here with you. Then there would have been no need for you to die."

The helmet slipped off of the dead man's head and thick gray hair spilled out of it. This particular guard had been an older man, probably only holding his status as a guard in a ceremonial position. But the old man's hair had covered the face of another victim beneath him. Ilfedo's tears roll down his cheeks as he pulled the hair away from the second face.

The face that stared back at him made his blood feel like ice. She had blond hair and her skin was as soft as silk, and Ilfedo knew her. He dropped to his knees, sheathed his sword, and pulled the little girl's body out of the heap. He clutched her to his chest, weeping uncontrollably as her little legs dangled over his arm.

A wailing rose behind him and he did not need to turn around to know that the women of the Hemmed Land were sharing his sorrow. Few of them had ever seen death on this scale, and fewer had witnessed it so close at hand.

Oganna stepped beside him, crouching close to the floor. He glanced at her through his blurred vision. Such deep sadness filled her face and her brow knit as if confused on some matter. But she let him weep for a long while, her own gentle sobs melding with his deeper ones.

Even the viper Neneila did not offer comment. The creature swiveled its head, its beady eyes taking in the scene as it wrapped its tail a bit tighter around Oganna's neck.

At last he stood, still clutching the little girl's body, and strode back toward the double door.

Ombre appeared in the doorway, hesitating as his eyes took in the grisly sight. His gaze rested on Ilfedo and he walked into the hall, meeting his friend halfway. Grasping Ilfedo by the arms, Ombre stared down at the little girl's body. "For now let the dead remain in here, brother. The sight of you like this would only trouble your men if you go outside."

Ilfedo shook his head. Ombre was right. Frustratingly, he was right. Ilfedo turned to the heap and started to return the child's body to it. His arms shook beyond his control and her body began to slip limply, threatening to dash her head on the floor. Oganna's gentle hands pressed the little girl back into Ilfedo's arms. Her blue-gold eyes seemed to look right through his chest, seeing his heart and soul.

Ombre grasped her shoulder. "Let him put the body back, Oganna. We must search for survivors of this massacre." He let out a long breath. "If indeed there are any survivors."

Oganna shook her head, eyes still focused on Ilfedo. "What is it, Father? Why?" She paused to glance around the room. "Of all these people, why did you pull out this little girl?"

Ilfedo drew back from his friend and from his daughter. He slung the girl's body over his shoulder and felt for the sword of the dragon. When his fingers found it he let it absorb his rage. "Remember, my sword. Remember and be prepared to deal to him as he has dealt with them."

The sword burned with living fire, simmering in its sheath, but offered no response. The flies in Ilfedo's vicinity dropped dead as his armor of living fire radiated heat around him.

Oganna's eyes widened. She pointed at the little girl's body. "Is this the child you saved from the haunted house?" Her question shot out with more energy than perhaps she had intended it to, but when Ilfedo responded by gritting his teeth even Ombre took a step back.

"Oh no. Not that little girl." Ombre put his hand to his forehead. "Of all the people in this city, Oldwell killed that one. Brother, is that really her?"

Ilfedo closed the distance between them. "I came to this city and God granted me the strength to save this one soul, yet now Brunster Thadius Oldwell has done this wickedness. Take her body and see that it is wrapped for burial," he commanded. As a stunned Ombre took the body into his arms, Ilfedo walked out of City Hall.

Standing atop the hall steps, Ilfedo ignored the women weeping there. His voice augmented by the sword's energy, he shouted for Commander Veil. When the man barreled to the bottom of the steps, Ilfedo pointed his sword around the city. "Have the men found anything to report?"

"They have not, my lord."

Ilfedo nodded and pointed his sword behind the city hall. "Back that way and to the left you will find the mayor's residence.

Send a division of twenty men to search it." He lowered the sword's point to the step and held up his fist. "No one, and I mean not a single person, is to venture deeper into the cavern without my express consent."

Veil saluted, then said, "What of your men who are searching the homes for survivors?"

"Let them finish their search of buildings in this vicinity, then I want them to pull back to the main highway." Ilfedo sheathed his sword again. "They will await further commands from me at that time."

With another salute, Commander Veil marched off up the road with a body of forty warriors behind him.

Ilfedo summoned Oganna out of the hall and a messenger soon arrived to inform them that the mayor's residence had been searched and found empty. "Bring the women there," Ilfedo told his daughter. "There is no need for them to remain here." He descended the steps and faced the unexplored parts of the city.

Behind him the women gathered their supplies and bustled away from the city hall, following Oganna and the messenger toward the mayor's residence. "Dry your tears, ladies," he heard her say to them. "You do not want to be the enemy's means of demoralizing our troops. For now we must forget the dead in order to care for the living."

As Ilfedo began to walk toward the unexplored southwest corner of the city, where he knew the library to be, a shout arose from his men. Panting, a warrior of light skidded to a halt beside him and bowed. A grin filled his features. "My lord, I bring good news! We have found survivors."

THE REST OF
THE STORY

The gray home in front of Ilfedo was familiar to him. For the first time since entering Dresdyn, he allowed his body to rest. His glowing warriors stood row upon row behind him and their ranks filled the narrow street, spilling into the side roads and the highways of the city. The search continued for more survivors of Oldwell's slaughter, giving him hope that what he was now witnessing was only the beginning of his findings.

A young man hobbled away from the house along the stone walk that led away from the porch, a large book tucked under his arm. His cane struck the path with a *rit-a-tat, rit-a-tat* and his peg leg inserted a *thud* into the rhythm. *Rit-a-tat, rit-a-tat, thud!*

Ilfedo remembered fondly when he had first walked by this home and Everett had pointed out this same young man. A teacher of "history and literature and math at High Glory Academy. Or, as it is commonly known, his house," Everett had said.

A line of boys and girls followed the young man out of the house. They appeared to range in age from ten to sixteen years old. When the young man stopped in front of Ilfedo, the boys and girls gathered behind him.

"Ardius, it is good to see you." Ilfedo spread his arms wide. "God be praised. It is good to see all of you!"

Ardius took another step forward on his peg leg. His green eyes evaluated Ilfedo from head to toe, then rested on the sword still flaming in Ilfedo's hand. He did not say a word as he limped sideways to gaze up and down the lines of warriors who, to him, must have seemed to fill the city.

The warriors of light divided beside Ilfedo as Oganna stepped through their midst. The warriors closed ranks behind her. Avenger was still in Oganna's sheath, so her body was not garbed in silver but her countenance filled with radiance as she looked at the children. She did not take note of Ardius, instead she stepped past him and pulled two of the children to her in a warm embrace. She knelt in their midst.

Ilfedo did a quick count of the little heads. There were around thirty children in the group. Ardius shifted again on his peg leg, this time half-turning his back to Ilfedo. He watched as the youngest children broke into tears. Watched as Oganna offered words of comfort and healing.

"You are safe now. Do not cry. We are here to rescue all of you." Her assurances washed over the children in a flood of warmth.

Soon the children put questions to Oganna. Where were their parents? Had she found them? Why had the dewobins gone dark for a long while and why had they at last come back to light the city?

Oganna shushed their questions, stroking one child's hair. "What is important at this moment is that you are safe at last." She stood, though her hands lingered on the children's shoulders. She turned to Ardius and smiled at him. "I am afraid we have not been introduced," she said.

For a few long moments Ardius stood statue-like. He might as well have been frozen in place. The line of his mouth set straight so that it neither smiled nor frowned. Finally his mouth twitched amusedly and he shook his head. "Wow, woman, you are a wonder," he said. "Do you practice how to turn every situation into a winning political move, or is it just habit?"

Ilfedo glared down at Ardius. The man's response seemed so indiscriminate. Indeed, he had inferred that Oganna had selfish motives for comforting the children. His words were an infuriating insult to the woman of character that she had proven herself to be. He imagined, just for a moment, that it would be permissible for him as the Lord Warrior to punch this pompous teacher in the side of his pompous face.

From the ranks of warriors Ombre stepped out. He stormed toward Ardius, fists clenched. "You fool, you will not speak in such a manner toward her."

Ilfedo held out his arm against Ombre's chest, bringing him to a halt before he could reach Ardius.

Ardius ignored the commotion. His gaze had fixated on Oganna, holding to her as if the world would crack under him if he did not. He widened his stance, hands comfortably resting on his cane.

Oganna smiled in an amused way and gave Ardius a slight nod. "Thank you," she said.

Ardius chuckled as he took her hand in one of his. "My name is Ardius, my lady."

"Well, Ardius, you should speak with my father. He has important questions, and perhaps you can help him find answers."

Ardius bowed, kissed her hand, then slowly turned to Ilfedo. He dipped a lower bow. "Welcome back, my Lord Warrior. Your presence here has been sorely missed. The people of this city suffered a great evil on the day you left them, and now it would appear that I and these children are all that remains of our civilization."

"Do not be quick to assume that, Ardius." Ilfedo put his hand on Ombre's shoulder. "Ombre, please bring Ardius and his students to the mayor's residence. I want you to personally see to their comfort until I join you."

Ombre nodded, then stepped past Ardius and smiled down at a little girl. He offered his hand and she took it, smiling back up at him.

"I like your sword," the child said.

"Well, thank you!" Ombre shrugged his shoulders. "Do you want something to eat?"

Ardius and the children formed a line behind Ombre as he led them through the ranks of soldiers. The children stared at the warriors' glowing white armor and Ilfedo heard one of them say to Ardius, "Is that what sunlight looks like?"

"I do not know," Ardius replied.

When the children were out of sight, Ilfedo

summoned Commander Veil. "Well done, commander. Now, if you will, instruct the men to resume the search but not to enter the southern portion of this city. Fan the divisions out and have them block off the southern portion. No one enters those areas until I give the word."

"Understood," Veil said. "Sir, what of the bodies that you found impaled atop the church?"

Ilfedo felt his shoulders slump. He had almost forgotten the fate of those dear men. "Have the bodies taken down immediately and bury them in the cemetery by the church."

Veil saluted and barreled over to three of his captains. With his arms he gestured, indicating where he wanted the troops deployed.

Oganna grabbed Ilfedo's hands and grinned up at him. "Father, it is wonderful. At least we found survivors! You must feel relieved."

Ilfedo hardened his expression. "Why did you let Ardius speak to you in such a manner? He treated you with the utmost discourtesy and you seemed to enjoy it."

Oganna laughed as she let go of his hands and started to walk with him back to the heart of the city. "Oh, I did enjoy it! Ardius regarded us with suspicion when we arrived. I think he was testing my character. He wanted to see if I would defend my pride, but he also wanted to see how people who know me would react when he addressed me in such a manner. When Uncle Ombre came to my defense Ardius noticed and appreciated it."

Ilfedo put his arm around his daughter's shoulders. "You believe Ardius wanted to understand your character, and he wanted to evaluate you based on that? Cunning fellow, that one. I will have to keep my eye on him."

"Cunning?" Oganna glanced at a small house as they walked by. A seesaw rested in the front yard, a little doll sat on its raised seat. "I suppose you could say that Ardius is cunning. But intelligent seems a better word for him. He is even sensitive in a unique way. The children certainly trust him."

Ilfedo sheathed his sword so that his glowing aura vanished. He looked up at the cavern ceiling, that pink dewobin 'sky,' and he sighed. "I believe you are right," he said. "When I was here the last time, Everett spoke to me about Ardius. It was his assertion that among all of my new subjects Ardius was the one whom I should trust the most, but one whose trust I would have to work hard to earn."

"That seems strange," Oganna said. "I would have thought that Everett would have said that about Elhandra the prophetess."

Ilfedo wore a thoughtful expression as they turned onto the highway leading to the heart of the city. "I do not think Everett meant it as an affront to either himself or Elhandra. Everett took for granted that Elhandra was above reproach and he knew that I fully trusted him. If I were to pick two people in this city to trust with you, I would have picked them."

"You say that, Father, and yet," her laugh tinkled on the still air of the cavern, "and yet I cannot help but point out that the only people that we have found alive in this city are those who were under Ardius's protection."

Ilfedo looked at her and frowned. It was true. He

could not deny it. Strange as it seemed, the only people who had escaped the slaughter had been the children under Ardius's tutelage. Perhaps he had been wrong about the younger man. Everett had seen beyond Ardius's physical limitations and judged him of strong character and a sound mind. In the end, Ardius had preserved a remnant of his people and delivered them safely into Ilfedo's care.

"I will have to get to know this Ardius fellow better," Ilfedo admitted. "Or I will let you do so. His admiration for you was almost immediate and that sort of connection to him is stronger, I would think, than his loyalty to any Lord Warrior."

"Or, maybe you misjudge him again." Oganna drew out her sword, letting it sheathe her body in the silver dress. "If Ardius is of strong character then he will put the security of his people above his personal preferences. You are his Lord Warrior. He will defer to your judgment and not to mine."

Ilfedo grunted. "It does not matter. If opportunity presents itself, and if you are inclined to do so, engage him in conversation. I would very much like to understand him better."

For a while longer they walked without speaking. Every now and then the dewobin light would shift as groups of the birds shifted position to other portions of the cavern's ceiling.

Under her breath, Oganna spoke, yet it was so soft that Ilfedo could not hear. The only words he picked out were, "Ardius . . . what a fascinating mind."

"Oganna," he asked gently, "I could not hear what you said."

"It is nothing. I was only thinking aloud." She

smiled up at him and changed the subject. "Did you want to go to the mayor's mansion? I was surprised at the extent of luxury some of these people have managed to maintain despite their living underground. I think even Vortain would have been comfortable staying here, if there had been a little sunlight."

They walked together down the streets of Dresdyn. The dewobins fluttered in the cavern high above, shedding soft pink light on the path. Throughout the city Ilfedo's warriors spread their light into its darkened buildings, yet the only survivors they found were those whom Ardius had so wisely hidden in his home. Ilfedo had set his mind with a sober determination. He prayed that Ardius would be able to clear some of the mystery surrounding the people's disappearance.

When he arrived at the mayor's mansion Ilfedo hesitated. He felt drained and ready to rest. This had been a long journey. He shook off the feeling and walked down the stone path to the front doors. Pulling them open he entered the hallway on the lower level. Pink carpeting covered the floor and continued up the wide stairway to the second floor. Three boys from Ardius's class darted out of a door at the hall's end, laughing as they opened a door on the hallway's opposite side. The boys darted through and shut the door behind them.

They found Ardius sitting at the long dining room table with ten of his students. Two of the women from the Hemmed Land walked the perimeter, calling into the adjoining kitchen when a child wanted more food. A chandelier hung from the ceiling and a mirror had been inset above it so as to reflect the light of its soft-burning lamps. Ilfedo glanced into the kitchen and found five other women working inside. They chatted as they cooked and stoked the twin stoves with more logs. The logs were not wood in the same sense as people in the Hemmed Land were accustomed to, for the people of Dresdyn burned logs they had cut from tree-size mushrooms that grew in the tunnels and other caverns of the underground world.

Ilfedo left the women to their work while he sat at the table with Ardius. Oganna sat with him and both of them listened closely as Ardius began to tell what had happened to the people of the city on the day that Ilfedo was taken away from them.

* * *

Ardius pushed his plate to the side, and rested his fork on it. He took a final sip from his cup. "I was there that day," he said. "And I remember the rage in Bromstead's eyes. He looked like a man truly possessed by the evil spirit of our long-dead Lord Warrior. To tell the truth, when word first reached me that an evil spirit had possessed the body of Bromstead, I did not believe it." Ardius held up a finger, pausing for effect. "Lord Ilfedo, you had given our people the opportunity to win the fight that came from that event. You even gave us a new ally, the black beast from the Observatory. But the spirit had full control of the body of our powerful captain of the city guard and we were no match for that combination, though some of the people thought otherwise at first."

Ilfedo faced the possessed body of Bromstead on the street in front of the Observatory. In Bromstead's hand was the evil blade of Brunster Thadius Oldwell, for the spirit of that long-dead Lord Warrior had possessed Bromstead's body. The blade glowed with an unfamiliar green light.

Ilfedo tackled Bromstead from behind, throwing him to

the ground. He rolled and poised his fists to strike, but somehow Bromstead got to his feet first and held forth his green blade poised to stab Ilfedo's neck. From above their heads Ilfedo's loyal nuvitor dove through the air, dealing Bromstead a wound. The man dropped his sword and grasped the bird by its neck.

It was then that Ilfedo had grabbed the green blade and attempted to use it on the man, but it had turned against Ilfedo instead. The blade stabbed itself through Ilfedo's lower ribcage, pinning him to the ground, for just as the sword of the dragon could not be turned against Ilfedo the sword of Brunster Thadius Oldwell could not be used against its master.

As Ilfedo lay wounded on the ground, Bromstead drew the sword out of Ilfedo's flesh and turned it against the city guards. He slew many of them. Ten fell. Twenty fell. Thirty of them fell to the street helpless before the sorcerer's weapon. For whenever a sword was raised against it, the green blade cut it in two.

Bromstead was a giant of a man. He charged toward the heart of the city. Ardius, tears running down his face, hobbled after the infuriated mob of men and women who pursued the possessed man.

Clad in their heavy armor the city guards met him en mass on the steps of the city hall. Bromstead slipped into their midst, his blade flashing green. Before long their blood covered his blade and the mass of their bodies twisted on the steps around him.

Pink-clad monks from the Church of the Seekers urged the people back as the glowing figure of Ilfedo miraculously appeared, striding toward Bromstead with the flaming sword in his hand. The people huddled in the side streets and watched as Ilfedo called to the madman. "Bromstead, hearken to me… You are in there still. Surely you have not been destroyed. You are a man of honor, so how did this spirit come to reside in you? How can you let him use you?"

Ardius sighed deeply and stared down at the table. "You know this part of the story already, my lord. I do not mean to bore you with details of that which is past, but now we come to the part that changed everything. For when you came forth to meet Brunster Thadius Oldwell in battle and brought the black creature Arvidane to fight with you, I believed you would win. Oldwell seemed to gain the upper hand, and perhaps you wanted him to believe that, for when the black creature came to your aid it took Oldwell by surprise.

"The creature took the green sword out of his hands and threw it so that it stuck in a distant building. The people rushed out of their hiding places, so many of them that it took my breath away. They took the sword and spirited it away from Oldwell's reach. Rarely have I seen my people act so decisively and never have I known them to rally in such a way. Oldwell's slaughter had been demoralizing, to say the least, but the people had rallied to you. Some even ran up the steps to the city hall doors and put out the flames so that the building did not burn down.

"Then something happened that changed everything, for the ring upon your finger grew into enormous proportions so that it appeared to be a living dragon made of yellow gold. Oldwell attacked the black creature, but it threw him back with little effort.

"The dragon of gold dragged you away from us. It moved with uncanny speed straight up the wall of our cavern and vanished with you." Ardius hung his head as he described the expressions on the faces of the people when Ilfedo was taken away from them at such a critical moment. His shoulders shook, forcing him to stop the telling as he reigned in his emotions.

Ilfedo reached out and grasped Ardius's shoulder. "I am so sorry. It was not as I wished it, but as the prophets had determined it should be. For me there was no choice in the matter. My task here was dropped in the urgency of another matter, one of far greater consequence, and the ring set me back on that path. It drove me mad not knowing what had happened to you here, and further that I could not immediately return to you."

Ardius gently pushed back Ilfedo's hand. "I do not lay the blame on you. It was the evil of Brunster Thadius Oldwell that brought this upon us." He waved his hand as if dismissing the very notion. "Now, please give me a moment more to speak, as this is difficult but I do wish you to know what I saw. When the spirit in Bromstead realized that you had been removed from the battle, it caused its host to pick up two swords from those that had fallen with the city guards. With these weapons in his hands Oldwell attacked the black beast first, driving both blades through its chest, instantly dropping it to the ground."

Ilfedo trembled upon hearing these words and covered his face with his hands, leaning forward. "This is too much to bear," he said. "Poor Arvidane. His life should have begun on that day. Not ended."

"I do not believe the beast is dead," Ardius offered, and in his voice Ilfedo heard the first hint of a hope that had been preserved.

Ilfedo uncovered his face. "Tell me of him."

"As Oldwell began to slay all of those within his reach, the black beast tried to rise. Its claws came within inches of impaling Oldwell's back. But it must have lost much blood for a veritable pool of red covered the stones upon which it lay. I did not see what ultimately happened to the beast, for a contingent of city guards marched out of the southern half of our city and held back Oldwell. Though he, like a madman, laid his attacks upon them as thickly as dust.

"I spotted Elhandra the prophetess as well as Everett in the midst of the fray. They appeared to be approaching the fallen black beast, though the sight of them was soon cut off from me. More of the city's guard rushed upon the scene, but at their head was Nomand, a troublesome, red-haired politician turned soldier. He had always spoken in great admiration of our former Lord Warrior and his face was filled with purpose in that moment.

"Nomand rallied his guardsmen to the aid of Oldwell, and declared for all to hear that he would stand alone if necessary to see the return of so great a leader as Brunster Thadius Oldwell. The fighting ceased as people evaluated him and his allies, but another man ran up and threw himself at Oldwell's feet. 'I also will serve you, great one,' the man said.

"At that moment Nomand pulled Oldwell's green sword from under his cape, dropped on one knee, and held it forth. Oldwell grasped it in his hands, and such a wicked smile played across his features that I never will forget it. The blade glowed harshly as he turned it upon those who remained faithful to you.

"I could not bear to watch what I knew would be a slaughter, so I hurried away from that place. The fathers and mothers of my students noticed my departure and they followed me. I turned to them with great sorrow and admitted that I believed the battle to be lost. They begged me to take the children with me, saying that they trusted only me to see to their well-being. As they shoved their children into a huddle around me, they declared that they believed that you, Ilfedo, would one day return to rescue the remnant of our people from Oldwell's madness.

"I took their children back to my home and we have hidden there ever since, venturing out only to find food and to dispose of our waste." He took a fork and stabbed it into the table. "I do not know what became of my people. The city streets have been deserted and the dewobins went dark the day after the metal dragon dragged you off."

Ilfedo smote his fist on the table. "You have no idea where Oldwell is! Or the people, or if Arvidane is alive. What of Everett and Elhandra?" He shoved back his chair and rose. "My apologies, Ardius, but if that is all the information that you can provide I must be going. Time is a precious commodity when the lives of people are at stake."

As Ilfedo left the room he heard Ogannna thank Ardius for the information. Then she excused herself from the table and ran up beside Ilfedo.

"Give me time to think," Ilfedo said to her. "Remain here for now and I will return shortly. A quiet walk should help to clear my mind."

"I could walk with you," she said.

"No, my daughter. That would be a distraction at the moment. I must walk this city alone." He opened the house door and stepped outside. The moss lawn was thick around his feet and the air slightly moist and cool.

Oganna's face tightened as he directed his steps southward. "Where will you walk?"

"Stay here," he said to her and he held up his hand. He settled his gaze upon her and was pleased when she lowered her gaze to the ground. She would do as he asked. There was no question in his mind.

He walked along the city streets, circling the vicinity of City Hall. A line of glowing warriors stood between him and the southeastern portion of the city. His sword was still in its scabbard as he wrapped his fingers over its smooth, crystalline hilt, and connected its power to his body. White armor grew over his body, flames licking along its surface. Like a second skin it moved with him, never impeding his movements, always feeding his limbs with extra energy.

Ilfedo waved his warriors aside and they parted before him. When he had passed through their midst, they closed ranks behind him again and a short officer took several steps toward him, raising his arm in salute.

"My lord, shall we commence a search of the lower parts of the city?"

"No, you shall not." Ilfedo kept his gaze upon the unexplored buildings and quickened his pace. "If anyone asks, tell them not to follow. Understood?"

He heard the clink of armor as the man saluted again. "As you wish, my lord."

Ilfedo proceeded down streets that he remembered well from his first visit to Dresdyn. The lonely buildings offered silence for company and he reveled in it. He let his fingers trail off of the sword of the dragon and, once the connection had been broken, the armor peeled away from his body, fizzing out of existence as it returned into the sword.

He passed a toy shop, its tall windows filled with various dolls, wooden soldiers, and colorful blocks. On the other side of the street the door to a barber shop hung open and inside were two chairs and a long counter with a pair of scissors and a razor atop it. Farther on stood a blacksmith's shop with an open front and living quarters built above it.

Turning down a side road, Ilfedo found other deserted homes. He ignored the mystery each of them offered, for he had set his mind on one goal. One building that might be of use to him in his search for survivors. There were paths out of this city that led into other underworld places and the people of this city had known those paths. He needed a map. He could have asked Ardius to draw one, but that would have been a mostly futile effort. Ardius might know where the paths were, but he would not understand their intricacies as well as someone who had traveled them. His peg leg had prevented him from joining the city guard and only the city guard ventured far beyond Dresdyn's boundaries.

Reaching the end of the street, Ilfedo stepped onto a broader road and continued to walk. His destination was close. He could almost smell the old volumes and scrolls in the archive.

PATH INTO
THE UNDERWORLD

The pink dewobin sky began to wink out as the tiny birds went to sleep. Ilfedo stood on the street in front of the library, his fingers stroking the hilt of his sword. He left it in its sheath but let its power flow out to cover his body in the radiant armor. His aura of light illuminated the street and buildings around him for thirty paces or more.

The library was a high wood-faced structure, buttressed at its corners with pillars of red brick. Two round windows were set half-way up its face, their glistening panes separated by lead latticework. Fat iron letters over the entry door spelled out *Records Library* and twin pillars of blue marble rose on either side of the door, supporting a beam that ran the length of the building. A large clock, which had been set in the face of the building and a few feet beneath its peak, ticked away the seconds.

Ilfedo looked away from the library, then looked back up at the clock. Yes, it was still ticking. He had thought at first he was imagining it, for he thought that such a mechanism needed to be wound on a regular basis.

He strode up to the door and grasped the latch. The door swung inward with a cumbersome groan and he stepped through, shutting it gently behind him. A mere few yards separated the outer wall from a secondary, inner one that curved away from him on both sides. The space between the walls, like an enclosed breezeway, served little purpose and the air smelled of musty wood. A narrow stair stood off to one side with a thin handrail that he imagined would break should he attempt to use it for support, and the stairway proceeded to a small door high overhead. Very likely the door opened into a cleaning closet or storage space of some kind.

He looked away from the stair and faced the library door ahead of him. As he opened it and stepped through the inner wall the round library room opened before him. A broad stone desk stood to the side with a lantern on top of it. This he lit with a flash of fire from the hilt of his sword, then he followed the front wall, lighting four more lanterns that hung there. Mirrors had been placed strategically behind each of the lanterns so as to reflect the light out into the wide aisles of shelves. Books, parchments, and scrolls filled many of the shelves.

Twin staircases offered access to shelves built high in the walls on either side of the room. He climbed one of them, lighting a couple more lanterns that he found before returning to ground level. He searched the aisles but found no other sources of light. However, the lamps he had lit proved to be adequate enough. He released his hand from the sword. His aura vanished, replaced by the warm flickers of the library lanterns.

The semi-shadows that the lanterns cast down the aisles comforted him somehow. He retreated into the shadows. The books' spines were etched in gold on a black background and some of them were carved out of wood. He walked his fingers over the spines as he read their titles. *Oral Historical Traditions, The Isle of Privit, Prophecies of the Three.* He switched to the other side of the aisle. *The Many Uses of Mushroom Trees, Underworld Herbs for Healing, The Dewobin Cookbook.* Ilfedo chuckled as he re-read the last title. Those poor little birds had proved useful beyond measure to the people of Dresdyn, for clothing and for food.

He stood back and crossed his arms. What he was looking for was not on these shelves, but where would it be? He walked to the aisle's end, standing there and taking in the whole of his surroundings. The book volumes filled the middle aisles some twelve feet high. Off to the sides parchments had been stacked on narrow tables up against the staircases.

Ilfedo climbed one of the staircases and stood atop its landing. Like a broad shelf the landing jutted out from the wall. Shelves lined the wall, shelves that rose high above him and could only be accessed via a ladder. The ladder had wood rails, but its steps were fashioned of iron, and iron clamps connected it to a rod overhead that ran the length of the wall.

Climbing the ladder, Ilfedo scoured the shelves. Scrolls filled much of them. He descended the ladder and shifted it a few feet to the side before climbing it again. The search might have consumed many minutes or several hours. He did not care. The room was quiet, wonderfully so. During his search the only thing that disturbed him was an occasional scraping sound from high in the wall. No doubt a mouse busy in its nest.

He found a pile of rolled papers that had been tied with leather ribbons. Down the ladder again, this time with the rolled papers under his arm. Descending the stairs to the main floor, he stacked the papers on the stone desk and sat down. He unrolled the first paper and found a diagram of an unknown building. The next papers were pretty much the same, only of different structures. He had to make a trip up the other stairway and bring back a fresh stack of papers before he found what he was looking for.

Maps! These papers had been covered with detailed sketches of the layout of the City of Dresdyn. What mattered more was that other papers contained sketches of underground routes out of the city. Access points through tunnels that led into caverns, some enormous and some very small. The underground realm was an intricate network of passageways connecting Dresdyn to underground rivers, a lake, mushroom forests, and a place called Kraylan Abyss.

The mapmakers had laid out in great detail where some paths proved treacherous, for many paths skirted deep pits and passed over natural stone bridges. The underground was a treacherous place to travel, yet travel the people had been forced to do. Without these maps they easily could have been lost in the dark, left to wander forever without hope of rescue. Ilfedo shuddered at the thought and wondered, briefly, if the rash warrior James McCormick was in any of the places these maps covered. More than likely his body lay at the bottom of a pit in some cavern. Perhaps in the lair of the monkey beast.

Ilfedo sorted the maps that interested him from those that did not. He needed to narrow the parameters of his search if he was to figure out what had happened to the people of Dresdyn. In his heart he knew that, through an as-yet-unknown motivation, Brunster Thadius Oldwell had led the people out of their city and into the dark tunnels. Perhaps there was something out there that he wanted to retrieve, or something that he wanted of them?

Tucking a few of the maps under his arm, Ilfedo stood from the desk. It was time for him to go. He opened the library door and accidentally slammed it against the wall, sending a shockwave through the building. He glanced over his shoulder at the many books, scrolls, and maps stacked on the shelves. He would form a special group out of the force that had followed him into the city and they would collect all of this, then transport it back to the Hemmed Land. History, art, folklore. Everything should go with him if he wished to merge his two peoples into one nation.

As he closed the door behind him, he touched the hilt of his sword again, drawing the armor of light around his body. Something scraped along the floor above him. He narrowed his eyes, scanning the dim rafters overhead. That was no mouse. Not unless some grotesquely large version of a mouse lived in this underworld.

The building was deathly quiet again, yet his eyes roved to the narrow stair leading upstairs. He set the maps against one wall, keeping his eyes on the stair.

Stepping with great care so as not to disturb the silence he made his way up it. To his surprise the narrow steps did not even creak under his weight.

At the top of the stairs he opened the little door and found a long hallway that bent around the inner wall of the round library. A dozen paces down the hall, a door stood to the left and another still farther on. He opened the first door. A closet—a large one—with brooms, long-handle dusters, and a mop leaned against the wall. Buckets had been stacked in the corner. Otherwise the closet was empty.

Shutting the first door he proceeded to the next. This opened into a long, wide room. A desk stood against the far wall with a worn old book splayed open atop of it. Various tools had been spread on the desk, along with a spool of thread beside the book. Someone had used this space to effect repairs for the library. A lone shelf occupied the room's opposing wall and its shelves were filled with broken and torn books.

The hallway continued to curve around the library. He followed it, checking a few more doors that he found along the way. He found nothing else of interest until he spied a flicker of light around the last bend in the hallway. He quickened his pace. The door around the bend came into view, a warm yellow light flickering around its seams.

Disconnecting himself from the sword so that his glow would not startle anyone inside, he let out a long breath and grasped the door latch. The room beyond was larger than any of those previous. A lantern burned on a nightstand beside the door, and a cot rested against the wall. A torn pink blanket lay over the cot, covering the thin form of a woman. Her long red hair fell in thin waves over the edge of the bed and her face was turned away from him. The room was too warm and smelled strongly of oil.

Could it be her? Ilfedo trembled a bit as he walked toward the bed. He knelt beside it and spoke as softly as he could, "Elhandra, is that you?"

The woman shivered, raising herself a few inches off the cot before collapsing. Ilfedo touched her shoulder and leaned over so that he could see her face. Elhandra's eyes were squeezed shut. Beads of sweat covered her brow and her cheeks. Her lips had swollen.

Ilfedo wiped the sweat from his forehead as he looked at her. The room was not just warm. It was hot. Yet she shivered as if she was freezing.

"Elhandra, wake up. It is I, Ilfedo. The time for your people's exodus from this place is at hand."

She stirred just enough to open her eyes. They were a beautiful, sober gray. If he could have painted a cozy beach with her eye color it would have been a piece of paradise. She opened her lips as if to speak, then closed them again. The creases on her brow softened as she reached a trembling hand to her shoulder and touched his hand. She knit her fingers with his and gently squeezed.

Ilfedo stroked her forehead with the back of his fingers. Again she visibly relaxed, though he had to pull his hand away. Her skin burned his as if with fire. "Elhandra, what happened to you?"

The woman pulled his hand under the blanket. She was very weak so he had to keep their fingers knit. He swallowed as she placed his hand on her bare abdomen. "Help me," she rasped out in a hoarse whisper.

"What is wrong?" he replied. But then his fingers

felt the slick of half-dried blood on her skin. He looked into her eyes. "I am sorry, my lady, I think you will agree that this is no time for decency?"

She smiled weakly, biting her lower lip and gazing back into his eyes. Then she turned onto her back and closed her eyes again.

Ilfedo was grateful that she did for as he pulled back the blanket below her belly he discovered that she was only half-clothed. Her skin was soaked in sweat and she grasped his hand tighter as he ran his fingers over her belly, touching the edge of a gash some six inches long.

The wound oozed blood and puss, but even more worrisome was the slight glow her flesh had taken on. A shiver of dread ran up his spine as he stared at it. A thread of neon green wove through the flesh exposed by her wound.

"The green blade?" Ilfedo clenched his teeth and looked at her face. "He did this to you, didn't he?"

Elhandra opened her eyes. She bit her lower lip and nodded, her eyes filling with tears.

Ilfedo set her hand on the bed and stood. He drew the sword of the dragon from its sheath, feeling her hopeful eyes on him all the while. He touched the blade to her abdomen. Elhandra's body jerked as the cool steel touched her skin. Ilfedo closed his eyes. Connecting to the living fire, he willed it to draw the poison out of the woman and to heal her. Nothing happened. He looked down and found that the wound had remained the same.

The prophetess stared down at her wound, fresh tears springing from her eyes. She began to weep.

Ilfedo tried again and again, but to no avail. The

living fire lapped at the wound, yet could not draw out the poison in her flesh.

He sheathed his sword and gazed down into her eyes. She responded with a slight smile but he could see that she forced it out despite her pain.

Her lips moved painfully slow as she whispered, "You have returned, my lord. That is all I ask. That you have returned so that I may look once more on your noble face, for truly I have never known a nobler man than you."

Ilfedo knelt at her bedside, grasping her thin hand in his own. "One last time? Have you so little faith that you think the Creator will not provide a cure?"

She laughed ever so quietly. "It hurts to——." The strength leaving her voice, Elhandra managed, "Please . . . my leg."

He covered her upper body with the blanket, for which she gave his hand an appreciative squeeze. Then he uncovered her legs. He felt his mind connecting to the rage that normally occurred during battle. He had to force his hand to not reach for his sword. Elhandra's legs looked as if they'd been dipped in acid.

"Who did this to you?" Ilfedo stood, his wrath still on the brink of releasing. "It was Bromstead, wasn't it? That vile spirit of Brunster Thadius Oldwell has driven him to insanity."

Elhandra's eyes were wide and she seemed to shake her head.

"No? Then who! I will rip his heart out with my own bare hand and serve it to you."

The woman lay there, her pitiable legs exposed and her lips moving in a feeble effort to speak. Still she could say nothing.

At that moment the door slammed shut behind him. Ilfedo spun to face whomever had surprised him, his hand dropping to the hilt of his sword. His aggressive posture did not prepare him for the greeting that followed.

Everett stared up at him, mouth agape. "You are back!" The short little man's face was even more grizzled than before. Now he looked like a dwarf with his beard wider than his face and six inches of it dragging on the floor. Everett set a tin bucket he'd been carrying on the floor. His eyes shifted from Ilfedo's face to his sword, poised as it was as if to strike. "Do you intend to cut me down? Brunster Thadius Oldwell would save you the trouble if you hand me over to him."

"Everett." Ilfedo said the pastor's name as if it were sacred. "You are not dead? Praise be!" Sheathing his sword, Ilfedo closed the distance between them and they clasped each other's arms.

For a few moments they both were quiet. Everett released Ilfedo's arms, retrieved the bucket, and slapped Ilfedo's bicep as he moved past him to Elhandra's bedside. He sat beside her and began dabbing at her forehead with a moist cloth. "This lady always held her faith in your return. Yes she did. She said that you would not abandon our people and that Brunster Thadius Oldwell would rue the day when you returned for him." Everett rinsed the cloth and moved to Elhandra's legs. She opened her mouth as if letting out some of the pain as he dabbed at her wounds.

"She is in a bad condition," Ilfedo said, standing behind the man. "And my sword could do nothing for her."

Everett sighed. "She is dying, Ilfedo. There is no

cure for this. She knew this before I did. I refused to accept it at first, but I have watched this evil sickness slowly consume her body and I know that it has already won the battle."

"Oldwell's work?" Ilfedo asked the question even though he dreaded the answer, for he knew it would be yes.

Everett confirmed it with a slow shake of his head. "Elhandra believes a viper also bit her legs, yet I was here when her condition greatly deteriorated and the poison of Oldwell's blade has caused her to halluci-nate several times. This fate would have been easier to accept had our demise come at the hands of someone else. Someone whom we did not know as a friend. I saw the pain in the faces of the people who trusted Brom-stead, and I felt it, too. Bromstead is not the man we once knew. His body only has survived, and survived as a vessel for one of the most evil spirits that I have ever encountered. I do not know if the spirit is truly our long-dead Lord Warrior or if it is merely claiming to be him. It matters not. Our people are being destroyed. Every soul in this city is being sickened by his evil."

"All, perhaps, with the exception of Ardius," Il-fedo said. When Everett looked back at him, surprise on his face, Ilfedo told him how his men had found the children safely hidden in Ardius's house.

Everett chuckled and wrung the cloth over the bucket. "I did tell you that you could trust him. Didn't I?" He pointed at the burning lantern. "Can you bring that closer?"

Ilfedo fetched it for the little man, holding it up so that he could better see Elhandra's mauled legs.

"You must be full of questions," Everett said. "I

know I would be if I were in your boots." He chuckled again and glanced back up at Ilfedo. "Or, I guess I could say, if I were in your armor." Appreciating the man's attempt to lighten the mood, Ilfedo smiled. "You would not fit in my armor." He caught Elhandra's gray eyes staring up at him and he reached down, stroking her forehead. "Her need is immediate, so tell me first what happened to her."

Everett spoke softly. "Ilfedo, you need to accept that she is beyond your help."

"Do not tell me what I must accept." Ilfedo held Elhandra's gaze even as he spoke to Everett. Elhandra was really a beautiful woman. The beauty of her soul filled her countenance so that even in sickness her physical beauty was only dimmed. "The only poison that cannot be countered," he said more to Everett than to her, "is a poison of the soul. And we know that her soul is selfless and pure."

"True." Everett smiled down at Elhandra and addressed his next words to her. "The Lord Warrior has great confidence in you, it would seem." Then he walked away from the bed and crossed his arms, leaning back against the wall. His grizzled face took on a severe expression, the lines of his mouth tight. "How much do you already know of what happened to us after you were dragged away by that metal beast?"

"Only what Ardius knew," Ilfedo said. "Some of the city guard allied with Oldwell. In particular a man whose name I have vowed to remember until I find him and bring him to a bitter death."

"Nomand." Everett spoke the name as a venomous admittal.

"Yes, that is the one." Ilfedo crossed his arms

over his chest and paced across the room. "Ardius said that he saw you two," he pointed two of his fingers at Everett and Elhandra, "as you went to the aid of Arvidane the megatrath. But he saw little else as he was forced to get his students safely away from the slaughter." He growled out his next words, wishing that he did not have to say them. "I found the bodies piled as they were in City Hall."

"No," Elhandra rasped, she started to tumble and Ilfedo jumped to her bedside. He gently pushed her back so that she would not fall onto the floor. The woman tried to say more but the words whistled incoherently out of her mouth.

From his side of the room Everett smiled to himself. "So, Ardius managed to stay here in the city." He let out a long sigh. "Cunning fellow he is. That is the best bit of news I have heard apart from your return." He returned to the subject of the discussion. "Oldwell and Nomand killed many," Everett said. "Armed again with his green blade, that demon turned the battle in favor of his allies—"

"If only I had been there," Ilfedo began to say.

Everett waved his hand dismissively. "You were not, and only fools will blame you for what happened to us. Elhandra and I assisted the wounded megatrath in crawling away from the battle. We hid the megatrath in a nearby building and then returned, hoping to join the fight even if it meant dying in the process. But the battle was already over. The multitude that remained alive had knelt in the streets and, though tears rolled down their faces to do so, they declared allegiance to Brunster Thadius Oldwell.

"Oldwell stood by the City Hall, the glowing

green blade in his hand. Beside him stood Nomand, such a grin on his face that I would have been grateful if someone had shoved him into Kraylan Abyss.

"Elhandra had reached the scene a dozen yards ahead of me and she started to wail at the sight of all those who had died. Oldwell turned and I swear his eyes lit up like stars. He raised his sword like a javelin in his hand and threw it. A sword should not fly as that one did. It slashed Elhandra's belly and, as she fell, a substance leaked out of the sword. It must have been an acid because it burned through her skirt and," he pointed at her legs, "you can see the result. I managed to drag her away. I must admit that fear lent my body a strength I have never known, for I could hear Oldwell screaming for me to stop and return with his 'prize.' But I kept going.

"Eventually the dewobins went dark. It was the strangest thing. Just before that happened I managed to hide us here, and ever since I have bounced between tending to Arvidane and tending to her. In the moments between I have kept the clock here in the archive wound, so that I will not lose track of the time that has passed."

Ilfedo let out a breath upon hearing those words. "Then the megatrath is alive."

"And recovering," Everett replied. "His wounds were deep, yet at least the blades that Bromstead used on him contained none of the strange infectious properties that were in the green blade. He will live." The little man leaned forward and folded his hands to his chin. "Have you brought help?"

Ilfedo laughed and grasped the monk's shoulder. "I do not make idle promises, Everett. If Oldwell comes again into this city, even if he has the aid of the entire city guard, he will be overwhelmed."

Everett frowned. "Not that I distrust you but I don't think you understand the power of the city guard. They have been fighting in the dark tunnels for many long years."

"Against the black megatraths?" Ilfedo said.

"Indeed." Everett took up the cloth and the bucket again, dabbing at Elhandra's forehead. "Do not underestimate those creatures. It is not a constant battle that we have fought against them, but they execute sneak attacks and intersperse them with larger assaults. If it were not for the fact that the creatures' bulky bodies limit their movement through the smaller tunnels, the city guard would have been overwhelmed."

"Do not fear the megatraths, my friend." Ilfedo stroked the hilt of his sword, allowing a smile to warm his face. "Though they do not answer to me, they do answer to an ally of mine. The megatraths are uniting under Vectra, a fine and noble creature. Perhaps one day you will have the pleasure of meeting her." Ilfedo strode to the bed, ignoring Everett's furrowed brow. "Now, my friends, we are leaving this place. Everett! Hold the other end of this cot."

Everett shook his head, wagging a finger down at it. "Too heavy."

Ilfedo looked upon him severely. "Pick up that end and I will take care of the rest. I only need you to balance it. If her life is to be saved we must get her away from here as quickly as possible. There must be no more delay."

As Everett grunted with the effort of lifting just one end of the cot, Ilfedo grabbed the other with one hand. He could see the skepticism on the monk's face until the living fire snaked out, covering Ilfedo in the armor of light.

Living fire fed Ilfedo's body with inhuman strength. The entire weight of the cot rested on him as he carried it out of the room and down the hall, then through the small door. Everett concentrated all his efforts on keeping the cot balanced so that Elhandra would not tip out of it.

When they exited the library and stepped onto the street, Ilfedo guided them back into the heart of Dresdyn. He had taken point so that neither of them could see the concern on his face, for in truth he had no confidence that Elhandra could be healed.

What plagued her was of evil. But at least he could get her comfortable in a place surrounded by good people. His people.

Then he could return for the maps. They would prove invaluable in understanding what he was up against. He would need a plan in order to find Oldwell, and in his mind that plan was already forming.

THE BLACK BEAST'S ERRAND

The lights of the dewobins winked out far overhead. Ilfedo was sitting on the roof of the mayor's mansion. A cooler air filled the cavern, driving ahead of it the more humid conditions that had prevailed since his arrival. There was no wind, just a subtle shift in temperature and a reduction in moisture.

He straddled one of the dormer windows that fronted the building on its upper floor. From this vantage point he could see other sections of the city. Though, without dewobin light, deep shadows soon covered its structures. Night had fallen upon Dresdyn.

He had left his daughter and his friends asleep in the mayor's mansion. Even Elhandra was asleep on one of the beds, though her condition had not improved. Her morale had certainly risen, but her body was dying.

A column of fifty men marched up the street in front of the mansion, holding their glowing white swords against their shoulders so that the blades pointed harmlessly upward. In the distance he could see other columns weaving their way between buildings, down streets, and peering into various structures. The purpose of the patrols was simple. He wanted no slippage in security. Somewhere down here lurked the spirit of Brunster Thadius Oldwell with a thirst for blood.

Ilfedo's army now controlled the upper half of the city. His force was strong. He had sent a hundred of the Elite to surround and guard the library until he could have its contents safely packed and transported to the Hemmed Land. That in itself would be an enormous undertaking, yet he had faith that if he delegated the responsibility to Oganna she would have no trouble seeing to its efficient execution.

Ilfedo stood and climbed down around the dormer that sheltered the room he had chosen. He let himself in through the window and slid it shut behind him. He had left one lantern burning on a nightstand, so he picked it up before quietly opening the door and slipping into the hallway. He descended the stairs and sneaked out the back door through the kitchen.

He needed space to meditate and he had an idea where to find that. Out in the cavern's open air again, he walked down the graveled road until he found the Church of the Seekers. The sanctuary doors opened for him without much effort and Ilfedo entered the lonely building. He tried not to think of the bodies of the monks that had been killed. His men had buried those monks and had said many prayers over them, especially asking God to grant life to the people of Dresdyn who still remained unaccounted for.

The pews on either side of the sanctuary were

empty, of course, as was the pulpit that faced away from the entry doors.

But he could not help feeling as if the souls of those that had been slain by Oldwell were filling the seats. Their eyes would be turned to him. Unseen they would beg him to release him from their sorrow, to allow no delay in finding their loved ones who had survived.

At the head of the room, the brass pipes of the great organ gleamed in the light of his armor. He knelt at the head of the aisle and laid his sword on the floor, yet still held it in his grasp. The sword thrummed against his fingers as he closed his eyes, letting his mind wander to what an eternity with God would be like. He could not imagine his life or the world for that matter, without faith. Yet he remembered Bromstead stating convictions along those lines. That the Creator did not even exist. It was an absurdity to Ilfedo, but who could convince such a one that his worldview was wrong. Even, that it would cost him his soul.

Ilfedo's aura of light vanished and the sword simmered down to a faint flicker of fire in the blade and a tiny spark in the crystalline hilt. In the darkness Ilfedo found the focus he needed to lay out his heart, praying for the redemption of Dresdyn. He did not know how long he remained there, but he did feel peace fill his soul.

"What shall be done with Elhandra?" Ilfedo pounded his fist on the floor, some of his frustration returning for a moment. "Please do not let this woman die. From what I have seen and heard of her, no one in this city is more selfless, for she has devoted her life to guiding people in your wisdom."

Though he prayed long and sometimes in agony, Ilfedo received no answer. But he remained on his knees, head bowed.

After a long while he looked up and found the room lighted by lanterns along the wall. "Forgive me, my lord," Everett said from behind him, "I did not realize you were here." The little man was standing by one of the pillars, a torch in his hand. "I thought this place should not be dark any longer."

Ilfedo remained on his knees and gazed at the floor. "I can do nothing for the prophetess," he said.

Everett replied in a gentle voice, "That I already know."

Ilfedo exhaled and inhaled deeply. "As the shepherd of this church what would you say to me?"

"You want my advice?" the man asked.

Ilfedo forced a chuckle. "I have had many counselors, Everett, and I have found that there is wisdom in keeping many counselors."

"Very well." Everett shuffled to the head of the room and the organ bench creaked as he sat in it.

Soon the deep tones of the organ filled the room. Majestic, urgent, the music seemed to embrace the city's dire condition and Ilfedo's sense of purpose. Ilfedo closed his eyes and imagined that he was sitting before the imposing bright throne of the Creator. There would be angels on either side, the floor would be made of gold, the pillars would be cut from diamonds. The pipe organ's music drove the helplessness out of him, replacing it with the strength and resolve that his quest for justice bequeathed him.

When a long while had passed, Ilfedo rose and headed out of the church. Everett followed him down the streets. "Ilfedo, how can I be of help?" the man asked.

Ilfedo walked with him all of the way to the library. The Elite warriors bowed out of his path as he stepped up to the door and opened it. He picked up a stack of maps and laid them in Everett's arms, then picked up the remainder and put them under his arm. "Come with me, Everett. You will help me plot out a search to find Oldwell."

The little man slowed his steps. "But I have never ventured into the tunnels."

"Oh, I know that, my friend. Yet you are better informed of the people of Dresdyn than I am and I need that intuition." Ilfedo looked down at the man. "Please, for the sake of the people who are lost I ask that you help me with this task."

"Very well, my lord. I will help gladly." Everett stepped up his pace and soon they entered the mayor's mansion.

Clearing papers off the dining table they laid out the maps and sat down. They opened the maps a couple at a time, looking them over again and again so as to begin memorizing the layout of the underworld paths. At last they looked up.

Everett was shaking his head and his beard brushed the table as he did so. "This is impossible, even for you. These paths are extensive and the caverns they traverse are even more so. Would you send your men on a quest to look into every dark corner of our underground world? Bromstead will have all the time he needs to do—" He threw up his hands. "Whatever it is that the demon possessing him desires to do with the people of our city."

"This is true," Ilfedo replied as he rolled up another map and placed it to the side. He unrolled another and studied the routes sketched on the yellowed parchment. It depicted a small mountain at the center of a cavern, which must have been enormous, and surrounding the mountain was a series of buildings. Three paths led north on the compass, a fourth snaked southwest. A few long buildings were marked toward the bottom of the map with words in red ink: "Abandoned," he read aloud.

"Ilfedo, you need to listen to me," Everett urged. "You have brought your army here and you would need to scatter them in a few hundred directions if you wanted to narrow the search in even a small degree. It is absurd! How can you search such large tracts of pitch-black underground?"

Pulling another map from the stack in front of him, Ilfedo said, "Do you know where the tunnels are that lead to the black beasts? The megatraths?"

"Yes. I do." Everett narrowed his eyes, folded his hands on the table, and leaned forward. "Why?"

"Because that is where we will start our search," Ilfedo said. "We need the help of those who know these paths, or, at the very least, I need to know if they will aid us in our search."

"They would never," Everett began to say.

But Ilfedo regarded him with a furrowed brow, letting a touch of cold steel creep into his demeanor. "Do not misjudge my commitment to this task, cousin. Finding these people is not an option for me. It is a necessity. By their word they have committed themselves to me and I will not turn away from them now."

Everett regarded him silently for a time, then Ilfedo stood from the table and dismissed the pile of maps with a gesture of his hand. "Come with me, Everett. Lead me to the black beast, for I have business with him."

That night Ilfedo and Everett met with Arvidane. The black megatrath had hidden in the basement of one of the abandoned homes.

Everett preceded Ilfedo down the cellar stairs, holding a lantern in front of him. "Arvidane, you have a visitor."

"Ah, monk, I had feared something happened to you," the deep voice rumbled back. A great bulk shifted in the darkness and the long snout of the creature edged into the light. "How is the sick lady?"

"Still as ill as ever, I am sorry to say," Everett said.

Arvidane growled a bit at that. "You are too kind, monk. You should have focused your efforts on her and not I. The world needs more like her, yet instead I am the one restored to health." The creature's round eyes glared out of the darkness. "Now tell me, who have you brought? Another survivor?"

Ilfedo stepped into the lamplight and smiled into the creature's scaly face.

Arvidane let his tooth-ridden jaws open fully. "You have survived human! And you have returned?" With a skip of its six feet the creature swung around the men, rumbling laughter from deep in its throat. It pranced around them, then its claws grabbed the stone floor in a shower of sparks. It looked Ilfedo up and down. "The demigods of the underworld have granted us mercy through your arrival. Now you can hide with us until this evil passes."

"Hide?" Ilfedo chuckled as he rested his fingers on the hilt of his sword. The living fire played over his fingers, begging him not to tease it, but to let it cover his body again in the magnificent armor. "There is no need to hide, Arvidane. No need at all. I am not alone, for I have brought with me a force that even Brunster Thadius Oldwell and his few hundred men cannot hope to defeat." As the creature stared at him, Ilfedo reached out and stroked its snout. "Are you well again, Arvidane?"

"I am indeed," the creature replied.

Ilfedo firmed his expression. "I have met your father Regulus."

"My father!" the creature let out a relieved sigh. "How do you know him?"

"We fought in the stone arena where the surface megatraths rule," Ilfedo said. "Regulus promised to protect my people in Dresdyn until I returned for them. To this day I know not what he meant by that, yet there should no longer be conflict between the black beasts and the humans of Dresdyn. Though I fear the possibility that Oldwell has angered your kin yet again against the people of Dresdyn. If that is the situation then I need to reach Regulus as quickly as possible to avert his wrath on my people in this city."

Ilfedo paused, letting the deluge of information settle in Arvidane's mind. "I need you, megatrath. I need you to get a message to your father that Lord Ilfedo, both his ally and Vectra's, has returned to reclaim his people from the evil of Brunster Thadius Oldwell."

Arvidane's long mouth showed all his teeth in the characteristically vicious grin of his species. "It has been a long time since last I was home. A very long time. Yet those paths are emblazoned in my mind so that I will never forget them." The creature shook its thick hide, then bowed to Ilfedo. "The journey is not a short one but I will go now and carry your message."

Everett stroked the creature's foreleg. "You are sure you feel strong enough?"

A laugh rumbled deep in the creature's chest, then released out its mouth. Its silver eyes glinted with purpose as it carefully climbed the cellar stairs. The stairs creaked and visibly bent under the strain of Arvidane's long bulk and six legs, yet it held.

Ilfedo and Everett followed the young megatrath outside and in the street they said farewell. Arvidane thanked both of them for their kindness and promised to do all in his power to relay Ilfedo's message to Regulus with all possible speed. Then, with a gleeful growl, the megatrath set off at a run toward the distant southwestern part of the city. Ilfedo watched until darkness swallowed the creature. High overhead the dewobins awoke, sending waves of pink light down upon the city.

The dim light of the dewobin dawn glinted off of the knifelike spikes on the black megatrath's back as it tore down the streets, each of its feet sending dull thuds to Ilfedo's ears. Ilfedo watched until the creature turned out of sight round the corner of a building, then he and Everett directed their steps back to the mayor's residence. Oganna would be waking soon, and Ilfedo's counselors would need his next instructions.

By Oldwell's Instruction

Oganna had been unable to sleep for the last hour or so. As she sat on the edge of her bed she loosened the front of her robe a bit more. She had just finished a cold shower, and the underworld air did not seem to allow her skin to fully dry. A muffled conversation was taking place in one of the rooms below her and occasionally she could pick out her father's voice.

Staring out of the window, she shuddered a bit. The darkness down here was absolute with not even a hint of shadows. How could people have lived like this for such a long time?

A glowing line appeared through the window. It wove down a street, then turned out of sight behind a building. The warriors of light were keeping up their patrols and she was certain that they were keeping alert for signs of more survivors.

Oganna set her bare feet on the rug and shuffled over to the dresser. On top of the dresser the oil lamp that she had brought with her into the room continued to burn low, letting out just enough light to help her find her way.

Raising the lamp's chimney, Oganna blew it out. She returned to the bed and sat on its edge again. She leaned her face into her hands and closed her eyes. Maybe sleep would come to her again if she could shake off this strange sense of foreboding.

Her heart beat in her chest with the strength of hammer blows. She could feel the strength of her pulse, her dragon blood flowing through her veins. Something inate called her to stay alert. She could almost feel the hot breath of the mightly Albino dragon himself as it washed over her neck. Yet the room was quiet and nothing appeared amiss. Only a hum of conversation from the room beneath her broke the silence.

The chatter in the room below stopped and a door opened and then closed. Apparently her father was having trouble sleeping, too. If anything, he would be working out a plan to find the people of this city.

She lay back in the bed and felt Neneila slither around her ankle with a gentle hiss. It was a comforting realization to know that she was not alone in the darkness. If the creature were not so tired Oganna knew it would tell her to get more sleep. Morning would come soon enough and the search would begin in earnest.

Oganna drew the covers around her body and closed her eyes, and a hand clamped over her mouth. With one strong pull her assailant wrapped her in the blankets. She opened her mouth to protest but a cloth was forced between her teeth.

Bodily she was lifted off the bed and set on the floor. A wood pole was laid against her back and her body was lashed to it with a rope wrapped around her torso and legs. Neneila awakened, slithering down her legs, avoiding the tightening ropes, and coiled around her feet. The blanket had sealed both of them in.

With a manly grunt of effort, Oganna's captor heaved her onto his shoulders. He fitted her through the window and set her on the roof outside before picking her up again. Oganna summoned the fury in her dragon blood but there was nowhere to throw the energy. Her hands, pinned as they were to her thighs, would have directed the attack against herself.

"Hey there!" a familiar and friendly voice called out.

Oganna grinned despite the gag. Dear Ombre. It seemed that even in the middle of the night he had managed to keep an eye on her.

"Uh, hi." Her captor shifted his burden. "The Lord Warrior asked me to bring him these."

Ombre laughed. "He made you carry them alone and out of the second floor window no less? I will have to talk to him about this." Gravel crunched under feet. "Do not worry about the package. You should worry more about your face."

Her captor shifted on his feet. "Uh, my face?"

Oganna heard the blow that followed, and she landed hard on the ground as the man released his hold. Ombre growled as he cut apart the ropes and unraveled Oganna. He pulled her to her feet as Neneila slithered onto the mossy lawn. A lantern rested on the ground where Ombre had set it down. "Are you all right?"

"Thanks to you, Uncle. Wow that was unnerving." She knelt beside the abductor and studied his face. "He does not seem familiar."

"To me, either," Ombre said. "Which makes me wonder why another player has entered the game."

"He could have been sent by that old Lord Warrior," Oganna said. She stood and pulled her robe up around her neck.

Ombre stepped on the man's knee and leaned hard on it. "If he was sent, then how did he know to come to your chamber? I don't like this at all. It stinks of treachery. Someone must have betrayed your location to another party."

"Not necessarily," Oganna assured him. "It is possible that he targeted me by chance. Maybe who he acquired as a hostage did not matter to him as long as he took someone."

"Good point. He could have wanted information about us." Ombre kicked the man's ribcage and the man groaned. "Oh yeah, you are waking up, fellow. Now you are going to answer our questions, in particular mine! But before we get into those, if you ever lay a hand on her again," he pointed emphatically at Oganna while holding the man's gaze, "I will skin you alive. And I am not making this threat lightly."

Oganna smiled but just then her arms were pinned to her sides as someone else grabbed her from behind. A blade of cold steel pressed against her throat. Ombre turned, mouth agape. Beside the man that held Oganna, two others stepped into the lamplight. They wore a bulky armor of red and bronze and their heads were helmed. Plumes of pink feathers swayed on top of their helmets. They drew bronze short swords from their sides and held the points to Ombre's chest.

Another man emerged from the darkness, holding a large lantern in his fist. He wore the same armor, yet no helm. His other fist held on to the ponytail of a small child. The child's eyes stared vacantly ahead. Her chubby cheeks were stained with tears.

"Let us all be extremely quiet," the man with the lantern said. He did not smile, yet satisfaction showed in his face as he eyed first Oganna and then Ombre.

"Oh? And why would I be silent?" Ombre had a deadly look in his eye. "You are a stone's throw from my men, and they far outnumber yours."

The man patted the little girl's head. "Because I have been ordered to kill this child if our meeting does not go our way."

Ombre bit back the words Oganna could see he wished to utter. Another soldier in red and bronze armor stepped into the light and knocked Ombre up the side of his head with the pommel of his sword. As Ombre collapsed to the ground, the man with the lantern said, "Bring the lady and keep it quiet. We need to slip past their patrols."

"Cursed glowing armor," one man said under his breath. "It makes them easy to spot. Did they think it would be an advantage to them?"

The man with the lantern abruptly pitched forward. He released his hold on the little girl as he fell to the ground, the lantern shattering in the moss. His face blanched and he tried to talk but his swollen tongue filled his mouth.

The other swordsmen glanced at each other. One of them knelt beside him and picked up Ombre's lantern. "He's been poisoned!"

"Poisoned? How?" The warrior holding Oganna grunted out a command. "Enough delay. Send word that we have acquired the hostage and bring—" The man's hold slackened and he dropped beside Oganna.

The telltale hiss as Neneila wrapped herself around Oganna's ankle, brought a relieved smile to Oganna's face. The viper wound its way up around Oganna's neck and purred words in her ear. "Sweeeet missssstresss. I am sssooo sorry. It seemsss they intended you harm."

A line of men circled her, drawing their swords and raising bronze shields before their faces. They formed a wall around her.

"Surrender the serpent!"

"It is all of you that are in grave danger," Oganna said, her concentration deepening. "Surrender to me now. If you do not, I will slay all of you with the exception of one. And I assure you that the survivor will wish he had not."

They tightened the circle around her but her hand flew up, glowing blue. A beam of energy shot from her palm, smashing into the wall of shields, and driving the men back several steps. They locked their formation and advanced again. She raised her other hand, which now glowed stronger than the first, and discharged the energy against those nearest her.

The blast rang against the shields, impacting with such force that it shattered three of them and cracked two others. "Stand back! Please do not force me to do this," she said.

Their circle divided to allow the passage of one man. He also wore the armor, yet he took the helm off his head and regarded her soberly. "Surrender now, or the life that will be claimed will be that of the child we brought."

Oganna glanced at the man's hair, for it was red. Then her eyes followed his sword to where it drew a trickle of blood from the little girl beside him. A fresh tear bubbled in the girl's eye. Oganna might have attempted to strike the man with the power in her blood, just as she had struck his soldiers, but with his blade pressed as it was against the little girl's throat.

No. She would not risk it. She could as easily make the man's blade slip and kill the girl.

Neneila hissed from her shoulder. "Shall I disss-patch of him, mistress?"

"If you are thinking of throwing your pet snake at me, think again." The man shook his head. "Yes, it could probably poison me, but not before this child dies. Unless, of course, her life means nothing to you. Besides I am quick with my sword arm and could lop of your pet's head before it reached my neck."

"You are called Nomand," Oganna said.

His eyes narrowed. "Baiting me for information will not work. You will accompany us." He tossed a leather bag into her arms. "Put your snake in there so that we can transport it, otherwise we will kill it."

"Try it," the viper hissed.

Nomand frowned, the muscles in his arm tightened as he pressed the blade an inch into the little girl's neck. The child coughed on her blood and collapsed in a faint.

Leaping at Nomand, Oganna covered his head with the leather bag. She paid no heed to the fact that little more than a robe covered her womanly form. Her thought was for the child and to deal with the traitor before he had a chance to take her to his master. Her hands radiated with blue light, forcing every swordsman in the vicinity to cover their faces and turn away.

The move bought her a few seconds, nothing more. But it was enough. The energy she released slammed into Nomand's chest, flattening him to the ground. By the time he had recovered enough to strike back, Oganna was holding his sword's point to his throat. She lifted her face and screamed out, "We are under attack!"

Lights flared into existence in every window of the mayor's mansion and a dozen Elite warriors came at a run around the corner of the building. They brandished their glowing weapons toward the enemy force.

The viper flung itself at Nomand's face and the man batted it aside. His legs ensnared Oganna's, dropping her to the ground. Oganna rolled with the fall, coming back to one knee. His sword was still in her hand and poised for his chest.

"You slippery thing," Nomand spat. "Do you really think you can escape me?"

The sword in Oganna's hand felt as a leaden weight. She gripped its handle with both hands.

Nearby the Elite warriors engaged the city guardsmen in combat. Steel clashed with bronze and the city guard seemed to hold their ground at first, but when the swords of light began to cleave the bronze weapons in twain Nomand's force began a strategic retreat. They struck back at the Elite with their shields instead and those heavy pieces of armor held against the swords' magic.

Nomand cursed as he saw the battle grinding to a standstill. He grabbed the shield of a man close to him and raised it over his head. Oganna struck at him as he charged her, but he moved with such unexpected speed that she tripped on her robe and fell to the ground. She raised the sword to block the blow as he smashed the shield upon her. At first she succeeded, for his blow glanced off the sword. But his booted foot kicked toward her chin and she had no defense against it.

When his boot uppercut her chin, everything turned black and she felt the world spin. She knew that she had miscalculated. Through the hazy sounds that reached her ears she heard her father's men cry out, even as she felt strong arms lift her up and carry her toward the unsecured depths of the city.

THE TRAITOR'S ADMISSION

The sword of the dragon was still in its sheath as Ilfedo walked with Everett up the city street on his return trip to the mayor's residence. But at that moment a line of heavily armed men trooped across his path, and he recognized their red and bronze armor. They were members of the missing city guard, and immediately Ilfedo and Everett stopped their walk.

The dewobin light intensified far above them, and Ilfedo was able to make out the grim expressions on the faces of the men. With professional ease they had drawn their swords and now pointed the sharp tips toward him.

"Oldwell did not come out to face you himself," Everett muttered with disgust.

Ilfedo acknowledged the man's assessment of the situation with a slight nod of his head. Oldwell had indeed sent men after him, but the tall man whose body Oldwell had possessed was not among them. Ilfedo scanned the city guards, looking for even a slight hint of hesitation as they surrounded him and Everett. As the guards' heavy armor clanked with their movements, their hands embraced the handles of their swords with an unnerving steadiness.

These men knew what Ilfedo was capable of and yet they showed no fear of him. They closed the circle, keeping their swords pointed at his neck.

A guard with very broad shoulders addressed him in a steady tone. "Lord Ilfedo, I am Captain Therman. The mighty Brunster Thadius Oldwell has instructed us to bring you to him. I have been instructed that your sword is to remain behind. You may take the clothes you are wearing and nothing more."

Ilfedo reacted before the fellow had an opportunity to come any nearer. He felt pure rage at being dealt with in this fashion and he needed these men to recognize what a foolish attempt this was. The living fire drew magnetically to his hand and the sword followed, shooting its handle to his palm. As his fingers curled around the handle, he raised his arm so that the crystalline hilt was over his head. The hilt flashed with blinding light, the guards looked away from him, and the living fire spilled onto the ground all around him even as it garbed him in his regal armor.

"Lord Ilfedo, please come peaceably," Captain Therman pleaded. "You don't understand the consequences of not doing as Oldwell instructs. Our families are his hostages! Even your own daughter has been taken into custody."

But there was no turning back the rage that fed

the sword's fury and the living fire blasted outward in an expanding ring of searing heat. When the fire faded with the sword's diminishing glow the city guards lay in the street, their armor smoldering. A couple of them had been thrown against neighboring buildings, their shoulders slumped and their chins resting against their breastplates.

Ilfedo had eyes only for one of them. The leader. Captain Therman trembled on the ground as Ilfedo approached. His leather gloves had protected his hands but his neck and chin had blistered from the flames.

Therman's eyes did not plead but his voice almost wept as he said, "You have doomed our wives and our children to the hands of that madman. You have doomed your own daughter. Truly you do not have the heart of a Lord Warrior, which would be selfless."

"Everett," Ilfedo said, "can you find some rope? I would like these traitors to be bound until they are taken into the custody of my own forces."

The little man shuffled off into a nearby building, disappearing inside. Before long he returned with a short stretch of rope. Ilfedo took it and rolled Therman onto his stomach, lashing the rope around the man's wrists. Everett, in the meanwhile, slipped into a few other buildings and retrieved an extensive length of thick rope. He tied each man in turn, linking them all together.

When the task was done Ilfedo counted forty men bound upon the ground.

"You have doomed us all," Therman said again as his head remained bowed to the dirt.

Ilfedo kept his sword out of its sheath as he placed his booted foot on Therman's neck. "Evil spirits the likes of Brunster Thadius Oldwell do not merit negotiation. If I had gone with your solution then Oldwell would have killed me and then done as he liked with your women and children, and my own precious daughter. You are a fool to play at bargaining with a madman who cares not for the welfare of those you love. He would as soon kill them when their use to him is through."

Ilfedo pressed the tip of his sword against the man's neck. "If any harm has come to my daughter, the perpetrators will reap my revenge a hundred times over. Yet I merit Oldwell had not the slightest clue what he tackled when he issued orders to take her. He is a fool to think that she could be lightly taken."

He eased the pressure he was applying and glanced up the street toward the mayor's mansion. Oganna was there with Ombre and a contingent of the Elite warriors. Surely Oldwell's force could not have fulfilled its task. But his heart told him that Therman was telling him the truth. Oganna had been taken.

Ilfedo glanced down at the humbled man upon the ground. "Stay here. I will have need of you shortly. For now, stay put. Otherwise you will get to Oldwell before I do, and I'm certain he will be ill disposed toward you and would take his wrath out on your family. You must pray that God grants me the upper hand in the coming confrontation, for if I fail the people are condemned to a life in slavery under that madman." He turned, issuing an order to the others. "This advice I give to all of you. Submit yourselves to my command. Commit yourselves to repentance for submitting to such a tyrant, as I fight on behalf of those you love. Your only hope rests in my protection and the strength the Creator has given me in this task."

The captain stayed quiet on the ground and so did his men as Ilfedo and Everett resumed their path back to the mayor's mansion. A sense of urgency built inside of Ilfedo and he ran.

A patrol of glowing warriors turned across their path and challenged them. As soon as Ilfedo was recognized the Elite bowed a few paces away from him. Ilfedo instructed them to retrieve the traitors whom he had found and inquired if anything of note had occurred in his absence. The answer, which was a 'No,' should have calmed him. Instead he found himself visualizing a night raid on the mayor's mansion where everyone slept. "The city guards who attacked me are led by a Captain Therman. Bring him to me as soon as you have secured his men," Ilfedo said.

The warriors spread out down the street, their captain signaling them to form three loose columns to sweep the area ahead. As the warriors did his bidding, Ilfedo led Everett the remaining distance to the mayor's mansion, but Ilfedo's gaze could have burned through an iron wall when he came within sight of the place, for the warriors of light had engaged in battle with many of the city guard.

"More of Dresdyn's people betray me?" Ilfedo looked first at Everett, then ran to the scene. A hundred or more of the city guard fought on behalf of Oldwell, their numbers insufficient to hold out against the swelling force of Ilfedo's men. Yet still they held their ground as if they were accomplishing something by doing so.

As a living torch of vengeance Ilfedo fell upon them. He moved quickly, felling the men of the city guard with blasts of fire and hammer-hard blows from the broad side of his sword. He let the living fire feed his muscles with unassailable strength. He darted between the men, knocking them from side to side, battering their helmets until they fell to the ground. They fell around him until upon their battered bodies he stood. He had killed none of them, for he wished no permanent harm upon them. Not now. Not when he could feel that the long arm of Brunster Thadius Oldwell had finally revealed itself in the form of these pawns.

Ilfedo's glowing warriors of light poured through the streets, surrounding the area. The city guards, however, held on to their swords as if the battle had not yet begun. Ilfedo smote the ground with his sword as the battle ended. "The people who I have come to save now seek my death! Yet, if I were to offer you a pardon for this treason would you have the courage to accept it? I know what Oldwell has done. How your families are at his mercy. You cannot face his evil! But I can and I am going to do so, with or without your aid. This city has lain in darkness for too long. Let the light be shone upon it. I have come to offer you and your families an escape from this underground world. From this time on you will leave Dresdyn in the volumes of history, for it is time to lead your wives and your children to a better life. A life under the sun!"

Staggering through the ring of glowing warriors that had surrounded Ilfedo and his subdued opponents, Ombre grasped Ilfedo by the arm. "They have taken her, Ilfedo! I don't know how, but I could not stop him. Oldwell sent that traitor Nomand and he has Oganna."

By the look in Ombre's eyes Ilfedo knew that rage over the deed had filled his friend's heart, so he returned his gaze with the strength of his own resolve. "Then let us pray they lead us to Oldwell," Ilfedo said as he looked around at his swordsmen. "Send word to Commander Veil. Five hundred warriors of light will follow Lord Ombre and myself into the caverns, while the remainder of the host shall remain to safeguard the city and those within it."

Ilfedo clasped his hand on Ombre's shoulder, looking back into his eyes. "Others of the Dresdyn city guard waylaid me as I walked the city. Their leader is a man called Captain Therman and I believe he knows how we can find Oganna, and probably Brunster Thadius Oldwell," he said. "I left him and his men wounded and Everett bound their wrists so that they could not escape. I sent men to secure them, as well as to bring Therman back to me. We will await his arrival before proceeding."

Before long Ilfedo's warriors of light parted ranks to admit a prisoner through. The man, Captain Therman, upturned his face to Ilfedo and said, "Slay me now, my lord, for I wanted nothing but to serve under your gracious rule. Yet I see that my hand was turned against you. In your time of need I joined with the enemy because I lacked faith in your strength to preserve those whom I love. I am unworthy in your presence." Thus saying, the man bowed his head until his chin touched his chest.

Grabbing the captain's chin, Ilfedo forced him to look up into his eyes. "You will have this one chance to redeem yourself in my eyes," he said in a foreboding tone. "Answer me this: do you know where Bromstead and the demon that possesses him have hidden?"

Therman swallowed so hard that his adam's apple stood out prominently on his neck. "Yes, my lord. I do."

Relaxing his stance, Ilfedo stood back a few paces. "Stand to your feet, captain, and lead the way."

As Therman stood, Everett shuffled through the glowing warriors' ranks. He placed his hand on Therman's shoulder. "So that we will know where you have taken him…"

Therman cut him off. "Bromstead has taken our people to the mines at Kraylan Abyss."

Ilfedo saw Everett stumble back a step and heard him say, "Lord God, have mercy on our people. That is no place for women and children." Ilfedo ignored him. All he could think about was Oganna's safety. Captain Therman walked down the highway, heading deeper into the cavern and to the very edge of the city. Ilfedo followed and Ombre marched behind him with five hundred of their grim-faced, veteran swordsmen. Whatever this Kraylan Abyss place was, Ilfedo did not care. He would pry Oldwell out of there even if he had to do it with his bare hands.

THE CAVERNS BETWEEN

The dewobins only shed their light inside of the cavern which contained the city of Dresdyn. Beyond that the tunnels, chambers, and caverns of the underworld were ruled only by darkness. At least, to Ilfedo's knowledge.

He remembered with startling clarity his journey out of Dresdyn to the realm of Vectra the megatrath. Many things of strange wonder and terror had met his eyes. He still saw in his mind's eye the many heads of the serpent dragon and he felt the pulse of the strange ancient weapon that had shot a shaft of light from its barrel. Stranger still was the metal vessel that had been stuck deep in the walls of stone where he had found that weapon. It had felt like a journey into the stars. Or, rather, a plunge into the darkness that lay between the stars.

Then there had been the city with a strange creature haunting it. Something so terrifying that everything he had ever encountered seemed to pale in comparison, even the mighty water skeel who called himself Cromlin did not seem to compare.

Vectra the megatrath had told Ilfedo that the city he had seen must have long ago belonged to her ancestors. Ilfedo marveled at that. How could the megatraths have survived so deep in the world? In such darkness life's existence seemed a foolish absurdity. For to live down here was to court the favor of death and the harsh denizens who had ruled it for untold generations of mankind.

Now Ilfedo was venturing outside of the city again. This would be his final journey into this part of the world. He reaffirmed that with every blaze of the fire that flared from his upheld sword. Bromstead had taken the people of the city to a place called Kraylan Abyss. The evil spirit of Brunster Thadius Oldwell had seen to that.

Ilfedo felt nothing but hatred for Oldwell. The spirit of that long-dead Lord Warrior had proved himself to be full of pure evil and had caused these people nothing but terror and bondage, as well as corruption to those willing to serve him. Now he had Oganna under his power as well. For that, he must be slain, even if that meant killing Bromstead, the demon's host and former captain of the city guard.

Turning briefly, Ilfedo grabbed Captain Therman by the collar and hauled him to the front of the column. The man stumbled at first under the sudden change in pace, then caught himself. He matched his pace to Ilfedo's.

No words were needed in order to convey Ilfedo's continuing displeasure. Therman kept his gaze ahead as sweat dripped from the end of his nose.

The road out of the city ended at a tunnel broad enough for six men to walk abreast. Captain Therman cleared his throat to gain Ilfedo's attention just long enough to point to the tunnel wall. By the light of Ilfedo's armor the tunnel was revealed. Its walls were smooth and glossy. Torches as long as a man's arm had been placed in iron fittings at ten foot intervals along the wall.

Ilfedo reached up with his sword and lighted the first torch as Therman held up a cautionary hand. "These lanterns are nearly spent, for we have not taken the long journey necessary to replenish our oil supply. I estimate they can burn adequately for no more than eight hours, maybe less. Without them no one will be able to come through this tunnel again."

Ilfedo proceeded to the next torch and lit it as well, then he glared over his shoulder at Therman.

Behind the traitor marched the Warriors of Light, their swords fervently glowing, pushing aside the darkness. Ombre, marching at their head, stepped around Therman and looked the traitor in the eyes. "Perhaps you need to consider that these torches will never be used again. If I know my Lord Ilfedo, and I assure you that I do, he intends that your people will return along this path and never have cause to walk it again. The door will not be left open when you leave this place. Lord Ilfedo will lock every door and no one will ever come back." He turned his back on the man and caught up with Ilfedo, saying out loud as he did so,

"This place gives me the shivers. How could you people survive down here?"

The question was posed but needed no answer. Therman seemed to understand this. "As you say, my Lord," he said and he nodded his head with respect to Ombre.

"Move onward!" Ilfedo gestured for the man to pick up his pace again. Another torch was revealed ahead of him and Ilfedo touched the flaming tip of his sword to that torch as well. The fire sputtered into existence, then burned with a steady flame as Ilfedo and Ombre proceeded farther into the darkness.

Before long, the tunnel opened into a cavern. Stalagmites of large proportions rose from the floor and the steady dripping of water from somewhere overhead echoed eerily into the otherwise silent chamber.

Captain Therman grabbed a torch from inside the tunnel as he emerged into the cavern, then he took the lead, guiding Ilfedo and Ombre through the strange territory. The Warriors of Light formed like a thread behind them, carefully matching the route Therman laid out for them. The air felt exceedingly cool and damp and Therman warned Ilfedo to keep his men on the path, for pits and cracks were hidden throughout the area.

After a couple of hour's marching, they reached the opposite side of the cavern and Ilfedo called a halt. Therman pointed to a break in the cavern wall where it appeared to open into yet another cavern. The break was divided by a stalagmite.

Therman spoke in a low voice. "Beyond this divide is a smaller cavern from which we will have access to a tunnel that leads to Kraylan Abyss. But we must step quietly through this place. Also, in the past this has been our staging ground for our defense into other tunnels against the black beasts. They are cunning and vicious. Though I have not seen one in some time, I would still advise caution. Besides this, Oldwell is certain to have left men guarding those tunnels in case the beasts return. We do not want him forewarned of our arrival."

Ilfedo stepped past the man and stared into the dark cavern beyond. "We will first subdue the guards in the tunnels and replace them with my own men. Then I will bring the bulk of my force to the abyss."

"But if a beast comes upon your sentry, that man will surely be killed," Therman said.

With a wave of his hand Ilfedo dismissed the man's supposition. "I have no time to school you in this matter, captain. Suffice it to say that the black beasts are not enemies of mine, nor do I intend to treat them as such. Oldwell's guards would surely ignite a fresh fight with the beasts, but my men know better. You will lead us to their access tunnels, first. Only then will we prepare our approach to Kraylan Abyss."

* * *

Oganna awoke to the gentle sway of her captor's shoulders, for he had slung her across them. The air was exceedingly damp and the light of a dozen lanterns revealed the small column of men around her as they made their way between two giant stalagmites. Her wrists had been bound together with a chain, and another had been lashed around her ankles. The metal felt cold on her skin.

They were in a cavern, of that she was certain. The steady dripping of water from somewhere overhead echoed methodically off the chamber walls. The stalagmites glistened with moisture as the red-headed man in the lead of the column walked around one of them, torch lifted high in his hands. He glanced back for a mere moment and she closed her eyes to slits, yet she had recognized his face. It was the same man that had led the raid to capture her. What was his name again? Her head throbbed from the blow his boot had delivered to her and her thoughts pieced together with difficulty. She could not at first recall.

The man carrying her grunted as he shifted her robed body in his big hands. He was not very tall yet he was broad and strong, judging by the ease with which he seemed to hold her weight. "Nomand!" the big fellow called to the redhead leading their march. "Someone take this load off of me for a moment. I need to stretch my shoulders."

Nomand either did not hear him or, more likely, chose not to answer. He led the column another ten feet, then turned them around another stalagmite before straightening his course. The floor of stone and dirt stretched on seemingly without end. Oganna wondered at the certainty of Nomand's steps. It demonstrated a confidence in reaching his destination, which no doubt included plans for handing her over to Brunster Thadius Oldwell.

A soldier next to her captor spoke in a low voice as they continued their march. "You can carry her the rest of the way. Do not complain or the master will be told of it."

Her captor grunted and his arm muscles flexed. "Shut your mouth, or I will shut it for you."

Oganna evaluated the group. They were proceeding deeper into the cavern and already she was completely at a loss as to which direction led back to the city of Dresdyn. Her father would fear for her, and she imagined his rage at her kidnapping would be dreadful. She could well imagine Ombre's downcast face. He had failed to protect her, or so he had felt. She had seen it in his eyes. Yet the truth of it was that she had failed to protect herself. Yes, she blamed herself. She had let her guard down somewhat and now had paid the price. Fortunately for her these fools that had taken her captive had underestimated her.

The man who carried her had a bronze short sword in a sheath at his waist and a heavy shield slung over his back. To attempt to wield one of the shields would have proved foolhardy for her. She needed to be swift if she was to succeed.

The floor of the cavern alternated between hard stone and patches of shallow sand. She waited until her captor stepped onto one of the sandy patches, and then she acted. She mentally drew upon the energy in her blood, calling forth the strength of her dragon side. She was the descendant of the mighty Albino, the dragon prophet, and his power swelled in her veins now.

Blinding blue light flashed from her bound hands as she directed her fingers to her captor's head. Latching onto his face, bands of energy caressed his skin, then surged against him. His cheeks billowed like sails on a boat as her power discharged into him with the force of a dozen punches.

The man stumbled, then fell forward, crashing on the ground.

Oganna thudded onto the hard floor of the cavern, rolling as well as she was able. She had been wise to delay her attempted escape, for she fell on a patch of sand instead of unforgiving stone.

As she rose to her knees the column of armed men reacted with practiced speed. Nomand, at their head, reversed their march so that they began to surround her. "She must not be killed," he ordered. "Oldwell's instructions were clear." Nomand's red hair seemed even more fiery in the light of the men's torches. "What did you think you were going to do, miss?" he mocked, spreading his arms wide with sword upheld in one hand. "You cannot defeat us all, nor can you escape from this cavern, for you do not know the way back. Do you?"

"No, I do not know the way back," she admitted as the line of men closed around her. "But this is foolish. You should all be protecting me, not kidnapping me. Your lord has returned and it is not this evil Brunster Thadius Oldwell. It is my father, Lord Ilfedo of the Hemmed Land." She gave a long moment of pause, hoping dread might set in some of the men at the thought of Ilfedo's wrath. "My father will not show mercy to any of you if you do not protect me. Is that what you want?"

"We support the rise of the old Lord Warrior, miss. Your father is a phony who could not stand against the true ruler of Dresdyn." In a flash, Nomand brought the point of his sword within inches of her throat. "Will you walk or be carried again?" He nodded at the collapsed form of the large man who had carried her.

One of his men knelt to check the fallen guard's pulse. When he stood again he shook his head.

Nomand balled his fist and spoke through gritted teeth, "You have cost me a good soldier. It is fortunate for you that Oldwell wants you intact."

"Yes," she admitted with a smile, "it is!" She

thrust her hands upward so that the link of her chain snared the tip of his blade.

Nomand grabbed at her bound wrists but she rolled away from him and kicked the knees of the man behind her. She heard the snap of bones as the man cried out and collapsed, his knees broken.

Oganna wrenched the sword out of the wounded man's hand. She could not quite stand without assistance. The chains prevented her. So she thrust one of the other men through his thigh. She released her hold on the sword, letting it clatter to the ground as she blasted more blue light into the faces of those around her. The men, including Nomand, stumbled back, shielding their eyes with their arms. In the moments that her attack bought her she grasped the sword with her bound hands. Using it as a cane she pulled herself to her feet and slipped into the surrounding darkness. She felt her way around a stalagmite and hid in its shadow.

It would take a minute for the men's vision to clear.

She could hear Nomand and his men expressing their frustrations at losing her. By the shifting light of their torches she knew that they were spreading out. She dared not move at first. The chains around her ankles would have revealed her to them. But the men knew that she could not have gone far in chains and they began a systematic search of all the nearby stalagmites. Fortunately they were few in number, which greatly slowed their progress.

Nomand grabbed a torch from one of his men and fanned out his men to check another stalagmite some twelve paces from her location.

When she felt sure that she was no longer in their

line of sight, Oganna sat on the floor of the cavern. She bent over and held the chains in her hands. Her hands glowed but she balled them together around the chain holding her ankles together so that the brilliant storm of energy taking place between her palms was mostly hidden from view. Hot metal dripped onto her skin as the chain melted. She bit her lip to keep from crying out.

The chain snapped from around her ankles and she stood to her feet, relief flooding her body. She spit on her palms to sooth the burns left there, then picked up the bronze sword. She held it awkwardly, for her wrists were still bound and she could think of no way to free them. But she found comfort in having the weapon in her possession.

"She is nearby," Nomand said from behind her stalagmite. "She is bound by her hands and her feet. Find her!"

Oganna smiled as she walked away from the stalagmite and deeper into the cavern's darkness. She held the sword in front of her, using its blade to feel out the terrain ahead. When she looked over her shoulder Nomand and his force were regrouping a considerable distance off.

"Quit trembling, you fools," Nomand said. "The girl cannot go far. We will return for her." He walked a circle around his men, then shouted out into the cavern. "You cannot get far, girl. You will never find your way back to Dresdyn, and I will be back soon to hunt you out. That I promise."

As the column of men marched off, Oganna knelt and burned imprints of her glowing hands into the stone floor. Then she scratched an arrow beside her handprints before tightening the strap of her robe. At least it was a warm garment, she thought, even if it was not proper attire for a lady to wear in the presence of strangers.

Softly she trailed Nomand's men, keeping always at a distance. She had little confidence that she could escape again if they captured her. Nomand was the fool, not her. She had no desire to return to Dresdyn at this moment. Her father needed to find both Brunster Thadius Oldwell and Dresdyn's missing inhabitants—and Nomand was going to show her the way.

TO THE BRINK OF KRAYLAN ABYSS

For a long while Oganna trailed Nomand's men. The chains around her wrists became increasingly painful to bear, yet she reminded herself of whose child she was and pressed onward through caverns and tunnels. When at last Nomand called a halt, it was so that they could stand before the entrance to another tunnel. He and his men sat on the ground for a rest, little knowing that not a hundred paces away Oganna watched from the shadows.

This tunnel was different than those they had previously entered. Hewn white stones rimmed the edge of the entrance and red bricks paved its narrow floor. The opening was broad enough for four men to walk abreast. It seemed a strange thing that it was situated such a distance from the city. Had the people of Dresdyn done this? Or had they borrowed the tunnel from other, more ancient masters of this underground world?

She sat on the ground, pulling her robe tighter around her neck. The damp air began to send chills to her bones. How she missed the warmth of the fire in the mayor's mansion.

She caught a whiff of something sweet in the cavern air. Hmm, it reminded her of the flowers back home on a warm and sunny day. A bed of roses and phlox by the kitchen window.

The smell intensified as she glanced around into the darkness. Her head felt dizzy. She fought the sensation, forcing her tired eyes to stay open. If she fell asleep now she would lose track of Nomand and his men. Her mind pushed back. "You don't need to stay awake. Just follow them through that tunnel when you awaken," she whispered to herself.

She lifted her hands to her face, and the chains clinked with the motion. Dimly she recognized a strange little voice squeal from behind her.

"Spit! She aint an easy catch. Why is she still awake?"

"Here," another replied. "Give me the wand so I can try. You really are an inept brother sometimes. Why do I put up with you?"

The first squealed back, "Aye? And yet mine is the only wand still available. Take that, you skinny mouse hunter. Spit! You continue to abide by me, then I'll abide by you. We is partners in our endeavors. Now close your fishy lips and watch the human while I search her."

Oganna felt her hands fall back into her lap. Her vision began to blur, yet through the blur she distinguished a tiny little man with a glowing white wand in his fist. He sprinted up her leg and stood on her knee, staring at her face. She managed to blink back at him, though the rest of her body refused to move.

"Spit!" the little man said. "She's seen me. This aint ever happened before."

Another figure sprinted up her other leg and stood there. A pair of wings fluttered from his back as he punched the other fairy on the shoulder. "You have the wand. Get on with it! Let's see if she's carrying anything worth having and get outa here. And stop saying 'spit.'"

"Ah, don't get your wings in a crinkle," the first said, punching back. He began inspecting Oganna's clothes, poking occasionally with his wand. He started to pull aside the fold of her robe. At the same time Oganna's vision sharpened, her dragon blood warming as it warded off the bit of fairy magic that restrained her movement.

The little fairy's face was narrow with a long nose. His white skin flushed a deep red as he hastily withdrew his wand from the fold of her robe. "Uh, Avra?"

The second fairy swiped at the wand, but missed. "Yeah, what? Has she got something good?"

The first shook his head. "Spit! Let's get outa here, Avra, this girl has nothing except the robe she's wearing and the sword she's holding. And I do mean she has nothing."

Avra froze, looking Oganna up and down as if really noticing for the first time. "Now this does not make sense. What sane woman would be down here dressed, or not dressed, like this? Answer me that!"

The first fairy, Oganna had assigned him the nickname of Spit, twirled a strand of her hair with his wand. "She has be-a-uti-ful hair." Spit grinned as the color returned to his face. "Nice eyes, too. Maybe she wouldn't mind if I shrink her down to my size so we can go courting."

"You have such lame ideas sometimes," Avra said. "Quickly, check and see if she has any jewelry around her neck. Then we can split before she regains control of her body."

"Uh," Spit said, "hold off a moment."

Avra hopped to his brother's side and punched him lightly in the stomach. "What?"

"Spit! Avra, we can't do this to her. Look." He aimed his wand at Oganna's wrists and the chain that was binding them.

Avra punched Spit's stomach again.

"What's that for?" Spit demanded as he bunched over, patting his bruised gut.

Avra jumped to the ground and kicked a pebble so that it rolled into the surrounding darkness. "You always have to turn a moral corner when it comes to making a living. First you're all for robbing this girl. Now you discover she's a prisoner and want to give up the idea."

"Well!" Spit gestured at Oganna's face. "Look at her." He put his tiny hand on his hip and with his other hand waggled his wand at his brother. "Do you still wish to proceed?"

"Of course not." Avra swept a chivalrous bow. "Free her of the shackles and let's get outa here."

Spit grinned up at Oganna. "See? We is not bad men. You're in trouble, and we will help you. We wish you the best on your—" He laughed. "Whatever it is you intend to do or where you intend to go." He twirled, balancing on one dainty foot as he held his wand high. Then he tapped her chain with the wand and a hot glow formed inside of the metal. It expanded a fraction and the chain snapped off.

As her hands fell free, her palms were exposed. The fairies both gasped as a strand of red glowed from beneath her skin, one in each palm. Oganna remembered a time when she was captured by the fairies of the underground city of Avejewel. They, too, had marveled when her palms had glowed like this.

Just as they had in the fairy city of Avejewel, her palms now sprouted a glowing miniature tree. Oganna dared not attempt to move. She wanted to see if these fairies would jump into the tree, just as the others had done. If they did, then she had no doubt that they, too, would vanish as if through a portal.

Spit and Avra shrieked in unison. Avra took off running into the darkness while Spit's wings hummed to life and sped him out of sight after his brother.

The threads of red dimmed in Oganna's palms and the tree gently collapsed in on itself. The light faded completely as she stretched her fingers and found the bronze sword's handle. At last the fairies' hold on her evaporated and she started to stand.

But then strong fingers grasped her shoulder and Nomand's familiar voice whispered in her ear, "Those little critters might have made tasty snacks over a campfire if they had not run off. Too bad, I will have to settle for having you in my clutches yet again." He chuckled. "My master will be eager to meet you, princess."

Something struck Oganna's head with such force that she felt a wave of dizziness overcoming her. She fought it, knowing that to succumb would put her in Oldwell's clutches. But her tired body refused as several torches rose in the hands of the men who now surrounded her.

In the midst of Nomand's men Oganna collapsed in a faint. The blow to her head had sapped her available energy. Nomand reached out and grabbed a fistful of her blond hair. His laugh echoed in the cavern and perhaps into those beyond.

Yet in that moment she heard the ringing of steel from many swords and a wall of light flared into existence around Nomand and his men. Swords blazed white in the hands of the Hemmed Land's finest warriors and the light of their swords revealed the sober purpose of vengeance in their eyes.

Nomand tightened his grip on Oganna's hair and pulled her head back. He pointed his sword toward her throat and looked around at the warriors, waiting for them to back off. Instead an ordinary sword stabbed out of the darkness. Its blade swept downward and severed his sword hand above the wrist.

With a cry Nomand fell to one knee, blood rushing out of his stub of an arm. Four of his own soldiers dropped their torches and prostrated themselves on the ground as the tall figure of Lord Ilfedo strode between them. His armor seethed with flames. He was terrible to look upon. The fire licked Ilfedo's body as if with kisses of pain and his helm was a geyser of flame.

Ilfedo's eyes passed over Nomand to the princess. Then he grasped Nomand by the shoulder while he brought the sword of the dragon down. Nomand screamed like he had never screamed in his life. A cry of terror that tore out of his throat as the sword of Ilfedo cut off his other hand. He rolled onto the ground, screaming all the while.

AFFLICTION OF THE GREEN BLADE

Ilfedo stepped back from Nomand, leaving him to thrash and scream upon the ground. He held out his hand as Ombre raised his sword again, this time to take off the traitor's head. For it had been Ombre's ordinary sword that had cut off the first of Nomand's hands.

Returning Ilfedo's gaze, Ombre shook his head. "Let me take what is left to him so that we may be rid of him."

"No," Ilfedo heard himself say in a calm tone. "Nomand will live without his hands. This is punishment enough. Let him serve as an example to those who follow him and, more particularly, to those who follow Brunster Thadius Oldwell. Stay your hand and save that wrath for the master behind the puppet's strings."

"As you wish, my brother." Ombre took a step

away from Nomand. His hands trembled with the effort as he lowered his sword.

Ilfedo knelt beside Nomand and grabbed one of his arms. Nomand shook with fear as Ilfedo touched the burning sword of the dragon to the severed limb. His flesh cauterized as the sword touched it and he screamed yet again. Ilfedo grasped the man's other arm and pressed the burning sword again to his wounded flesh. This time Ombre shoved a cloth into Nomand's mouth.

Ombre tore his glare away from Nomand. "What now, brother?"

"Now?" Ilfedo stood and wiped the blood off his blade. The living fire subsided somewhat as he spoke. "Now we have a humble guide to show us the path to Brunster Thadius Oldwell." He looked down at Nomand. "Unless the said guide chooses to lose his feet instead."

Ombre ripped the cloth out of the man's mouth and tossed it onto the cavern's floor.

"Forgive me," Nomand rasped out. His eyes darted from Ombre to Ilfedo, back to Ombre, and back again to Ilfedo. "I did not realize your greatness, my lord. Truly you can lead our people out of darkness. Oldwell would do well to tremble when you find him. It is you who shall rule over us as the true Lord Warrior. Not him."

Ilfedo gave a slow nod. "You will guide us, Nomand, and if I am pleased with your work then I will let you and your men remain in this underground world. You shall be living, yet outcasts marooned in this darkness. I do not have to kill you and I do not have to bring you to my homeland. I deem you too great a threat to bring into my land, therefore you will follow me while I remain in this realm. You shall be a slave to me until I leave this place. It should be your hope that my mercy will continue to be extended to you. Does this seem acceptable to you?"

Nomand did not say a word. His gaze went to the ground and his shoulders shook as he sobbed.

Ilfedo kicked the man aside and knelt beside Oganna. She was unconscious. "Ombre, will you bring her back to Dresdyn?"

Ombre did not hesitate. He stabbed his sword into its sheath and crouched beside Oganna. His stoic expression caused the warriors of light to step out of his path as he lifted her in his arms and turned to walk back the way he had come.

"And Ombre," Ilfedo added, "instruct Commander Veil to secure the path through these caverns. There will soon be many women and children returning to the city."

"Our men will hold this path," Ombre grunted as he walked off.

With a wave of his hand Ilfedo issued a command to his men and a dozen of them formed a protective ring around Ombre. They accompanied Ombre into the darkness on the route back to the city of Dresdyn, their glowing armor lighting his path.

Another man stepped forward from behind the line of Elite warriors and Nomand's eyes widened as he recognized him. "Captain Therman, what are you doing here? They did not kill you?" Therman knelt in front of Nomand and shook his head. "Ilfedo is a man of wrath, but also a man of justice. I have watched him stay his hand against me and my men. I stood by as he directed his men to take Oldwell's tunnel guards prisoner, being careful not to kill any of them." Therman's eyes did not even blink as he held Nomand's gaze. "Unlike myself and my men, you were not coerced into these deeds. If not for you our people might still be free."

Nomand trembled afresh. "You have received mercy? Even forgiveness? I beg of you! Ask for mercy on my behalf. I could be an ally to Lord Ilfedo. You have seen how useful I can be."

When Therman stood, he turned his back to the man and lowered his gaze as Ilfedo looked at him.

"Do you wish mercy for him?" Ilfedo asked.

"My lord, you are wise," Therman said. "I will not ask for you to do either good or ill to this man. I only ask how I may next serve you."

Ilfedo waved the sword of the dragon's burning blade toward Nomand's men. Their faces scrunched up as if trying to shield themselves from the light. He pivoted his blade so that its point aimed at the stonework tunnel. "Is this the path we must follow?"

Stifling a last sob, Nomand struggled to his feet. He kept his arm stubs crossed over his chest. "If you wish to find the people of Dresdyn and Bromstead also, then yes. That is the way," he said.

Ilfedo grasped Captain Therman's shoulder. As the man glanced up at him, Ilfedo relaxed his expression. "I do see goodness in you, and you have acquitted yourself well for your past deed by helping me find my daughter. Return with Lord Ombre to the city and wait for me there." He squeezed the man's shoulder. "Have hope, captain. The Creator will grant us strength this day and show our people out of this dark world."

Therman's eyes glistened and a lone tear fell

from his eye. "You called them 'our' people. Go now, I beg of you. For my wife and children are among those that were taken." He straightened, saluted, and followed after the warriors of light who were accompanying Ombre.

Ilfedo turned to Nomand, prodding him with the tip of his sword. "Lead onward. Your men will remain here. Captain Therman guided me well. Let us hope that you are as cooperative." He gave another command and the warriors of light forced Nomand's men to their knees, binding their hands behind their backs. Nomand trembled a bit as he turned to face the tunnel. Though he feared Ilfedo, a fear of his old master must have still remained as he forced his legs to move. He led Ilfedo through the arched opening.

The warriors of light filed into the tunnel behind Ilfedo. He kept his sword's point keenly pressed to the small of Nomand's back. Without his hands the man posed no threat, yet Ilfedo did not want to risk that the man would lead him astray. He needed fear in the man's heart. Fear in his mind that would drive him onward despite any fear he had of displeasing his master Brunster Thadius Oldwell. It had cost the man his pride and his hands, certainly this would be enough to make him take Ilfedo's threat with sincerity.

The tunnel proved to be a long one. When at last Ilfedo emerged into another cavern it was to look upon a new and stranger sight than that of the wooden city of Dresdyn. The chamber was half as large as that which housed the city and it did have its own light. Yet the source of that light was quite different from the gentle pink dewobins.

Molten lava cascaded from dozens of fissures

high in the cavern, spilling a few hundred feet before plunging out of sight down the edge of a cliff which overlooked an abyss. The abyss stretched in a half circle so that it appeared to have swallowed much of the cavern's floor.

Under the golden glow of the lava falls, a row of stone structures was visible along the edge of the precipice. These buildings had been built of hewn stone. No visible windows or doors. Just empty holes in the stone that allowed access like a colony of ants. Women and children huddled in front of the buildings, warming their hands over fires built from mushroom logs. Not a man was in sight.

Ilfedo grasped his sword by its blade and struck Nomand across the back of his head with its pommel so that he dropped to the earth. "Bind his feet and bring him back through the tunnel," he said to the men beside him. Four of them stooped to obey as Ilfedo turned his back to the abyss.

The tunnel through which he had come was packed with a few hundred glowing swordsmen. He issued a command and at once the men sheathed their weapons. Like snuffed candles the men melded into the darkness of the tunnel. Those nearest him flattened themselves against the tunnel walls as their brothers in arms carried the unconscious body of Nomand the betrayer back from whence he had brought them.

Sheathing the sword of the dragon so that it, too, went dark, Ilfedo ordered the soldiers to hold their position. At first one of his captains objected. "Send one of your scouts, my lord."

Yet Ilfedo needed only to cast one angry glance and the man averted his gaze. "I was tracking the wild beasts of the Hemmed Land long before I led armies into battle, lad. There are few scouts better than I."

"We will remain here as you wish, my lord," the captain said.

Turning his back to his men, Ilfedo walked up the sloping floor of the cavern toward the huddled women and children. The path was a large shelf of stone that was blocked on his left by the walls of the cavern. On the other side the path dropped off into the abyss. He approached the edge of the abyss, advancing close enough to peer over the precipice. The flows of lava fell from the distant side of the pit. Their glows should have illuminated the depths, but instead the lava vanished into a fog of utter blackness. Something about it made his spine chill so he turned away and approached the fires.

For more than an hour he studied the scene before him. The fires were spaced about twenty to thirty paces apart. Young children huddled to their mothers' skirts. The women, their faces smeared with dirt and their clothing frayed, tossed fresh logs onto the fires. Ilfedo studied them, noting the pallor of silence that seemed to hover over them all. No wonder. They must have given up hope of deliverance from Oldwell's madness.

But where were the men? Could they be working the 'mines' at Kraylan Abyss? There were perhaps fifty individuals camped along the abyss, which left hundreds more unaccounted for. Where had Oldwell taken them?

Suddenly the sword burned in its sheath and the living fire lashed out. The sudden flash of light elicited screams from the women and the children. Ilfedo grabbed the handle of his sword, half-closing his eyes as he cursed his weapon for giving away his presence prematurely. The sword started to float out of its sheath, yet he slammed it back in and glanced around at the small hills of stone that lay behind the stone buildings.

The sword fought him. It sprang out of its sheath, striking his hand aside as it did so. It hovered a few feet in front of him and a soft voice spoke from the flaming blade. It was the words of the prophecy Ilfedo had heard Elhandra the prophetess utter. "When darkness has fully fallen, and the spirits of the children are weak, then let their Lord Warrior speak. Let him bind and shackle, hew and spear. His arm is against them, his arm is for them. The Lord Warrior comes to doom them. The Lord Warrior comes to save them."

Ilfedo snatched the sword by its handle and slid it back into its sheath as the stone buildings erupted with people. Like ants piling out of holes in the ground the lost women and children of Dresdyn came toward him. They screamed, they cried. The children crowded him so closely that he could not have drawn his weapon again even if he had wanted to.

In the midst of this chaos Ilfedo felt dread rise with the vengeance of a bear robbed of its cubs. The tall figure of a man stepped into the lava glow. He stood atop the stone buildings and gazed down upon Ilfedo and the people that thronged him.

"Bromstead," Ilfedo said in a near whisper, for the figure was the possessed body of his former ally.

Bromstead stood as still as a giant sculpture. A few hundred yards separated him from Ilfedo and he nodded as he returned Ilfedo's stare. At his side the deadly blade of an ancient Lord Warrior shimmered with an emerald glow. The same blade that had hacked apart innocent men in Dresdyn.

Bromstead raised his arms and beckoned to Ilfedo with both of his hands. His eyes remained locked on Ilfedo's.

Gently Ilfedo parted the children in front of him. They, with furtive glances at the looming figure of Bromstead, shuffled around Ilfedo and huddled behind him. A majority of the women stood beside their children, shushing their cries. But a few of the mothers blocked Ilfedo's path. He frowned as an older woman spoke to him in trembling tones.

"You are the true master of our people, Lord Ilfedo of the Hemmed Land, and we have secretly prayed to God for your swift return. But you cannot face that man, for he is a man no longer but a demon," the old woman said. She reached out a trembling hand and touched his cheek. "Take the children back with you. Take them now. We would sooner sacrifice our lives to keep this monster away from our children and put them safely in your hands. Take the children! Do not wait. For if you delay the demon will conquer us all."

From the stony rise Brunster Thadius Oldwell laughed with the voice of Bromstead. "It is too late for escape, woman, and your dear 'lord' knows this full well." He paused long enough to close the distance between them by several dozen paces. His long legs propelled him with uncanny ease. "Tell her the truth, Lord Warrior. For I believe that you know as well as I do that this duel must come about. It was fated from the moment you took my scepter in your hand."

Ilfedo gently held the old woman by her shoulders and guided her to stand aside. Then he strode toward Oldwell.

Oldwell stopped in mid-stride and, drawing out his glowing sword, raised it above his head. The sword pulsed with harsh green light, and with each pulse filaments of black rippled from the sword's point. Oldwell grinned as smoky human forms rose from the cavern floor all around them. There were hundreds of them. Staggering along, they groped their way with claw-like fingers.

The throng of women and children constricted around Ilfedo with the force of quicksand as they tried to stay away from the demonic forms that were moving in on them. Some of them fainted as the demons drew within inches of touching them. The ground turned to ice under the demons' feet and the sound of their vile hissing and whispers rose in a sinful din.

Ilfedo's arms were forced to his sides by the press of bodies. He could not move. He could not free his sword. He shouted for the women and children to give him room, even as fear closed their ears to his plea.

Oldwell waved his sword and the demons halted their advance, forming a ring to prevent the women and children from releasing Ilfedo.

"You should have stayed away, Lord Ilfedo," Oldwell mocked. "The dark world is no place for a son of the world above. Down here, I am immortal."

Ilfedo thought to himself that he had been a fool to venture into the cavern on his own. Over the writhing mass of corrupted spirits he glimpsed the entrance to the tunnel where his men lay hidden. He attempted to mentally summon the living fire from the sword of the dragon, but Oldwell seemed to guess his intent. The tall figure pointed his vindictive blade toward Ilfedo. A green vapor spilled from the sword, covering the ground around Ilfedo and around the women and children. The vapor thickened, rising to his chest, and he could establish no connection to his sword.

* * *

Oganna's head ached as she regained consciousness. She raised her face away from the chest of the man carrying her, fists ready for a fight, but it was not an enemy who returned her gaze. "Uncle Ombre?" she asked. "How? When did you find me?"

His gentle arms set her feet on the cold ground as he gave her a grim smile. "I found you just before I severed the hand of that vile Nomand, and I would willingly have done it to the rest of his men, too." He clasped her hands together and looked her up and down. "You seem to have the use of all your limbs. Are you hurt anywhere that I should know about?"

She forced a chuckle, clapping her hand to her head. "This hurts more than a little, but I am otherwise unharmed." All around her stood the warriors of her father in their brilliant glowing armor. But the tall figure that she had hoped to see blazing with fire did not stand among them. "Where is father?" she asked at last.

"He is bent on finding the master perpetrator behind your kidnapping, Brunster Thadius Oldwell himself." Ombre forced a grin. "Of course, he did not go alone."

Oganna gazed off into the darkness of the cavern behind her father's men. Then she squeezed Ombre's hand and looked him in the eyes. "I can see that you have feared for me since the kidnapping, yet I am safe now and I do fear for my father. Please, send your fastest runner to retrieve my sword and my clothing from my room in the mayor's mansion. Please accompany me back to where you left my father. I do not want him to face this enemy alone."

"Neither do I," Ombre said. "But I will not allow you to venture back there."

Oganna rested her fingers on his cheek. "Uncle, we cannot afford to risk more of our family. I cannot lose Father, too."

"And we won't," Ombre assured her, but his gaze darted back the way he'd come.

Oganna knew that he was thinking of his loss of the beautiful Caritha. Out of her five aunts, Ombre had held Caritha in supreme regard and affection. For an instant Oganna wondered where her aunts were at in this moment. Had their trip on the Maiden Voyage ended in tragedy, or perhaps they had returned by now to the Hemmed Land?

"We have almost reached the tunnel that takes us to the city of Dresdyn," Ombre said as he pointed off into the darkness behind her. "If you wish to go after your father then so be it. I am not going to stop you. Yet I will stand by you and you will not venture off on your own." He held out his hand and regarded her out of the corner of his eye. "Agree to this, Oganna, as if you were binding your soul with an eternal oath."

She might have smiled as she shook his hand, but his eyes riveted on her with uncharacteristic soberness. She lowered her gaze a bit as she said, "You have my promise."

SHATTERING THE DARKNESS

It had proved quicker for Oganna to return on her own to the mayor's mansion to retrieve her clothes and her sword. She had apologized for putting her father's men in such an uncomfortable position when she had realized that her request to send one of them for her garments had turned many a valiant face a deep shade of red.

Ombre stood in the doorway to her quarters, his fingers tapping the pommel of his sheathed sword. He was eager to begin the search for her father.

She ignored his impatience as she pulled on her last leather boot. It felt so good to again have padding under her bare feet, and to be wearing her shirt and trousers. She braided her long blond hair in one long braid that hung to the backside of her knees. Some of her hair needed trimming, as attested to by the many split ends she struggled with.

Oganna smiled as she gazed down at the crystalline weapons laid on the feather bed. She grasped the blade boomerang, flipped it twice, and tucked it under her belt. Then she picked up her sword by its crystalline blade and slid it into the sheath belted to her other hip. The large ruby that formed the sword's pommel glowed softly under her fingertips.

From the disarrayed bed sheets Neneila the viper slithered forth to look up at her mistress. "Ssshall we go, mistress?"

"We shall indeed," Oganna said.

The viper hissed, then snaked around her outstretched arm, slithering up and around her neck. Its tongue brushed Oganna's neck as it said, "Sssink my fangsss into your enemies. That'sss what I shall do."

"Not unless my life is in danger," Oganna said as she turned to the door and nodded at Ombre. Under her breath she added a qualification to the viper. "Neneila, just do not put yourself in unnecessary danger. It would do me no good to see you hurt in my defense."

The viper nuzzled her neck with its head and Oganna knew that the creature was pleased by her concern. It comforted Oganna to have the viper so close. Other people might speak strangely about her relationship with the serpent. Some whispers back in her homeland suggested that Oganna fancied herself a sorceress and as such the viper was appropriate to her. Yet she knew the creature for what it was. A loyal and close companion. In its last effort to defend Oganna, the viper had been knocked out of the fight and had been forgotten by Ilfedo's men when Oganna was kidnapped. The loyal creature's pride had been hurt, yet when Oganna had returned to the mansion she had retrieved the viper and filled its ears with praise for its valiant deeds.

Neneila's forked tongue slicked in and out of her serpentine lips. Her fangs dripped thick venom, which she slurped back into her throat so that it did not land on her mistress's exposed neck.

"You sure you want to bring that creature with you this time?" Ombre asked. He shook his head as the viper hissed in defiance. "She's a spiteful thing . . . sometimes."

The serpent settled into its place, head resting on Oganna's shoulder, eyes half-closed.

Oganna danced up to Ombre and squeezed his arm. "You are kind, Uncle, but you underestimate Neneila. Were it not for her, I doubt I would still be alive."

Ombre almost chuckled as they walked down the hallway to the stairs. "I know," he said. "I do know. It's just that she is such an excitable creature that I can hardly help teasing her."

Oganna dropped her voice and spoke into his ear, "Please, do not do that."

In response Ombre gave her arm a quick squeeze, then he reached around her neck and, with two fingers, stroked the viper's head.

Neneila glanced at him. "Mistress, does thisss one think my friendship is ssso easily won?"

The question went unanswered as Ombre withdrew his hand and he and Oganna strode out of the mayor's mansion onto the moss yard which fronted it.

The brink of Kraylan Abyss awaited them, though of what they would find there she felt uneasy. As she marched out of the mayor's mansion she separated herself from Ombre and drew Avenger out of its sheath. A silver dress grew over her body, glowing with soft light as it did so. The sword's ruby pommel pulsed angry red and the sword's crystal blade faded in and out of visibility. She had fashioned this sword and appropriately named it for its purpose. Avenger had once been her mother's sword, yet her mother had not known to expand its potential as she had.

She marched down the highway out of the city, a dread purpose in her heart and her fingers tightly clasping the sword's handle. Something was reaching to her from the dark caverns and tunnels of this underground world. She could feel impending doom and at the same time a very great hope. But was the doom for her father, or for his enemy?

Behind her a line of ten swordsmen had formed. They kept pace with her, following her silvery form into the tunnel, all of them glowing white. Once they had entered the first adjoining cavern she grabbed Ombre's arm and smiled at him.

"What is it?" he asked.

Oganna pointed with her sword into the darkness ahead. "They are coming," she whispered. "Just as father asked of them, they are coming."

Ombre shook his head in frustration. There was an edge to his voice as he said, "Speak your mind. I've had enough with the riddles! Who is coming?"

His question was answered by the phosphorescent glow of a hundred eyes from the dark depths of the cavern. A scaly foot thudded into the ring of light emanating from Oganna and she smiled as the creature's claws tapped the stone floor.

A long snout riddled with teeth descended toward her and the men behind Oganna lowered their swords and bowed their heads as Vectra the megatrath smiled down upon Oganna. "Young one, it has been too long since our last meeting."

"Vectra." Ombre slapped the megatrath's foreleg. He smiled up at the creature for she stood more than ten feet tall. "I know not how you came to join us at this time, but I am very pleased to have your company."

"Indeed," Vectra rumbled in her deepest voice. She closed her eyes and dipped her long head politely. "The pleasure is mine, human. The paths of this underground world are long and, some would say, arduous. Yet thanks in part to Lord Ilfedo, my rule now extends a vast distance. The race of the megatraths is united now as they have not been since the days of my great grandfather."

Vectra turned herself about on her six powerful legs and grunted into the darkness. Flames spurted from a dozen toothridden snouts. The flames splashed against the cavern walls. In that moment the cavern and its occupants were fully revealed. The megatraths had truly arrived for there were hundreds of them cloistered behind Vectra and others thudding their way out of a pair of tunnel openings at the cavern's rear. A few black megatraths had even climbed high up the cavern walls. The nasty spikes on their backs glistened in the light of megatrath flames.

Oganna caught her breath as the last flames flashed out of existence and the cavern returned to darkness. The megatrath horde far exceeded the force that had accompanied her in the battle for the city of the giants, and even then they had been formidable.

Fire roiled behind Vectra's teeth as she gazed

upon Oganna. "The son of Regulus returned to him yesterday. He delivered your father's message, in my presence, and I formed this force of my kin to find and destroy the one called Brunster Thadius Oldwell. But Regulus did not listen to me, though by oath he is now bound to obey me. He left his son in the safety of his home cavern and ventured off alone. His last words were that vengeance upon Oldwell belonged to him, not to me."

A megatrath slid down the wall of the cavern, leaving a trail of sparks where its claws ripped the stones. As the creature thumped onto the cavern floor Vectra raised a fist and smote the ground. Oganna coughed on the resulting dust.

"Silence! I want absolute silence," Vectra bellowed into the darkness behind her.

Neneila slicked her tongue against Oganna's neck. "My, my, thisss creature's temper—"

Vectra's hand darted toward the viper and one claw slid out of a finger, lightly pressing Neneila's flesh. The viper swallowed its next words, staring at the megatrath's claw.

Oganna swatted Vectra's claw aside with her sword. Avenger's blade blazed crimson as if already drenched in blood. As Vectra's focus shifted to her, she nodded at Ombre. "We know where to find Brunster Thadius Oldwell."

The long corners of Vectra's mouth curled up at that. "When your father spoke that name he filled it with loathing. If he were a megatrath he could have dug his claws through diamond." The creature's snout came within inches of her face, and it spoke in a satisfied rumble. "Where can I find this man?" Then Vectra growled so deep that Oganna felt her spine rattle. "I should like to gnaw on him with my teeth."

Vectra scraped her claws along the stone floor, lighting the vicinity with an eruption of sparks. She swung her long body around the group of humans, all six of her legs powering her about so that she stood beside and behind them.

Oganna needed no other instruction. She understood Vectra was ready, even eager to find the lost people of Dresdyn. Oganna let the brilliant aura of her silver dress light the path as she led the way deep into the cavern and into the caverns beyond. Grunting their pleasure the megatrath horde followed. Their long, scaled bodies passed like shadows around her.

Beside Oganna, Ombre chuckled. "I believed we outnumbered Oldwell's force before. Now he had better run, for I think he has underestimated the following you and your father command."

The megatraths strode beside them, some of them fully ten feet tall at the shoulders. Some of them were gray, as Oganna was accustomed to seeing. Others had scales as black as pitch and long sharp spikes arrayed along their spines. They were formidable. The floor reverberated with the thudding of their clawed feet. Random sparks caught where their claws scraped stone, and now and again a glowing yellow vapor slipped from their long mouths.

She lifted Avenger, with both hands holding it so that the crimson blade rested before her eyes. She thought it burned with an eagerness equal to that of the megatraths.

The megatrath Vectra sent her followers into every dark corner of the caverns. This world could not hold an ambush for creatures as accustomed to it as they were.

Confidently the assembly moved toward the tunnel that would at last bring them to the edge of Kraylan Abyss. The warriors of light who had been left behind by Ilfedo to guard Oganna's kidnappers shone forth as a beacon in the darkness ahead. Their swords could be seen distinctly even at a distance and Oganna instructed the megatraths to slow their pace and allow her to precede them. She raised Avenger high, holding it with both hands, and called out to the warriors of light. They raised their swords in salute.

# THE HEART OF A FOOL

Bromstead no longer resembled himself. Ilfedo could see the look of a demon in his eye. The soul of the man he'd known and respected had been overwhelmed by this spirit.

Struggling against the press of women and children around him served little use. He could not get to his sword. Ilfedo felt only sorrow when he glanced again at Bromstead. The man's eyes were shadowed with the intent of the wicked spirit within him.

All around Ilfedo and the women and children, the wispy forms of the spirit beings tightened their circle. Three women at the outer edge of the huddle started to collapse as spirits touched their faces. The color faded from their faces, faded to stone gray. The demons had claimed their first victims.

The wrath of the sword of the dragon was tangible on his skin. The living fire felt as if it would burn through the scabbard against his leg. On any other battlefield he would have unleashed that energy with devastating accuracy.

His mind searching for a solution, Ilfedo at last turned his face toward Oldwell. He focused his mind, willing the sword to strengthen his lungs. He drew in as much air as he could, then let his voice rise above the mass of terrified women and children. When he spoke even Oldwell took a couple of steps backward.

"Everyone, fall to your knees," Ilfedo commanded. "Give me room so that I may defend you!"

The children knelt almost without hesitation. Some of the women did so as well as they turned their eyes up to gaze upon him. They had hope, at least a little, that their Lord Warrior was capable of stopping these abominations. Many women, however, stayed on their feet, frozen by the sight of hundreds of humanoid spirits advancing upon them. Yet the shift in humanity at last freed his sword arm. In a dramatic sweep he drew out his blade and, as the living fire clothed him, he pivoted, facing the mass of demonic forms. He did not fear them. He had faced their kind before when he had confronted the Grim Reaper. Through the power of living fire he had brought the Reaper to partial physical form, and in so doing had been able to sever its arm.

Eager children divided before him, their faces taking on stronger hope. They pushed their mothers and grandmothers out of his path. Their widening eyes settled on the funnel of fire and light that was him and his sword.

Ilfedo darted through their midst. He fixed his mind on recollections of his duel with the Reaper. Though that foul being had seemed as elusive as air, he had managed to defeat it. Now he must do similarly again.

The first demon he reached half-smiled as he drove his sword through its chest. As if time were slowing, Ilfedo watched as the living fire wrapped around the being's chest and gradually forced the being fully into the physical world. The sword met the resistance of flesh and drew blood, then tore the being in two. Now in the form of a man the being landed on the cavern floor. Not a muscle in its body even trembled and its eyes remained open.

Seeing the fate of their comrade the mass of demons withdrew a dozen paces. Relieved to have a reprieve, even if only for a moment, Ilfedo relaxed his sword arm. The women and children huddled behind him, some of them sobbing but most taking slow breaths to calm their nerves.

A green blade flashed across Ilfedo's vision, knocking the sword of the dragon from his grasp. He cursed his own foolishness for having relaxed his vigilance even for an instant as the sword clanged against the stone floor.

Bromstead stepped in front of him. Ilfedo reminded himself that the man was no longer in control of his body, for in truth Brunster Thadius Oldwell's spirit still possessed him. Oldwell pinned the sword of the dragon to the ground with the point of his green blade and that wicked sword bathed Ilfedo's weapon in a halo of its own energy.

No longer could Ilfedo feel a connection to the living fire. The power of the prophets seemed a distant memory as his glowing armor flashed out of existence, leaving him defenseless.

"You are prepared to meet your Maker?" Bromstead asked in Oldwell's voice.

Ilfedo glanced up at the man's face. "Forgive me, Bromstead," he said.

"The man you speak of is no longer a part of this body," Oldwell's voice bit back. "You think yourself a Lord Warrior, Ilfedo, and yet you know not what it means to carry that title. I do, and your forefathers did. I was among them when they abandoned the homeland in search of a new one."

"They did find a new homeland, you fool," Ilfedo said. "How else would I have been born from their blood?"

The big man sneered as he made a sweeping gesture with his free arm. "As you can see, even these damned souls serve my commands."

"Because they, like you, are a servant of the Devil." Ilfedo felt the urge to spit at Oldwell's feet, but he held his composure. Angering him would not help his own plight nor that of the women and children.

Suddenly Oldwell started to laugh. Not the maniacal response of a demon, but the response of one who finds genuine humor in something that was said. He smiled as he said to Ilfedo, "I want you to understand these things. It is important to me that you do, because, whether you like it or not, I am also your ancestor."

Ilfedo felt the blood rush from his face and his fingers grew cold. The demon's words must not be true. He did not want this heritage.

"I will tell thee my story, Ilfedo Matthaliah, and I expect you to listen. In distant memory your forefathers journeyed across the desert above and were driven deep underground by a sandstorm of unimaginable devastation. The storm prevailed for many long months and eventually they found the cavern wherein the dewobin birds dwelled.

"Unable to return to the surface world, they built the city of Dresdyn. They had brought with them many materials for building and supplies of food, as well as their collection of scrolls and books. Suffice it to say that the people were soon comfortable in their underground home and I urged them to remain here. Yet many of the people had no interest in staying. They would wait out the storm, they said, then move on to find a new land under the sun.

"The storm continued to hold its strength and then, quite mysteriously, several people were found dead. A couple of them had been slashed, as if with claws, yet not the claws of a beast. Another was found dead on her doorstep, her face ashen as if drained of life. After that a great fear settled among the people and many began the return journey to the surface world even though the storm still posed a great threat to their lives.

"Others in the city were soon killed in a likewise manner, even a child. My own family was divided on whether to remain in Dresdyn or to take their chances with the sandstorm. Many prayed to God for protection from the mysterious killers, yet Heaven did not intervene and the faith of many was shaken. My own wife was among those who ventured into the storm and not long afterward a couple of men returned to Dresdyn having found her body.

"I was devastated at her loss and realized for the first time that if there were a just god then I would not have lost her. I wandered deep into the caverns and found this place." Oldwell glanced around at their surroundings. "It was here that the demons tried to kill me as they had killed those people in Dresdyn. But my sword could touch them, and this they feared. It could kill them and send them to oblivion if I wished."

Oldwell leaned close and spoke softly. "There is one thing that I learned in my life and in my death. There is no God, but there is a Devil. And he wants to torture us. Humanity may wish for a being of infinite mercy and forgiveness, yet the only truth I have found is that evil exists and we are a part of it."

Oldwell stood straight again and chuckled amusedly to himself. "The people of Dresdyn did not at first receive me well at my return to the city. Many of them eventually left the city, including most of your family line. But with the demons at my command I manipulated the city into subjugation and held their loyalty through fear. Yes, I even orchestrated a few murders and other crimes so that I could appear as their hero and savior. The people never knew that I was behind the demons.

"But now, with so much time passed, I have no need for subtleties. You freed me from the scepter and now I can rule as never before. This body is younger than mine was, and stronger too."

Oldwell stepped back and gestured. Three of the city guard marched around the body of women and children. They took position behind Oldwell, hands to their sides. "Bind this man's wrists," Oldwell commanded.

One man produced a chain from his belt, the other two held Ilfedo's arms. Ilfedo thought of flipping the first man over his shoulder, but as he tensed his muscles Oldwell caught his eye. The villain nodded his head toward the demons behind him. "They will take another innocent life if you try it." Oldwell jutted his chin toward Ilfedo and whispered, "Do not let that hold you back. Amuse me, sir. Innocent lives mean nothing to me, but to you that is quite a different matter."

It was true. Ilfedo could save himself from this madman but not without destroying those he had come for. He relaxed his stance, allowing the guard to bind his wrists. He felt the guard hesitate upon finishing the task. The man slipped something smooth and cool into Ilfedo's hands, then herded him up the rough slope of stone.

Behind Ilfedo, Brunster Thadius Oldwell picked up the sword of the dragon. He paired it with his green blade. The green aura throbbed around both swords. Ilfedo could still feel no connection to his weapon, though he focused his mind wholly upon it. He wondered by what means the connection had been broken.

"March, lord of the Hemmed Land. One misstep and these children will watch their mothers die first." Oldwell laughed as he said it.

Ilfedo glanced over the faces of those he walked past. Many of the women's eyes brimmed with tears until they saw the gentle smile he gave them. The children watched as if waiting for a miracle and believing it could happen. When Oldwell's attention shifted from him to the buildings ahead of them, Ilfedo gave them a reassuring wink.

The children and the women, their faces betraying hope, let him depart from them without protest.

In his heart Ilfedo condemned his own foolishness. He had been captured. He had been foolish to allow this to happen. Perhaps he should have stormed into the cavern with the Elite Thousand. One thing only had held him back from summoning his men. The demons could not be touched by conventional swords and, though he hoped he was wrong, his bet lay that the swords of light would be ineffective against them as well.

As Oldwell's men led him past the stone structures, Ilfedo glanced over his shoulder. The taller man grinned at him, the knowing look of one who possesses all the keys on his face.

"Where are you taking me?" Ilfedo asked.

Oldwell swept his gaze over the swords in his hands. The green light swam in his eyes. "The abyss stands ready for you, lord of the Hemmed Land. The abyss asks for you and it will not be denied."

To the edge of the abyss they marched. The guards pushed Ilfedo to his knees and, drawing their bronze swords, held the blades against his neck. Oldwell, with the swords still paired in his hands, drew himself to the brink of the abyss, though out of Ilfedo's reach. The vast pit before them threw a steamy heat against Ilfedo's face as the lava falls blazed the air. The phosphorescent streams of yellow and red lighted the rough stone walls of the abyss, dropping hundreds of feet into darkness. For all he could see the pit had no bottom but opened to the core of Subterran itself.

Oldwell yelled into the abyss. "Come forth! I have a gift for thee."

TO HOLD THE DEVIL'S HAND

Ilfedo could still feel the smooth object between his hands. As he maneuvered it out of his palms and up to his fingers, he glanced down. It was a stone cut into the shape of a triangle. One edge had been honed sharp and a single word had been chiseled into the stone's face. In the dim light he had to squint in order to read it: *Help*.

While Oldwell peered down into Kraylan Abyss, Ilfedo allowed himself a smile as he brought his arms up. With the chain still binding his wrists, Ilfedo landed a blow to the side of the first guard's face. The second guard made as if to cut his blade into Ilfedo's neck but Ilfedo parried the blade with his chains and stood to his feet.

The remaining guard levied a kick to the man's back, sending him in a terrifying tumble into the abyss and thus proving his allegiance to Ilfedo. Blood ran from multiple punctures in the first guard's face as he swiped his sword within a hair's breadth of Ilfedo's chest, then pulled out a dagger and drove it into the shoulder of Ilfedo's ally.

With a sharp groan, Ilfedo's ally collapsed to the ground. "Go," he called to Ilfedo.

Ilfedo swung around, knocking the remaining guard to the ground. Then he threw himself at Brunster Thadius Oldwell. The tall man still held the prized swords in his hands and as Ilfedo leapt toward him, the man turned and lowered his green blade. The point drove through Ilfedo's arm and held him there.

"Fool!" Oldwell declared. "Did you think to throw me into the abyss?"

Fighting the blinding pain that ripped through his arm, Ilfedo forced his arms to move. With the green blade impaling one arm and the chain still binding his wrists he had to rely on his one arm to move, using it to pull along his wounded one. He grimaced with the effort as he clasped his other hand on the hilt of the sword of the dragon.

Oldwell glanced away from the green sword that was still stuck in Ilfedo's arm. His eyes riveted on the sword of the dragon in his other hand. Oldwell's mouth opened wide as the living fire swarmed over Ilfedo's arm and drew itself out of Oldwell's hand, resting itself firmly in Ilfedo's grasp. The man's face contorted with rage. Grasping his own sword with both hands, he raised Ilfedo bodily off the ground.

The armor of living fire began to grow over Ilfedo's body, but once it reached his wounded arm it stopped. The green blade sucked the living fire into Ilfedo's wound. Ilfedo cried out as the green blade cut deeper. Soothing warmth spread from the living fire, healing him, but the green blade leeched off of him like a poison.

Oldwell, still holding Ilfedo impaled on the green blade, turned so that he lifted Ilfedo out and over Kraylan Abyss. Ilfedo hung there, the green blade sucking the life out of him, while the sword of the dragon imparted its healing properties. Ilfedo's muscles tore as the green blade grated along his bone and again he cried out.

To his right he saw the guards. All three of them lay on the ground, though Ilfedo's ally was still breathing while the other two were not. The dagger that one guard had driven into his ally's shoulder now protruded from its wielder's head.

Something moved in the pit beneath his dangling feet and a pair of golden eyes glowed out of the shadows in the abyss. Tendrils of smoke rose from the lava falls and a winged beast crawled up the wall of stone. The scales on its body, wings, and long tail glistened with moisture. Grasping the cliff's edge it clambered up with ease and stood over the three guards.

Still impaled upon the green blade, Ilfedo found his eyes drawn to the beast's arched back where the ghostly figure of a woman sat. Her long legs straddled the beast and she wore a thin red dress that revealed a little of her semi-transparent form. Her cheeks were sunken and the flesh along her exposed arms was flaked and crusted. She held a pair of long leather reigns in her delicate fingers.

Oldwell heaved Ilfedo back to the cliff. He breathed heavily and sweat soaked his hair as he looked past Ilfedo to the woman on the beast. At last Ilfedo's feet rested on the ground.

"Is this the one you bring me?" the ghostly woman said, and her voice flowed like silk on the humid air.

Oldwell panted as he twisted his green blade in Ilfedo's flesh.

As renewed pain knifed through his shoulder, Ilfedo struck at the man with his own sword. Ilfedo clenched the handle with both of his bound hands as Oldwell pulled back, parrying the blow. The living fire covered the remainder of Ilfedo's body and the fiery helm grew on his head. The blade of living fire seemed to merge with its green nemesis every time they collided. The ring of metal against metal became deafening as the two men became fully absorbed in trying to subdue one another.

Between the clashes of their swords there arose the sound of gentle laughter. The two men continued their battle, moving away from the edge of the abyss as they did so. The beast from the pit circled them. It had a long narrow snout, somewhat like a megatrath's but thinner and glossy. Its small gold eyes glanced first at the men and then at the ground it walked upon. Unlike other beasts Ilfedo had encountered, this one had no claws on its fingers.

The woman's laughter abated as she rode the circling beast. With one hand she grasped the reins and with her other she stroked her long red hair. "Oldwell, your arm is strong yet this man's arm is stronger," she said. "Your effort is valiant, but this stranger is your equal with the blade." She laughed again. "Leave him to me."

Oldwell grunted and withdrew a few paces from Ilfedo. He spread his arms. "A truce, little lord of the

Hemmed Land?"

Ilfedo concentrated the living fire. Its flames melted the chain around his wrists so that they fell to the ground. He spun, pivoting his sword so that its point drove toward the demon woman and her strange beast. But the creature swayed away from his attack, dance-like it carried the woman toward the whimpering women and children of Dresdyn.

Now Ilfedo could see that the massed demons numbered in the hundreds. Their ghostly forms drove the women and children toward the edge of Kraylan Abyss, and when the woman on the beast raised her delicate hand the demons stopped their march.

"Now, Lord Ilfedo," Oldwell said as he strode to the side of the beast on which the woman rode. "How many lives are you willing to sacrifice today to save thy own?"

The women of Dresdyn murmured prayers and cried as they clutched their children to their sides. The demons hovered nearby as if waiting for the woman's signal to drive their would-be-victims over the cliff.

From over the rise in the cavern floor where the stone buildings stood, a strong line of bronze-clad guards from the city of Dresdyn marched into view. Their faces bore a stolid expression. They grouped behind Oldwell and the demon woman on her strange beast. Their swords were drawn.

Ilfedo slowly lowered his sword and his brow knit in an angry line as he faced Oldwell. "What do you want of me?" he asked.

"Want of you?" Oldwell spat on the ground. "You are of little concern to me. I want you out of my affairs. Out of my domain. But I would never trust you to stay away, so I must kill you."

"Enough of your foolishness!" Ilfedo said the words with such force and suddenness that Oldwell held up his sword defensively. Ilfedo used that moment to look into the faces of the many soldiers who remained from Dresdyn. "Enough of this foolishness! Stand and fight like men. Stand and fight with me. These women, these children are your flesh and blood. Will you stand by and let them die in despair?"

Several faces flinched and eyes glanced to the ground and then at their comrades. Suddenly one man stepped out of the assemblage. He shook his head and, with anger brooding on his face, he knelt. "Hail, the true Lord Warrior! Hail Ilfedo of the Hemmed Land."

Immediately the lines of men began to follow suit. A mere handful remained standing.

Oldwell pointed his green blade at them and said to those who remained standing, "Execute the traitors."

But those who knelt stood to their feet again and they far outnumbered Oldwell's supporters. Ilfedo watched as the city guards rose against their brethren and slew them in his name. Some fought back and, as they did so, the woman on the beast cried out for the other demons to slay Ilfedo's allies.

The demon horde swept toward the city guard with deadly purpose. The first line of men that met the demons in battle dropped without a sound, and their faces turned ashen white when they fell against the cold floor of the cavern.

Ilfedo rushed the woman on her beast and the beast swatted his arm, forcing him to roll on the ground. He stood and thrust the sword of the dragon toward the demon woman, but Oldwell rushed between them.

The green blade thrust aside the sword of the dragon and Ilfedo spun, seeking another point of entry.

Oldwell moved with precision. He did not attempt to overcome Ilfedo, instead he protected the woman. It was then that a doubt entered Ilfedo's mind, a doubt that gave him confidence to press his attack. For if Oldwell felt the need to protect this demon then she was vulnerable like any other creature in this world. Truly she and the others like her were unique, but they could be vanquished. She had allied herself with Oldwell, or he with her. Perhaps she was not truly a demon, only a being of great malevolence. Oldwell had laced lies with truth in his account.

Ilfedo glanced at the demon horde as they slew yet more of the city guards. These ghostly beings seemed invincible, yet through the strength of his sword Ilfedo knew that he could defeat them. The "demons" as Ilfedo had called them before, were not demons at all. They were creatures of a sort he had never known existed. Ruled over by this phantom queen.

If he could reach her—

Thrusting, parrying, driving his attack, still Ilfedo could not pass Brunster Thadius Oldwell. In the body of Bromstead the departed spirit had found a capable host.

Many of the city guards had slumped lifeless to the ground and still the demons advanced. The phantom queen rode her beast into their midst, urging her forces to slay every last guard. Her amused laugh fueled Ilfedo's anger as he glimpsed the futility of the guards' defense.

The women and children still huddled at the edge of the abyss, though the demons had abandoned them. At least in this the city guards had managed to make their sacrifices count for something.

Ilfedo retreated from Oldwell and raised the sword of the dragon in his hands. The living fire raged from the blade, forming a vortex of white light and flame that rose toward the cavern ceiling. In the blinding light the demons stumbled and shrank away from the city guards. Even the beast startled and threw the woman off of its back as it scrambled back toward the edge of Kraylan Abyss.

Out of the corner of his vision Ilfedo saw what he hoped to see. From the lower part of the cavern raced a line of warriors in glowing white armor. Oldwell turned toward them, a look of consternation filling his face. For Ilfedo's army poured into the cavern. Ilfedo's captains shouted orders, forming two spearheads. One formation herded the women and children away from the abyss and toward the exit tunnel, as the other broke upon the demons' rear flank.

Ilfedo let the living fire flood his body, amplifying his voice so that his men could hear his command. "Get the women and children out of this place, then leave! Do not let these creatures touch you."

The demons turned against the warriors of light. It was too late for a retreat. They swiped their ghostly hands toward the warriors' faces, but when Ilfedo's men struck out with the swords of light the demons shrank back, grabbing themselves as if they'd been stung.

Oldwell screamed his rage as he rushed Ilfedo. Ilfedo dodged the green blade, then struck back. But Oldwell rained blows upon him and drove him back to the edge of Kraylan Abyss. The green blade sliced his hand, then stabbed his thigh. Ilfedo staggered to the ground.

He blasted living fire from the blade, striking Oldwell's chest. Oldwell fell back, rolled to the side, then kicked Ilfedo in the ribs.

As Ilfedo clutched his side the living fire began to heal him, it tornadoed around his body.

Oldwell kicked him again, this time laying him flat on his back. Ilfedo cried out as the man raised the green blade and stabbed downward, the point driving through Ilfedo's chest, pinning him to the cold stone.

As Ilfedo's blood began to pool around him the woman on the beast rode up beside him. Her laughter again filled his ears, but this time it was suddenly silenced as a black form hulked out of Kraylan Abyss. A clawed hand slashed open the beast's side, spilling its innards on the cavern floor. Another set of claws clamped Brunster Thadius Oldwell's arms to his sides and the long form of Regulus rose behind him.

Regulus's voice rumbled as deep as thunder. "For the years you stole from my son." His silvery eyes found Ilfedo and gazed back. "We meet again, human." Then the megatrath effortlessly lifted Oldwell and smashed him on the ground, releasing its hold and circling him.

Oldwell struggled to his feet but the black megatrath lowered its long snout and snapped it back, driving its long horn through the man's shoulder. Blood spurted from the wound as Oldwell's legs collapsed under him.

Pulling the sword of the dragon against his chest and closing his eyes against a wave of dizziness, Ilfedo breathed deeply. The living fire slowly began to close his wounds but he had still lost much blood.

He heard the megatrath roar and so he opened his eyes. He wished he had not, for the demon woman stood beside the mightly black beast. Her hands raked down its sides, tearing off its scales and cutting into its exposed flesh. Regulus swiped his claws at her and they passed through her without effect, for she was nought but a ghost to him. Mercilessly she tore into his body. Pulling a bone blade from her belt she carved all six of his knees until he fell thrashing to the ground.

Though his arms trembled, Ilfedo raised the sword of the dragon and pointed it at the phantom queen. But he had lost too much blood. His arm fell limp and he was left gasping for deeper breaths.

He could still see Regulus, and he thought that the mighty beast looked back at him with its silvery eyes one last time as Brunster Thadius Oldwell stumbled to the woman's side and then drove his wicked green blade through the black megatrath's skull.

"No. Please, dear God, not him too." Ilfedo's words were merely whispered, yet the phantom queen swept toward him, her red hair flowing behind her.

Oldwell staggered along right behind her. "I am going to put this through your heart, Lord of the Hemmed Land." Oldwell spat blood as he spoke. "Say hello to oblivion for me."

He raised his sword to strike at Ilfedo's heart and the phantom queen nodded as he did so. But Oldwell screamed and swung his sword toward his side instead. A man had crawled there and now held a dagger in Oldwell's foot. The man smiled and Ilfedo recognized him as the guard that had first fought to free him at the edge of the abyss. "You are dead," Oldwell said to the guard.

In that moment the hand of a megatrath grasped Oldwell from behind, lifting him off his feet. The face of Vectra rose over Ilfedo as she plucked the green sword from Oldwell's hand. As it clattered to the ground she kicked it with her foot and sent it sliding over the cliff's edge into the depths of Kraylan Abyss.

"Vectra, stay clear of the demon—" Ilfedo uttered the words as the phantom queen charged the faithful megatrath.

Vectra smiled her long, toothy grin as she turned to reveal the young woman riding her back. Oganna, clothed in the glowing silver dress, slid off Vectra's back and poised her crimson blade between the demon and the megatrath. The demon laughed and stabbed at Oganna with the bone blade, but Oganna's Avenger severed the blade from its hilt and the phantom's hand from the body. The slimy belly of Neneila the viper slid around Oganna's shoulders and that creature's head rose.

Ilfedo stumbled to his feet. The living fire continued to strengthen him. He reached out, focusing his sword's power. It enabled him to grasp the phantom by the back of her neck. She screamed as he forced her body to enter a fully physical state. She tried to shake him off but Oganna held the Avenger to the phantom's throat, stilling her struggle.

"Sstay still," Neneila the viper hissed.

"I do not wish to execute you, woman. But, I will, if you force me to make that choice." Ilfedo paused long enough for her to gulp twice for air. "You command them?" He posed it more as a statement than a question. "End this. Now!"

The phantom queen at last raised her voice in a shrill call. The whispy forms of her fellows fell away from the warriors of light and retreated from the surviving members of the Dresdyn city guard. They swept toward Ilfedo and he saw in their gruesome faces a rising anger. They were not surrendering. They wanted to kill him. Oganna stood behind him. Vectra still held Oldwell so that his feet dangled a few feet off the ground.

Oldwell chuckled as the demons approached and, as Ilfedo glanced at him, the man's lips set in a confident scowl. "Die well, Ilfedo of the Hemmed Land," Oldwell said.

The demons closed within a dozen feet of their position. Some of the ghostly beings divided from the main group, sallying into the remaining guards from Dresdyn. Three of the bronzeclad warriors cried out as they fell helpless to the ground, their armor thudding to the stone floor of the cavern.

Ilfedo thought of the suffering these beings had unleashed on the people of Dresdyn. As if slowing time to a crawl, he recollected the first day he had entered the underground city. He had found a house haunted by these beings and there he had found one of their victims. A young girl. Her innocent face filled his mind as sweat ran down his face.

Ilfedo thrust the phantom queen to the ground, ignoring her startled cry. He kept the vision of the young girl in his mind as he sent a silent prayer to the Creator to grant him vengeance. The phantom queen, now loose from his grasp, began to revert to her previous form. She smiled and clawed at his leg, but her fingernails merely scraped along the armor of light. She looked up at him, eyes wide. Ilfedo struck off her head with the sword of the dragon, then grabbed her hair and tossed the grisly object into the path of the approaching demons.

The beings slowed their approach, regarding the rolling head, then they raced toward him. Ilfedo walked into their onslaught with the sword of the dragon burning in his hands. He held its point toward heaven, focusing his power to completely envelope him in flames. He struck off their heads and thrust many through their chests. The few that passed him met with Oganna, in whose hands the Avenger affirmed its deadly effect. Soon there lay about them a pile of bodies that appeared to be of no more substance than a morning mist.

From behind the demon horde line upon line of Elite swordsmen advanced, mowing the enemy down from behind. For the swords of light cut through the phantoms as well, reaching through their essence to slay them.

The beings before him opened their mouths in noiseless screams. Their bodies began to fade as they sought to escape. The beings vanished in droves, some of them floating off into the abyss and others merging with the darkness. Wisps that could not be seen.

Ilfedo raised his sword to resounding cheers from his men and those who remained of the city guard. As the cheers rose again, he glanced sideways at Oganna as she sheathed her sword. Vectra lowered her mighty head and Oganna climbed on. The creature rose to its full height and let out a roar that deafened him. From behind the warriors of light there arose a chorus of other roars until all of Ilfedo's men covered their ears. And then it was that Ilfedo saw for the first time the host of megatraths emerging from the shadows, for their numbers astounded him.

Turning to face Vectra's prisoner, Ilfedo said, "Now you see why I am the Lord Warrior. Brunster Thadius Oldwell, you are defeated."

"Defeated? I think thou art mistaken, Lord of the Hemmed Land," Oldwell said. "Look around at the

high cost of this victory, and still you cannot touch me."
He laughed as he said it. "It is a beautiful thing. You
can hurt the man I inhabit. Yet cannot touch me in the
slightest."

Ilfedo set his jaw in a firm line. "Then I will need
to find someone who can touch you."

TAKEN
FROM THE ABYSS

Ilfedo wiped the sweat from his forehead and smiled as four of his warriors of light marched by with young boys running around them. To his left Vectra stood atop the rise of stone homes that formed a parallel with Kraylan Abyss, Brunster Thadius Oldwell still clutched in the claws of one of her powerful hands.

The megrath growled. "You are pleased, my friend?"

"To have confronted an evil as great as this and then to emerge victorious?" Ilfedo chuckled and smiled again. "Vectra, this pleases me greatly."

The creature allowed herself a long, toothy grin. To many people the grin would have seemed threatening, but Ilfedo welcomed it. On many occasions Vectra had proved herself not only a trusted ally but a valued friend. "I have not often seen you this pleased," the creature said. "Yet it is a good change."

Ilfedo glanced over the sea of blazing white swords that were spreading through the cavern. His warriors probed every makeshift building and every crevice they could find, searching for survivors. Even now another man stood from the battlefield with the help of a warrior of light, while nearby two more soldiers of the Dresdyn city guard saluted Ilfedo in passing. Megatraths scoured the cavern as well, mingling with the humans. "You will see me smile more when I have safely escorted all of the survivors of Dresdyn out of this underground realm."

"As will I." Vectra lifted Oldwell and turned him over with the same ease that one would examine a curious toy. Oldwell grunted and began to mutter, yet he could offer no other protest. "What do you plan to do with this one?" Vectra asked.

Ilfedo shook his head, regarding the prisoner again. He had been asking himself that same question without success. "I will bring him to the monks, for I do not know how else to handle his condition. This spirit seems to have overwritten the soul of the man this body belongs to. I will bring him to them and see if the Creator will intercede on Bromstead's behalf."

"He is very large. Very strong," Vectra observed. "For a human, that is."

"And he was a good man to have by my side," Ilfedo said. "I will have him back if I can."

He looked again into the depths of the cavern. Among the swords of light, Oganna's silvery form danced from one survivor to the next, shepherding a line of women, men, and a small number of children toward the exit tunnel. The lava falls of Kraylan Abyss provided a mesmerizing backdrop to the entire scene.

Turning his back to Vectra, Ilfedo strode down the sloping stone floor until he reached the cadaver. The black scales on Regulus's body still glistened in the lava's glow. Ilfedo shook his head, then faced Vectra again. "I am sorry for his death."

"As am I," she replied in a soft rumble. "Regulus commands the respect of all megatraths. He was as cunning in politics as he was in battle. Only his rage in finally confronting his son's kidnapper could have driven him to so recklessly pursue this battle."

"What will become of Arvidane, now that his father is dead?" Ilfedo asked.

Vectra raised her head, snorting a plume of fire from her nostrils. "As any other megling, Arvidane will have the opportunity to prove himself to his kin and to me. If he rises to his father's greatness then so be it. If not, then his name will be allowed to fade into oblivion. No megatrath asks for any honor more than that which they earn, yet they can aspire to continue the legacy of their bloodline."

Ilfedo laid his hand on Regulus's horn. It still bore the stain of Oldwell's blood. No, not Oldwell's blood! The blood of Bromstead, captain of the city guard. Striding back to the megatrath and her captive, Ilfedo studied the man. His eyes flicked instantly up to meet Ilfedo's gaze. Ilfedo touched the man's hand. It was warm to the touch.

Oldwell scowled, a puzzled expression slipping through his disciplined features.

Vectra tilted her head a bit to the side. "Lord Ilfedo, are you looking for something?"

"No. All is well," Ilfedo said, and he turned away

from the prisoner and started walking down the slope toward the exit tunnel. He would soon return to the City of Dresdyn, this time with hundreds of survivors. He found comfort in the fact that during his struggle with Oldwell he had not permanently maimed the host's body. If Bromstead was still in there, may heaven and hell be moved to bring him back and dispel the evil spirit within him.

Before he was out of earshot, Vectra said to Oldwell in a low rumble, "I was a little worried that you might be carrying a disease."

Ilfedo smiled again upon hearing that. He had much to be thankful for on this day. Many lives had been saved, and in the midst of it all was the megatrath's humor.

"Brother," Ombre strode up and clapped him on the shoulder, "the foe is vanquished. Are you ready to take all of these people out of this darkness? I think a few of the survivors back in the city will be more than a little happy to see that so many have returned to their families."

Ilfedo drew to a stop. He shook his head. How could he have been so foolish as to forget? Elhandra!

Ombre blocked his path, crossing his arms over his chest. "That look tells me something is wrong."

"The prophetess." Ilfedo slapped his fist into his other hand. "The poison, or whatever is killing her, I have no hope of stopping it without the sword of Brunster Thadius Oldwell. It was he that infected her and he used the green sword."

"Okay, then where is that weapon?" Ombre asked him.

Ilfedo turned his back to the exit tunnel. He

would soon take the path back to the city of Dresdyn, but not now. He slapped Ombre's shoulder and started to run back toward Kraylan Abyss. "Come with me, brother." As Ombre ran alongside him, Ilfedo told him of the struggle that had ensued when Vectra and Oganna had joined his battle against Oldwell and the phantom queen. The last he had seen of Oldwell's green blade had been as Vectra kicked it over the edge of the abyss.

"What! You want to go down there?" Ombre gave a beleaguered frown as they stopped at Kraylan Abyss's edge. He leaned sideways to look down into the abyss's depths. "It's a little dark down there, don't you think? I don't see a hint of any glowing green sword."

"For all I know it could take a couple of days to climb down that cliff," Ilfedo said. "Or it has no bottom at all."

Ombre blew out his lips as he replied, "I think the later of your two guesses is the most likely. In fact, there is a third alternative."

"A third?" Ilfedo frowned.

"You could find a bottom to this pit, yet the lava falling down there could have buried the weapon by then," Ombre said. "Or it already has."

"I have to try," Ilfedo said. "Oldwell is already my prisoner. Perhaps I can figure out how to get him to withdraw the curse he placed on the prophetess. If not, maybe we can figure out a way to use it without his help."

Ombre shook his head, stepping back from the cliff. "She is worth a risk like this?"

Ilfedo recollected the day he'd entered Dresdyn. Elhandra had been there. She had stood by him.

He returned Ombre's gaze. "A more faithful counselor I would have difficulty finding, and I value the wisdom she can bring to our people. I will not abandon her unless I have failed in all that is within my power to do."

Ombre looked again down into the abyss. "Ilfedo, there is no way you are going down there." He held up his hand as if to dissuade Ilfedo from offering a rebuttal. "I know you are set on it, but can't you use your God-given brain to figure out a smarter way to search for that weapon?"

The thudding footfalls of a megatrath preceded Vectra's arrival. She grasped the edge of the abyss and stared down into it.

Ilfedo glanced at her empty hands. "Where is the prisoner?"

"Do not fear," Vectra said. "I have entrusted him to the choicest of my bodyguards. Even now they are bringing him back to the city of Dresdyn where he will be held until your arrival." Her big eyes probed the abyss.

In the rest of the cavern the survivors began their exit. They formed groups with the glowing warriors assisting the survivors through the stone-strewn terrain and between the stone buildings. Megatraths loped along beside them in greater numbers. The beasts did not join the humans through the exit tunnel, instead they split off from them, climbing into the dark recesses hidden high in the cavern walls.

Ilfedo pointed at the departing megatraths and looked to Vectra. "Do they know other ways out of this place?"

Vectra grinned. "Indeed they do," she said. "You must keep in mind, Ilfedo, that this underground world is our home. We know it better than most. If a human were trapped in here they would have a nearly impossible time discovering the tunnels that lie high in the cavern walls. Even if they could find them, they could not reach them." She swiveled to again look down into the abyss. "You are set on finding this weapon that I cast into the pit?"

"I must find it," he said. "I believe the life of a good woman depends on it."

Vectra blew out her nostrils, letting bits of flame out as she did so. "Let me seek it out for you. For it was I that discarded it, and my claws are surely capable of letting me down this cliff with much greater ease than are your arms."

"It is a generous offer, Vectra. And I thank you," he said. "However, when I first came to the city of Dresdyn I used my sword to lower myself down a high cliff face. It set me safely on the ground at the cliff's base."

"Mmm," the creature replied, "yet I think such an act carries great risk this time."

Ombre raised his hand. "I agree!"

Ilfedo shook his head. "It served me well before. Even faster than if you were to climb down it. I mean no disrespect."

The megatrath dipped the front of her long body in a slight bow. "Have you considered that molten rock and lava may have pooled at the base of this abyss?"

"Exactly what I was thinking," Ombre said as he rolled his eyes. "Ilfedo, you'd be a fried chicken. Or, I guess, a fried lord."

Ilfedo furrowed his brow. In actuality he had not considered the possibility. It made logical sense, yet he had been hasty and fixated on the task of retrieving the sword. "Your caution is valid," he said to Vectra.

"Then let me see to this task for you," Vectra said in a satisfied rumble. As Ilfedo started to nod his agreement, she pulled back her head and let out a deafening roar.

Ten megatraths turned away from climbing the cavern wall. In the dim light of the cavern it was hard to see them at first but when they approached Vectra they only stood as high as her shoulders. She instructed her companions to follow her down into the abyss and told them of the green sword. The creatures immediately let themselves over the cliff and began the descent. Vectra followed.

"Vectra, wait!" Ilfedo held out his hand and the creature hesitated, her big eyes returning his gaze. "That sword is a vile weapon of a power equal, it seems, to my own. Handle it with care and do not put any mental focus upon it. Keep your mind on the task of bringing the sword to me. I believe that by doing this you can avoid awakening its power."

Vectra growled, then let herself over the cliff's edge, her claws gripping the stone with confident strength. She backed down into the darkness of the abyss and in that moment the abyss seemed to swallow the megatrath and her companions. The lava falls reflected a little off the walls.

Kneeling at the precipice, Ilfedo watched the creature fade into the depths. "Can you still hear me?" he called after her.

Another growl preceded Vectra's reply. "Have patience, my ally."

Ilfedo waited and Ombre stood beside him. The people of Dresdyn continued to file out of the cavern behind them and many of the megatrath horde disappeared high into the walls through hidden tunnels and crevices. Oganna waved in his direction before she glided out of sight into the tunnel. Her silvery dress carved her image into the darkness with stark contrast.

A contingent of twenty Elite warriors stationed themselves half-way between his position and that of the exit tunnel. The warriors looked toward their position, but Ombre raised his hand in a silent command for the men to remain where they stood until called upon. Elsewhere in the cavern, megatraths and men were still bringing survivors toward the exit tunnel as Ilfedo waited for Vectra to return.

He waited a long time.

The heat of the lava falls brought large beads of sweat to Ilfedo's forehead. He wiped them away with his sleeve. Time seemed to move with the patience of a snail until, at long last, three forms lumbered up the cliff's face. Powerful arms reached out of the darkness and thick claws grasped the edge of the precipice as Vectra pulled herself onto the ground again. Her companions lumbered up behind her, perching themselves on the cliff's edge.

Vectra's face broke into a toothy grin as she dropped the sword of Brunster Thadius Oldwell onto the cavern floor. "The weapon is yours, my dear ally. Do with it whatever you wish." Then she loped off into a far corner of the cavern, her companions following, and climbed the walls of stone. Her thick hide swayed as she slipped out of sight behind a stony crevice.

Ilfedo fixed his eyes on Oldwell's weapon. It was a stunning design. An ivory two-handed piece with a blade four feet in length, and a gap that ran three-quarters of the way up its fuller. He knelt and reached his hand toward it. As soon as his fingers touched the hilt, the weapon glowed warm light again. He jerked his hand back.

"How are we going to take that thing with us?" Ombre asked. "I mean, it acts similar to the sword of the dragon. It could turn on you if you grab it."

"No," Ilfedo said. "Grabbing it would hurt me at best, kill me at worst. I would guess at the later consequence if I picked between the two. But Oldwell meshed the power of his sword to mine and they appeared to cancel each other out. If I do the same, it may neutralize the sword's threat."

Ilfedo held out the sword of the dragon and laid it on top of Oldwell's sword, allowing the living fire to encase it. With a slight hesitation he extended his fingers around the green blade's hilt so that he held the swords together. At last he lifted them and the living fire held the green blade captive in a vortex of white flames.

The assemblage of humans and megatraths leaving Kraylan Abyss grew in number. Every corner of the cavern had been searched. Hundreds of survivors had been located, many of them had been working to mine the precious metals that the abyss had to offer. Many others had been conscripted to fashion swords and spears from the metals. A few of Ilfedo's men were the first to discover forges that utilized the flowing lava to heat the metals. The megatraths found others. Though the wicked spirit of Brunster Thadius Oldwell had remained mute on the reasons behind his decision to bring the people to the abyss, Ilfedo surmised that Oldwell had intended to build a militaristic stockpile utilizing slave labor. He could only guess at whether the demon would have remained underground or sought to bring conquest to the surface world.

It no longer mattered.

Ilfedo waited for everyone to exit the tunnel to Kraylan Abyss, then he signaled to the warriors of light who had waited for him. The men marched behind him as he followed the last of Dresdyn's people through the exit tunnel. When he emerged into the cavern beyond, He called to those who guarded his prisoners. Ombre turned a hot glare upon Nomand as the warriors of light brought the traitor forward. Nomand raised his trembling arm stubs and cried for mercy. Ilfedo could not find it in his heart to hate the man. He pitied him. Ilfedo pitied Nomand the death he would die by Ilfedo's command. Yet for the sake of justice the deed must be done.

"You and your men will take up your abode in the mines at Kraylan Abyss," Ilfedo uttered in stolid tones as the man whimpered, begging again for an escape from his fate. "Nomand, I commit you into the caverns of the underworld. I pray that you seek forgiveness of your Creator and in these last days of your life find hope in that forgiveness. Otherwise your despair will consume you until madness fills your mind."

The warriors of light shoved Nomand and his companions through the tunnel, then stood back. Ilfedo laid the sword of Brunster Thadius Oldwell on the ground, then raised the sword of the dragon and blasted the tunnel entrance with fire. Stones and dirt thudded to the tunnel floor as it collapsed, sealing the traitors on the other side.

As dust billowed around Ilfedo, causing Ombre to cough, Ilfedo knelt and bonded the sword of the dragon once again to Oldwell's sword. With both hands he hefted the weapons and rested their blades against his shoulder as he turned his back on the tunnel to Kraylan Abyss and directed his steps on the return path to Dresdyn.

The warriors of light marched ahead of and behind him, illuminating many of the long stalagmites and stalactites inside the caverns. As they marched around one stalagmite that stood as high as Ilfedo's house, a tall megatrath emerged from the darkness and nodded to him.

It was Vectra, leading a dozen or more of her kind. The creatures sped ahead of Ilfedo's men, their long legs enabling them to eat the distance in easy strides. The thudding of their heavy feet echoed from one cavern into the next, along with the occasional rumbling growl.

As he strode forth, Ilfedo examined the sword he held beside his own. It was a magnificent weapon. Yet it had proved deadly, at least in the hands of its evil master. Somehow, by some means, he had to use it to undo the plague it had unleashed upon Elhandra the prophetess. He lowered the weapons so that he could focus on the path before him. "Hold on to life, my dear prophetess," he whispered into the underworld. "Dear Creator, please spare her and give me knowledge of how to do it."

THE OUTCAST'S TALE

When Ilfedo strode out of the tunnel and observed the wooden city in the cavern before him, he stood on the roadside and Vectra swung around him. The sword of the dragon still blazed in his hand, the living fire encompassing both it and the wicked green blade. Vectra stood behind him and rumbled in her satisfied way as a line of white armored swordsmen marched two abreast down the road and into the city. A megatrath rose out of the tunnel behind them and ambled off into the city, five more of the creatures following on its heels.

Hundreds strong, Ilfedo's men marched down the road where a contingent of soldiers awaited them. Commander Veil removed himself from the contingent and directed the returning warriors with a wave of his arm. The men split in two columns, making their way down separate streets toward the heart of the city.

The megatraths' numbers quickly grew. Vectra roared at them and swatted them aside with her tail. She herded them to the outer edges of the city and the commotion she made summoned the megatraths that had entered the city. They returned to her, emerging from the city to join the swarm of their kind that now hovered behind Vectra like bees gathering to their queen.

"At last," Ilfedo whispered to himself. The city of Dresdyn lay before him again, but this time he could seal its fate for the better.

Ombre emerged from the tunnel with a couple dozen warriors clad in bronze and holding torches. He separated from the group, letting them continue on to the city. Captain Therman was among the warriors that marched to the city and he gave Ilfedo a slight bow as he passed by.

"Brother, your arms must be getting tired of holding both swords," Ombre said.

Ilfedo nodded for it was indeed tiring his arms. The energy from the sword of the dragon would normally have given him a longer wind, yet now its power seemed wholly absorbed in negating the powers of Oldwell's blade.

"You need rest," Vectra said, rumbling deep in her chest. She held out one of her massive hands and let her claws slide into view. The living fire glinted off of her claws as she flexed her fingers. "Leave the weapon here," she said, tapping a claw on the cavern floor. "I will guard it."

Ilfedo set the wicked blade on the ground and then sheathed the sword of the dragon. He kept his hand on the handle for a long moment, half-expecting

Oldwell's weapon to burst with green flame.

Pinning the blade to the stone with the tip of her claw, Vectra nodded toward the city. "I sent four of my choicest guards into the heart of your city with the prisoner. They will be waiting on your command."

With a slight bow, Ilfedo turned away from the megatrath and started to walk down the road. Ombre kept pace alongside him. They left the megatrath horde behind them and made their way into the heart of the city. On the mossy lawn by the mayor's mansion stood the four megatraths, and in their center stood Brunster Thadius Oldwell.

The man glared down at the men as they approached him. He spat on the ground. His green eyes held an unnatural contrast to his darkened skin.

Ilfedo gazed up into those green eyes. He held them, unwavering. He felt the will of the possessing spirit boring down upon him. It was full of spite. "You wounded the prophetess Elhandra?" Ilfedo asked.

The green eyes stared back, though a look of amusement betrayed itself on the man's face.

"You cut her with your blade, somehow poisoning her," Ilfedo continued. "I need to know how to cure her."

"And you expect to learn this from me?" Oldwell chuckled. "Thou art truly a child in a world of monsters."

"Your poison is strong, Oldwell," Ilfedo said. "I will not deny it. But in harming her you accomplish nothing. Tell me what will save her."

Oldwell crossed his arms across his chest and looked out over the city. "In exchange for what? My freedom?"

Ilfedo chuckled at that. "I would not pose such a promise, for it would be a lie. You, Oldwell, are my prisoner until I discover a means of expelling you from the body you now possess."

Oldwell raised his eyebrows and gazed down upon Ilfedo again. The megatraths guarding him growled softly in their throats as he pointed a finger at Ilfedo. "Then let her die while you celebrate this victory."

With a shake of his head, Ilfedo firmed his jaw. "Do it to show your strength. You could save her as a display of your power and to demonstrate—in front of the people of Dresdyn, my men, and even the mega-traths—that your knowledge of these things is superior to mine. Surely that would bring you satisfaction."

Oldwell smiled at this. "Thy tactic is worthy of a true Lord Warrior, Ilfedo of the Hemmed Land. If I were a lesser man I would flaunt my knowledge, as you suggest. But I am not a lesser man. I will not give you what you want and you will not give me what I want. The prophetess shall remain until her soul is painfully removed from this life. God save her."

Ilfedo stepped back and glanced at the mega-traths. "Continue to hold him here. If he needs rest, let him sit where he stands. It is only the spirit within him that I loathe. The body still belongs to a man I would prefer to have returned to my service."

The creatures rumbled their response and dipped their long snouts in obeisance. Stepping past his pris-oner, Ilfedo entered the mansion and Ombre shut the door behind them. Hesitating, Ilfedo half-turned toward Ombre. "Give me some time alone, brother, please."

"You are going to visit her?" Ombre sighed. "Wait until morning. After you've rested your body and your mind. Even with the sword of the dragon sustaining you, you still need to rest."

Ilfedo started to climb the stairs. "She may not have long, brother." When he reached the top of the stairs he glanced back down. "I could use a good meal."

Exhaling in a frustrated way, Ombre said, "Then come down and get one! She is likely asleep anyway."

"I'll be down in a few minutes. Save some food for me." Ilfedo headed down the hall.

When he reached the bedroom he'd been looking for, he opened the door. Inside, on a fluffy bed, lay the prophetess. Everett sat in a chair beside the bed, his bearded chin touching his chest as he softly snored.

Stepping past the man, Ilfedo stood at Elhandra's bedside. He watched without saying a word. Only the silent room lit by a fading lantern's flame gave him company. The quiet was a welcome relief after the day's activities. After a long while he pulled back Elhandra's shirt to check the wound. She stirred yet did not waken. Now that he had Oldwell's weapon perhaps he could undo what was happening to her.

He felt his mind go blank. He could no longer remember what he had come here to do, so he prayed the Creator's blessing on her and then slipped out of the room, closing the door behind him.

Joining Ombre down in the parlor room on a long pink sofa. Ilfedo laid his sword on the coffee table. He closed his eyes and leaned back. Though he thought he'd failed to realize it before, his back ached and his eyes wanted to rest.

"Take it easy, brother." Ombre grasped his shoulder and leaned back his own head, closing his eyes.

"I cannot." Ilfedo leaned his elbows on his knees,

cradling his face in his hands. "She is dying, Ombre. The prophetess is dying while we think of rest."

Oganna stepped into the arched opening to the dining room. She leaned against the frame, sipping from a steaming cup. She smiled at her father and then glanced into the room behind her, beckoning with a hand.

A short, roundish woman bustled through the arched opening, a smile filled her face as she placed a hot cup on the coffee table. "I make the best meat broth you will ever taste, my lord!" She curtsied as he thanked her, then she bustled out of the room, humming a tune.

Ilfedo frowned at his daughter. "She seems almost cheerful. Does she not know that the battle has cost innocent lives?"

"Do not look down on her for it, Father. She has been of the greatest comfort to the women I brought with me. I understand that she is a widow with several of her own young children, all of them boys whom she loves dearer than anything in this life. Her husband died in the battle for Ar'lenon." Oganna hesitated, lowering her gaze to her cup. "Today, she has had the chance to serve her broth to the most eminent man in the Hemmed Land. You, Father, are a hero to her sons and she will be able to go home to them with the story that she personally served the Lord Warrior in his time of need."

Ilfedo glanced at Ombre.

His friend smiled back. "You raised her too smart, didn't you?" Ombre said with a chuckle.

Lifting the cup, Ilfedo sipped the broth. "Her intelligence came from her mother and was encouraged by her aunts I think, not I," he said. "Oganna, you have put me gently in my place with your words." He looked at her and she smiled back as he said, "Thank you, my daughter."

"What else is a princess for?" Oganna teased.

The broth was indeed delicious. Ilfedo requested a refill, much to the delight of the woman who had made it. Oganna called her back in and she again served Ilfedo. He made a particular effort to thank her, even taking her hand and thanking her for her husband's service. At his words the woman sobered.

"We have all lost much, I believe," she whispered. "But we have also gained much more, thanks to your care. May God continue to grant us your guidance." With that she left the room.

Ilfedo listened as Ombre and Oganna discussed the strange battle with the demons at Kraylan Abyss. Neither of them could fully grasp the role the phantom queen had played in Oldwell's reign, yet Oganna thought that in some way the queen had found Oldwell to be a kindred in the spirit of evil.

Their conversation melded into the background as Ilfedo leaned back on the sofa and closed his eyes. He fell asleep, determined that when he awoke he would go to Elhandra and again attempt to heal her.

* * *

When Ilfedo awoke the lanterns in the sitting room were burning low. Ombre snored on the other end of the couch and Oganna was no longer in the room. Silence filled the large rooms of the house. A peaceful silence that helped him close his eyes for a few moments more. His back ached again, this time from sleeping on the couch, but his mind was a little clearer than it had been.

He stood to his feet, grabbed the sword of the

dragon off of the coffee table and made his way upstairs to the bedrooms. He passed Oganna's closed door, proceeding to the next one. The door stood ajar and inside rested a large bed covered in sheets. Weary and yearning for the deep sleep that his body craved, he pulled aside the sheets, removed his boots, and lay on the soft mattress. He clutched the sword of the dragon to his chest, closed his eyes, and dreamed of the lush meadows in the forests around his Hemmed Land home.

Perhaps it was a couple hours later, Ilfedo could not be sure at first. He opened his eyes and stretched his arms. He felt somewhat rested but not yet to his former strength. He grasped the handle of the sword of the dragon and the weapon sparked with living fire. It shot up his arm and started to cover his body. Ilfedo focused his mind on only drawing strength from the weapon. He did not need it to clothe him in the armor of light.

As a candle in the night, the sword drove the darkness into the corners of the room. In the illumination he saw something that shot cold shock down his spine. For there, standing in the doorway, was the wispy form of a woman. She held her hand toward him and mouthed something through her cracked lips. Her long brown hair had long ago thinned and her eyes were a haunting gray. Ice spread over the floor as she took a soundless step toward him.

"Foul creature! You will have no part of me." Ilfedo rose to his knees on the bed, drawing the sword out of its sheath at the same time. The blade rang as he placed it between himself and the demon.

The demon clawed toward him, her face as hideous as death itself, and he drove his blade through her abdomen. Her face was within inches of his. As the living fire inundated the demon she began to take physical form. From her balding head to her tattered blue dress she appeared to transform into a human. Her mouth opened wide as her fingers grasped the blade that he had struck through her. She looked first at the blade, then up into Ilfedo's eyes.

She clamped her mouth shut and looked at the ceiling as her body spasmed. Blood oozed between her lips. Ilfedo could even see a portion of her jawbone through the fragments of skin that partially covered her skull.

"Be gone, demon," he said. "Return to your home in Hell and leave my people in peace."

The being looked down into his eyes. Her arms trembled as she reached out and held his shoulders. Suddenly she spoke, "It—is—not—as—you—think. P-please. I-I am no servant—of the—devil. I mean no harm—to you—to your people." The last words were spoken with the greatest of difficulty as blood gushed from her wound. Before Ilfedo could even think how he should respond to the demon's declaration, she fainted over his shoulder.

Death had nearly claimed her and part of Ilfedo wanted to allow her to die, but a doubt had entered his mind so he did not. He rolled her onto the bed and gently pulled the sword of the dragon out of her body. Then he ran into the hallway and banged on Oganna's door until she cracked it open.

"My daughter," he said in a gentle voice. "Take your sword and join me in the adjoining bedroom."

Her brow furrowed. "Father?"

"Hurry, my child!" He waited until she belted Avenger to her waist, over her robe.

Ilfedo brought Oganna to the bedroom he'd been using. "Father," she exclaimed as she looked upon the woman lain there, "what is this?"

He held the sword of the dragon over the woman's tattered form so that it shone upon her. "Oganna, she appeared to me just now in the form of a demon. I stabbed her here. I wanted to kill her, but she spoke to me."

"Spoke to you?" Oganna said. "Father, is she dead already?"

Ilfedo shook his head and said, "That is what I mean, my daughter. I want your help in saving her."

"Saving her? Father, these spirits are evil! Cursed already are they not? Why would I help you save her?"

Ilfedo looked down at the woman. Her form had fully materialized into the physical world. He could touch her hair and her gruesome face. At last he glanced back at his daughter and said, "Do it."

Oganna bowed slightly and drew Avenger from its sheath. The long blade glowed crimson and a silver dress magically grew over her body. Approaching the bedside Oganna laid the blade against the woman's back. "I will need your help to accomplish this, Father."

Grasping Oganna's shoulder, Ilfedo laid the sword of the dragon beside her blade, mentally focusing its energies on healing the woman before them. The wound he had dealt her was deep, having gone clear through her body. Yet beside this her skin appeared to have rotted, leaving places where flesh and even bone were exposed.

Before their eyes the woman's flesh knit back together. She heaved a few deep breaths and rolled onto her back, then sat on the bed. She smiled at Ilfedo, seeming to ignore Oganna. "You are the prophesied one, my lord. You have both destroyed and healed the souls in this dark world, as you have both destroyed and healed me."

As she spoke, the being's body transformed to a wispy form, as of smoke or vapor. This time, however, her face did not horrify him. She was by no means a great beauty but she was not an ugly woman. She smiled widely. "Thank you."

Ilfedo regarded her for a long moment, keeping the sword blazing in his hand. Beside him Oganna stood and circled to the far side of the bed. Avenger's crimson blade divided the darkness as she held it at the ready. Ilfedo stood and looked down on the demon. Then he reached out with a cautious hand and, when the woman nodded her approval, he swept his hand through her shoulders. He could find no substance. It was as if she were a ghost. "You are not a demon?"

"Though I heard you call me that," she said, "no, I am not."

Leaning over her, he stared hard into her eyes. "Convince me," he said.

She laughed softly. "I am relieved to be alive, Lord Ilfedo, for I thought when you thrust me through that my errand to you had ended in folly."

Ilfedo held up his hand, silencing her. "Do not turn this into a lengthy explanation. The hour is late and I spent the day killing demons like you."

"We are not demons," she said with a firm shake of her head. "Phantoms, I suppose. You could call us phantoms, yet herein lies the challenge. A demon serves the Devil himself, they are children of the afterlife of the accursed and followers of the Deceiver himself.

They have no physical life, so to speak, but are truly disembodied spirits."

Oganna circled to her father's side and pointed Avenger's blade at the woman's chest. "Considering the nightmares your kind just put us through—"

"Yes, of course," the woman said. "I regret that but there was nothing I could do to stop the others. Long ago my people lived in peace in the depths of these tunnels. We flitted through the darkness, never worrying about the beasts down here, for they cannot touch us. We are a special race, created I believe to live in solitude and peace. Our figures are indistinguishable from those of humanity, and our bodies maintained an appearance of youth for a thousand years.

"Then there came a day when one of us, the most beautiful among us and our queen, fell in love with a human man. She became obsessed with him, appearing to him and coaxing him until he revealed to her his perverted beliefs and his desires. He taught her a corrupted manner of things, promised her power over the rest of her kind—over us." The woman's face faded to total invisibility as she hung her head, then smoky wisps reconstituted her face as she looked up. The hint of a tear lay on her cheek.

Ilfedo lowered his sword's point to the floor and sat on the bed beside her. "This man you speak of. Was his name—?" He wanted to say Oldwell's name, but voicing it now seemed unsettling to him. It would imply that Oldwell was once a man just like himself, and had somehow become something else.

She looked up into his eyes and nodded. "Before his arrival we were a peaceful race. We had nothing to gain from an alliance with a human. We wanted nothing from him and nothing to do with him, but our queen continued to speak with him. We thought he had nothing to gain from us and so we let him speak with her. We were wrong."

Sitting on the floor, Oganna rested Avenger across her knees. "You mean Brunster Thadius Oldwell, don't you? He deceived you."

Again the woman nodded, then she reached out with one ghostly hand and held up a finger. "Have you an idea what it means for a race of peace-loving people to have one of their own turned into an agent of evil? He used our queen to gain control of us through torture and the like. His green blade became the conduit through which he and our queen could become one, and through which our people could be harmed."

"And none of you stood against him?" Ilfedo said.

The woman sighed and a ripple spread over her transparent form. "I did," she said. "I and many others. We were made to suffer for it. Using his sword he turned us into flesh and blood, then flayed the flesh from our bones before letting us return to our phantom forms. One by one the others converted to his cause, becoming his wraiths to inflict suffering and fear among the humans of Dresdyn.

"Others among us continued to refuse to submit and our queen turned on them, tearing their heads from their bodies. Among them I alone escaped that slaughter, making my way into the caverns where even she on her beast would have difficulty finding me. From that day on I have lived in secret, not revealing myself to any." She returned Ilfedo's gaze. "I am not a demon."

Ilfedo glanced at his daughter. As she sat on

the floor, Oganna's soft expression confirmed everything that he knew in his heart. The woman was telling the truth. The revelation that these phantoms were not from the spiritual world but instead were a species of the physical creation saddened him, for he had slain many of them. It was possible that she, through his actions, was the last of her kind. Meanwhile the phantom woman continued to gaze up into his eyes, waiting to see if he had believed her story.

Focusing the power of living fire within his blade, Ilfedo reached out and grasped her hand. As the flames gave her hand physical cohesion, he stroked her soft skin with his thumb and stared at her hand. "What is your name?"

"You believe me," she said with sudden hope brightening her countenance.

Ilfedo nodded. "I see no reason not to. Now, please, I would like to know what we may call you."

"I am Meleese," she said. "From a thousand years ago my name means the one who glides." She stared at his hand. "It has been a lonely eternity for me. I have not known the touch of a man for longer than you know."

Ilfedo squeezed her hand and then released it as he stood, sweeping his arm toward Oganna. "You know that I am called Ilfedo. This is my daughter, the princess Oganna."

Meleese glided to her feet. "Oganna and Ilfedo, I hope you will come to consider me a friend. You have shown great courage in not letting me die, for I know what fear my kindred have fostered among your people. But I hope that my errand to you will strengthen our friendship."

"And what errand is that?" Oganna asked.

Meleese grinned wide. "The prophetess was sickened by Oldwell's poison, and you have taken from him the blade that he used to harm her. I have come to try and help you heal her."

"How can you do that?" Ilfedo asked.

"I watched from hiding when he poisoned her with the green blade," Meleese said. "I saw what he did and how he did it. Bring me to her. Then when the deed is done I will return to the tunnels and float through them freely as I did long ago."

THE PHANTOM'S BLADE

Ilfedo awoke to dewobin light spilling through the bedroom windows. He vaguely remembered walking down the hall to Elhandra's room, only to collapse from exhaustion. Oganna had begged that he rest before again attempting to heal the prophetess. "You need your rest, Father. You will do little good for Elhandra if you are not mentally prepared for the task."

"Your daughter is right, I'm afraid," the phantom woman had said. "You must take your rest or you may further harm your friend instead of helping her."

He had stumbled back to his room, collapsing onto the bed as the phantom faded out of sight inside the doorway, and Oganna had returned to her room.

Morning had arrived. The people of Dresdyn had been rescued from Kraylan Abyss and Nomand the traitor had been left behind. Ilfedo's megatrath allies were still holding Brunster Thadius Oldwell prisoner.

Ilfedo stood from the bed, rolled his shoulders, and stretched his arms. He felt renewed. As he belted the sword of the dragon to his side there came a knock on the door.

"Father, you are awake?" Oganna asked.

He straightened his shirt and tucked it under his trousers. "You can open the door."

With a bright smile Oganna entered the room. Around her neck draped the viper Neneila. It raised its slimy head to regard him before it nuzzled back against Oganna's neck.

"I am glad you encouraged me to sleep last night, my daughter," Ilfedo admitted. "Thank you for that. My thoughts are clearer now to deal with the next matter at hand."

"Father, a few of the women who came with us have prepared a breakfast of dewobin eggs. Also bacon and a good wine. Uncle Ombre sent me up here and he insisted that you join him at the table."

"Wine with bacon?" Amusement filled Ilfedo's expression, then he sobered. "But first I must see to the prophetess. She is dying. I must see if there is anything that can be done for her." He glanced around the room. "Have you seen our phantom lady friend?"

Oganna shook her head. "Not since last night."

"Tell Ombre that I do not want to be disturbed except in case of immediate necessity. I will be in the room with Elhandra the prophetess." Ilfedo fingered the soft crystalline hilt of his sword. "Send for Everett. I would value his presence in Elhandra's room."

"He is already with her. He has not ceased to care for her since last night," Oganna told him. She glanced at the floor thoughtfully. "We can all hear his fervent prayers as he seeks divine intervention to save her."

"Good." Ilfedo smiled and stepped up to her, placing a reassuring hand on her shoulder. "Now join your uncle and the others. Enjoy a hearty breakfast and remember me in your prayers. I do not want us disturbed."

She curtsied and slipped out of the room and down the hall to descend the stairway.

"I assume you are in here somewhere," Ilfedo said to the empty room. "It will be necessary for you to reveal yourself if you are to hold to your promise and help me figure out how to heal Elhandra." He hesitated for a long moment. "I believe you said your name is Meleese."

He heard Meleese gently laugh. "Please forgive me, my lord. I am right here."

"I do not see you." Ilfedo glanced around the still-empty room.

"Oh." She laughed again. "My apologies. That is my fault. I am afraid I fell asleep beside your bed last night."

Ilfedo raised an eyebrow at that. "You fell asleep beside my bed?"

"I did. I do hope that makes you uncomfortable." Meleese coalesced on the floor beside the bed. She appeared as strands of smoke forming into the shape of a woman with long hair. She dusted off her dress and smiled up at him as she stood, her countenance was playful, perhaps flirtatious.

Ilfedo waved his hand dismissively. "I fail to see why you would hope that this makes me uncomfortable."

"It does not matter." She smiled as she walked past him. She leaned against the doorframe. "You amuse me by pretending that you do not notice the charms of a woman. But, as I said, it does not matter." She inclined her head toward the hallway. "We must go now if we are to save her. But please do me a kindness and warn your priestly friend that I am not the enemy. I'd rather the religious man not remind me of my fallen brothers and sisters." With a wave of his hand Ilfedo ushered Meleese into the hallway. The phantom followed and hung back a few steps as he opened the door. Everett sat inside on a chair beside the bed, dabbing a cloth on Elhandra's forehead. The room had one small window. A little pink light filtered through from the dewobins outside, while several lanterns scattered about the room provided the greater illumination.

"Cousin?" Ilfedo said and Everett glanced up at him. "I do not wish to alarm you," Ilfedo said. "I found someone who believes she can help the prophetess."

The little man stroked his beard and raised an eyebrow. "Who?"

Ilfedo stepped aside and the phantom woman glided to his side. Everett shot to his feet, eyes widening.

"She is not like the others, Everett," Ilfedo said in soft tones. "I'd like you to meet Meleese. She was afflicted with a rotting of her flesh, somehow by Oldwell's doing. But I and my daughter have healed her." In as few words as possible Ilfedo related to the man how the phantom had appeared to him, what had transpired between them, and the story that she had told him afterwards.

Everett did not say a word. "All is well if she is not a demon. I will not prejudge one of God's creatures." He nodded to Meleese and stood aside from the bed.

When Ilfedo stood beside Elhandra he bit his lower lip. A thin line of phosphorescent green showed on her neck, testifying to the spread of the poison.

The phantom glided to the opposite side of the bed, gazing down on the prophetess. "We must act swiftly. I believe she is very near death. Have you brought the green blade? The blade of Oldwell?"

Ilfedo excused himself from the room and found Oganna and Ombre in the dining room with Commander Veil and six Elite officers.

"Ah! You changed your mind and would like a bite to eat?" Ombre laughed as he wolfed down a forkful of eggs. But his face sobered upon looking into Ilfedo's eyes. "You need something, my brother?"

Oganna set down her own fork and wiped the corner of her mouth with a pink napkin. She, too, looked up at him, though she did not say a word. From Oganna's lap Neneila the viper raised her head over the table's edge, sinking her fangs into a thin strip of meat on the plate.

With a gesture Ilfedo brought Ombre to his side. "I trust only you with this errand," he whispered in the man's ear. "Last night I left the sword of Brunster Thadius Oldwell in the care of Vectra. Now, I need it."

Ombre's eyes flicked to Oganna. "Ilfedo, your daughter is familiar with weapons of power. I do not even wield a sword of light. In this matter I think you should send her."

"No. In this you are wrong," Ilfedo said. "You are capable of keeping your mind on the task and there is no magic in your blood, which I think would awaken

Oldwell's sword. Oganna is strong in dragon magic. I think it would be dangerous for her to handle it." He slapped Ombre's shoulder. "Will you bring it to me, my brother?"

With a determined expression Ombre replied, "I suppose breakfast should wait. Return to the prophetess and I will get you the sword." He turned to those at the breakfast table and dismissed himself, stepping through the door to the outside.

Ilfedo held up a hand so that Oganna remained in her place, then he strode back upstairs and down the hallway. Reaching Elhandra's room he waited for Ombre's return. The prophetess's breathing was shallow and sweat soaked her face. Everett dabbed at her face with a cool cloth, whispering prayers as he did so.

When at last Ombre returned he handed the green blade to Ilfedo, then he retreated to a dark corner of the room. Ombre folded his arms across his chest and leaned against the wall, frowning all the while.

Ilfedo balanced the blade on his palms and held it toward Meleese. The phantom lady faded a bit, then her form strengthened again. "You said you could help," he said. "How?"

She held up both hands. "Patience, sir. I am neither all-knowing nor infallible. I offered my help because I believe that I have insight into this thing."

"Make a suggestion then," Ilfedo said.

Meleese tilted her head to the side, keeping her gaze on the prophetess. "Put your own sword on the floor."

Setting Oldwell's blade on the floor, Ilfedo drew out the sword of the dragon and set it aside. Then he again took up Oldwell's blade.

"Good." The phantom pointed with one of her transparent fingers. "Lay the sword on her body." Ilfedo did so, then stood back.

The phantom eyed the prophetess up and down for a long moment. Then she shrugged her shoulders. "Take the sword's handle and try to awaken its power."

"What!" Ilfedo shook his head. "This is not a game, Meleese. Tell me now if you know how to heal this woman, or no."

She glared up at him. "Patience!"

Suppressing his frustration Ilfedo bowed slightly. The phantom turned her attention again to Elhandra. Her brow furrowed deeply as she put her finger to her lips. Smoke wafted around her finger. She leaned forward, considering for a long while. At last she smiled.

"You have an idea," Ilfedo said.

With a nod she said, "Your sword has great healing capacity. We should have thought of this before. You can use it to draw the poison out of her body."

Ilfedo clenched his fists. "I tried that."

"And?" she asked. "I must add that you have the patience of dewobin! Give me time to consider and let us figure this out together. I am trying to help you."

"The living fire has no effect," he said, and he felt thoroughly chastised. Meleese was right. Why was he being so harsh with her? She was doing this for him with no promise of anything in return. Finally, he said, "In fact, the powers of my sword and of the green blade cancel each other out."

"Then you should leave your sword alone and do as I said before. Grab hold of Oldwell's sword and awaken its power. Force it to draw the poison out of her body," Meleese offered.

"When I first encountered this weapon I made the mistake of trying to use it," Ilfedo replied. "I threw it at its master and it flew around his head and struck me instead. It could have ended my life but my own sword was able to heal me. I will not awaken that sword's power again."

The phantom wagged a finger dismissively in his direction. "The poison must be drawn out of her body, of this I am sure. And the only way to accomplish that is to use the power of the green sword. It must absorb the poison."

Ilfedo shook his head. "Then this woman is doomed. I can neither risk using the green sword's power, nor can I force it using my own because they would cancel each other out."

There was a long silence between them and Everett hung his head, holding Elhandra's hand in both of his.

Behind them Ombre cleared his throat. "If I may offer a thought, would it not make more sense to let the phantom lady use the sword to draw out the poison? After all, the weapon does seem to respond to her kind. Doesn't it? I mean, this madman Oldwell is a phantom also."

"Not like me!" Meleese spat out, and her words dripped with venom. "Do not dare compare him to me. Oldwell was loved by my queen, the queen of my race. She wanted him so badly that she transformed him into his current state. I do not exactly know how, yet he became like us and yet different, able even to possess the bodies of other men, like a demon. He is not of my race. He is a corruption and a vile scourge at that."

Waiting for her anger to cool, Ilfedo said, "Not

like you, Meleese, yet my friend has a valid argument. What if this weapon will respond to you because its master took on a form similar to your own? What if you can access its power to do good where its master meant it for evil?"

She shook her head. "I cannot manipulate physical things the way you can." Then she reached her hand toward the blade as it rested on Elhandra's chest. When she closed her fingers over the handle, her fingers passed through it as if through air. "Now you see," she said.

Ilfedo sighed and started to raise his voice in agreement, but Ombre spoke over him. "No, I don't think I do see." He slapped Ilfedo on the back. "Use the power in the sword of the dragon to turn her into a physical being, then she will be able to hold the sword."

The phantom's eyes opened and she glanced first at Ombre. Then she locked eyes with Ilfedo. "I like how he thinks," she said.

"It may work." Ilfedo grasped his sword, letting the living fire bathe his body. "But what if the sword turns on you and slays you?"

She laughed. "Release your hold on me and my body will return to its natural state before the sword can kill me. I do not think there is any risk for me in this."

Ilfedo looked hard at Oldwell's blade. "Except that I will be connecting you to a weapon of immense power, and an apparently corrupt power."

"It is a weapon," she said. "Not an entity! Let me try this." As she reached her hand toward him, Ilfedo said to Everett, "Pray with all your might." Then he grasped the phantom's hand.

Her body materialized and her eyes gleamed as she grabbed hold of Oldwell's sword. Her arm twitched as a connection was made. Strands of light wove out of the blade and it glowed a nasty green.

Outside there arose a human howl that sent a shiver down Ilfedo's spine, but he kept his focus on Meleese. She was smiling, her eyes half-closed.

Ombre darted to the window. "Wow," he said as he looked outside. "Ilfedo, Oldwell is on the ground struggling as if he's lost his best friend. The megatraths have him pinned to the dirt." He laughed. "Oh yeah, he is really struggling. Whatever is happening must be good if it is making him that mad." He laughed and opened the window. "Losing control, oh mighty one?" he shouted.

A bolt of energy snaked through the air from Oldwell's blade as if to strike Ilfedo. It came within inches of his nose, then snapped back into the blade. Meleese's subsequent smile filled her face. "I understand how to use it now, Lord Ilfedo," she said through her smile. "It is bound to my will now. No longer to that demon we so despise."

"Can you heal her now?" Ilfedo asked.

Meleese relaxed her expression, eyes focused on the body of the prophetess. "Heal her? No, but the poison is leaving her system. Look and see," she said.

The green glow receded from Elhandra's neck and her breathing eased. Her eyes opened and she sat up in the bed as Meleese pulled the sword away from her and rested its point on the floor. Ilfedo immediately released the phantom woman's hand.

The green blade slipped out of the phantom's grasp and her eyes followed it until it clattered on the floor. "I do not believe it is connected to Oldwell any longer," she said in a soft voice.

"Good. Then at last I can destroy it, or in the least lock it away where no one will ever use it again," Ilfedo said. He relaxed his shoulders, touched the sword of the dragon to the prophetess, and imparted some of its healing energy into her body. Then he slid the sword back into its sheath. He turned his gaze upon the prophetess and took her hand gently into his own. "I had thought your charm and your wisdom was lost to me forever, Elhandra."

"Lord Ilfedo of the Hemmed Land." Elhandra reached out her other hand and squeezed his shoulder. "It is good to see you. You are indeed fulfilling the prophecies spoken of you. The prophecies spoke of two Lord Warriors. Oldwell came to destroy us, and you came to save us." She laughed a gentle, joyful laugh.

Part of Ilfedo wanted to blush at her attention, while the other part felt completely at ease. He felt an attraction to her, yet unlike other women after his deceased wife, he felt no shame in it and he knew that the most she would be to him was a friend. Ah, but he needed her counsel and her friendship. He thought he would be glad of both in the coming years.

Elhandra looked around her at those with him, her eyes lingering on Meleese. She set her feet on the floor and shakily stood, leaning for support on Ilfedo's arm. She faced the phantom lady. "I overheard my Lord Ilfedo telling Everett about you and I am aware of the role you have played in freeing me of this curse." She inclined her head in the woman's direction. "For that I thank you."

The phantom said not a word. Her form wavered in and out of visibility, first one part of her body vanishing and then another, only to form again.

Ilfedo led Elhandra out of the room and Ombre took up the green sword. As the phantom started to vanish, Ilfedo paused and thanked her. "You have earned my gratitude, Meleese. Please know that you will be welcome should you ever choose to visit my people."

Meleese chuckled at that. "What would I do among your people? I am but a ghost to them and I do not share their customs or history. To them I am an object of curiosity and perhaps of fear." She waved her hand at him as she stepped back into a shadowed corner of the room. "Farewell." Then she vanished.

Walking Elhandra downstairs, Ilfedo shouted his joy to the captains as they sat at the table. Elhandra smiled as Commander Veil stood from his chair and held it for her. She took his invitation to sit down and gratefully accepted a hardboiled egg on a plate.

Oganna waited until Ombre and Everett emerged behind Ilfedo, Ombre still carrying the green blade. She stood from the table and curtsied toward Elhandra. "I have hoped for this moment to meet you. My father has spoken highly of you."

"You are kind," the prophetess replied. "And I assure you that your father spoke highly of you on his first visit among us."

Ilfedo spread his arms and everyone focused their attention his way. He bade all of them to give the prophetess time to gain strength and requested that they not fill her morning with questions. Then he excused himself out of the room and asked Ombre to follow him outside.

There he found two megatraths with their heavy clawed feet pinning Oldwell to the ground. "Curse you, lord of the Hemmed Land," the possessed man said.

"Perhaps you think you have gained a victory. Yet I will rise again and strike you dead."

Striding onto the street, Ilfedo ignored the man's cursing.

"Brother," Ombre asked as they walked out of earshot from Oldwell, "you have in mind a fate for this sword of his?"

"For now we will lock it away in the library, then I shall bring it to the Hemmed Land so that I may be assured of its destruction." Ilfedo waved to a contingent of warriors of light and they fell in step behind him and Ombre. He navigated the streets of the city, at last emerging in front of the library itself. The warriors he stationed around the building. "No one gets inside," he instructed.

He led Ombre through the outer doors into the building, then into the library room itself with its circular floorplan. The familiar scent of aged paper drew him into every corner of the room as Ombre set the green blade on a stone table and together they scoured the corners of the library.

It was Ombre who found it. A wooden box, long and shallow with brass fasteners. They set it on the table and laid the sword inside.

A knock on the door preceded a warrior in his glowing armor. He bowed to them. "Lord Ombre, Commander Veil sent me to fetch you, if you are able. He wishes to integrate the remaining members of the city guard with our forces in preparation for moving the people through the exit tunnel."

Ombre slapped Ilfedo's shoulder. "Unless you have further need of me."

"Thank you, no." Ilfedo waved him off. "I will

speak with you later." As his friend stepped to the door, Ilfedo added, "And Ombre, thank you for handling this weapon for me. I still have no confidence that I can handle it safely."

Ombre gave him a sober nod as he held the door.

Ilfedo stood by the sword, visually examining it. He contemplated breaking the blade, but part of him thought that doing so would divide its power as well, rather than destroying it. No, it must be sealed in this box and lost to the sands of time. As he mused on these things, a soft female voice spoke in his ear. "Troubled, Lord Ilfedo?"

Ombre darted back into the room, drawing his sword.

Before Ilfedo could react, Meleese congealed out of the air beside him. Startled, he stumbled backward. "I thought you had returned to the tunnels," he said.

She laughed and he realized that her arm extended into the box. He touched the pommel of the sword of the dragon as she closed her fingers over the green sword's handle. He expected her fingers to slip through the weapon. Instead she lifted it out of the box and held it aloft, smiling all the while.

"No!" Ilfedo grasped at her hand, trying to force her back to physical tangibility but a flash of green from her blade negated the power of living fire.

The phantom looked up at the sword in her hand, the smile still on her face. "You do not want me to have this?" she said.

"Indeed, I do not." Ilfedo faced her. He held his own sword at the ready. "That blade should be locked away or destroyed."

Meleese laughed again and winked at him. "It will

be a souvenir of my time with you, Lord Ilfedo. Now I am free to go where I wish and interact with physical beings, just as you do." She sighed in a resigned sort of way. "I regret that you fear me now and, if I am to reveal the truth to you, I will admit that it was not my intention to take this sword. But now just think of it! No longer is it connected to Oldwell. It is bound to my will. And I will take it deep into the tunnels that I have lived in for so long, far away from you and your prisoner. It will be no threat to you, but it will be a great comfort to me."

"Meleese, I will beg of you please do not do this," Ilfedo said. "We do not understand that blade's power. Even if your intention is to use it for good, who can say if it will instead do evil? Who is to say it will not be able to twist your mind?"

She laughed and reached out, stroking the side of his face with her ghostly fingers. "I have not sold my soul to the Devil, Lord Ilfedo. How do you think I have remained uncorrupted all of this time, even when most of my people joined with our queen and Oldwell in their oppression of the humans of this city?" She glanced at Ombre. "My thanks to you, kind sir, for both discovering how to heal the prophetess and for giving me such a mighty gift."

Meleese faded into invisibility and so did the sword that had belonged to Oldwell.

"Ilfedo, forgive me," Ombre started to say.

But Ilfedo cut him off. "There is nothing to be done now. I think we will never know if we empowered a new agent of evil, or gave rise to a new heroine. Whichever is the case, the phantom and her blade are now lost to us."

A City Left in Darkness

The streets of Dresdyn were not as quiet as they had been before. When Ilfedo stepped out of the library the sword of the dragon was belted to his side and let it array him in the armor of light. A slight chill hung in the cavern air. Ladies and men of Dresdyn smiled at him and bowed as they passed him. With glowing lanterns swinging from their hands they proceeded down the street. The fear that had been ever present in this place had vanished from everyone's faces, and the sight was a reward all its own for the difficulties he had faced.

Ilfedo turned to one of his Elite warriors who stood guard by the library door. "Warrior, what is going on here?"

The man made a slight bow. "I do not know, my

lord."

Ilfedo watched as a man guided a woman into a house down the street. They left the front door ajar, vanishing inside, and before long the man reappeared with a pile of goods in his arms.

He set them in the front yard, then slipped back inside the house. Soon the woman brought out a box of silverware, followed by blankets and a box whose contents he could not discern.

"Father!" Oganna called out as she slipped out of a side street to stand beside him. "The people were eager to leave this place, so Ombre and Commander Veil ordered them to gather what possessions they have and bring them to the base of the cliff."

"They can bring very little." Ilfedo put his hand on her shoulder. "Bringing them out of this cavern and up to the desert floor, then on into the Hemmed Land will require a lot of labor."

"A labor of hope." Oganna looked up at him. "But you cannot tear them away from their sentimental items. Imagine if you were to give up the bed mother used to sleep in, or the forks she ate with. What of the clothes that she wore?"

He sighed and stared down at her. She had grown up. She had become wise, like her mother before her.

"This is necessary," she said and she swept her arm toward the bustling people. "You are tearing them away from the only home they have known. Let us just be certain that we tear them away from the place and not from their fondest memories. Let the women keep their kitchenware and the paintings on their walls. Let the men bring their tools, armor, and weaponry."

"I have no intention of ripping them out by their

roots," Ilfedo said. "Very well then, if the people are focused on doing this then I will begin the most important process of preserving their history." He grasped her by the shoulders and turned her to face the library. "The books and the scrolls must all be packed away with great care. I trust that you will handpick ladies to help you in this task and recruit as many of our soldiers as you need to carry the volumes to the base of the cliff."

Oganna nodded as she gazed upon the library. "Do you want Oldwell's sword taken as well, or have you already destroyed it?"

"It will not be destroyed." As he said the words he feared their consequences. "Meleese the phantom woman followed me back here and took the blade. It seems that she now possesses the only weapon that rivals the sword of the dragon."

Oganna's eyes widened.

Resting a hand on her shoulder, Ilfedo reassured her. "Nothing will come of it. In truth I think there is a chance that the weapon is safer with her than with us."

She stood on her toes and softly kissed his cheek. "I pray it is as you hope. For my part, I do not know whether I trust that phantom." She shook her head as if to dispel her doubts. "I will organize the packing of the library. Do not fear. I know that the volumes and the scrolls in there are of immense value. I will see to it that they are packed into crates for the journey."

"Thank you," he said as he took a refreshingly deep breath. "Things are now moving along as they should. I will go speak with Vectra, for I need her help in the next phase of this migration."

Ilfedo left Oganna, even as she sent a warrior to summon the women she had brought from the

Hemmed Land. Without a doubt she would pack the volumes and the scrolls of this valuable data collection with great efficiency.

He marched down the streets of the city, hesitating only when Captain Therman of the Dresdyn city guard stepped into his path.

"Forgive my forthrightness, my lord," the man said.

"Speak," Ilfedo commanded.

Therman cleared his throat. "May I walk with you for a while?"

Resuming his brisk march, Ilfedo turned toward the lower portion of the city where he knew the mega-traths to be camped.

Stepping onto the street Therman kept pace beside him, his eyes trained on the road.

"Speak your mind, captain," Ilfedo said. "It must be important for you to approach me like this."

"It is, my lord." The man cleared his throat. "It's just that ever since you returned we have known that information was passed to Oldwell which led him to send my troop to capture your daughter. Yet I cannot imagine who that information could have come from."

Ilfedo nodded. The thought of it had troubled him as well. Oldwell had not only known when Ilfedo returned to Dresdyn, he had also learned of Ilfedo's daughter and of where he could find her. Information enough to send vile Nomand's force to kidnap her.

Therman continued. "Apart from Everett and the prophetess, only Ardius and the children under his care remained in this city."

"Are you suggesting that Ardius or one of the children spied on us for Oldwell?" Ilfedo said.

The man shrugged his shoulders. "Perhaps they were compelled to under threat of violence against them or a loved one. Can you think of another possibility?"

Ilfedo walked in silence for fifty paces, then he stood still and gazed at the ground. "You have done well to bring this to my attention, captain. For that I thank you. It had almost passed my notice. A man in my position cannot let this matter pass. The facts must be ascertained, if at all possible, and we must make inquiry now." He looked up at the distant ceiling of the cavern, awash with glowing waves of pink feathers. Thousands of dewobins flew across the stoney surface. "Bring Ardius to the mayor's mansion. I would speak with him alone and have no one besides the three of us know about it. I will join you soon but there is something I wish to do first."

Therman snapped a salute. "It will be as you wish my lord," he said, then he directed his steps toward the heart of the city.

Ilfedo strode toward the city's outer edge until the buildings gave way to a flat landscape of stone. Line upon line of megatraths stood there. They acknowledged his approach with dips of their long snouts. From their ranks a megatrath stomped forth to meet him.

"Human, do you seek my mistress?" he said in rumbling tones.

Vectra shouldered her way through her followers. As one they gave place to her and kept their heads bowed. She pivoted on her four rear legs, then dropped to all six. Her claws dug into the hard ground with ease as she whipped her long tail through the air, smashing it into the side of the megatrath who had spoken to Ilfedo. The megatrath fell on its side, grunted and crawled back to its feet, taking its place again in the line.

"Lord Ilfedo, forgive my subject his impertinence." Vectra gave a toothy grin as she lumbered toward Ilfedo. "He will remember next time to address you by your title and not merely as 'human.'"

Bowing to her, Ilfedo said, "I took no offence."

Vectra picked up a loose stone and crushed it in her claws, glancing back at the megatrath she'd struck.

Ilfedo chuckled as he turned away from the megatrath host and walked in pace with Vectra. "You do enjoy tormenting your subjects."

"Not really," she grunted. "Yet there are some males who I give more attention than others. That one pleases me greatly. Devoted, strong, yet lacking a desire for power. An unusual combination of traits for one of my species, as you saw with Regulus."

"I am sorry for the death of that megatrath," Ilfedo said. "You will be hard pressed to find a male as strong as he was."

Vectra puffed glowing yellow vapor from her nostrils. "Vengeance blinded Regulus. He should not have taken on Oldwell alone."

"I might not be alive if he had not." Ilfedo laid his hand on the megatrath's snout, holding her gaze. "I would bring him back from the dead, if it were possible."

Turning away from him, Vectra spat a flame from her mouth. "It was a good way for him to die, and now that he is gone I think his son will arise in his place. I sense great potential in that one, even though he is not yet grown."

Ilfedo half smiled as he remembered Arvidane. It was true. Regulus had left one like himself. The bloodline would continue.

"Thank you for everything you have done, Vectra." "We are allies, and we are friends," she rumbled.

Ilfedo spread his arms toward the city of Dresdyn. "The time has come to bring these people to the surface." He pointed toward the distant, high cliff. "There is a tunnel up there that can take these people to their new home."

"I see it," Vectra said.

"If I may impose again on your generosity, mighty Vectra," Ilfedo said. "We need to construct a stairs up that cliff. Otherwise it will be necessary to levy every person and their goods up there with ropes, and that would be a staggering undertaking."

Vectra grinned again. "If you wish, we megatraths will carve a stairs in the stone's face. She roared over her shoulder and half a dozen megatraths lumbered out of the ranks. "These are among my strongest tunnelers, Lord Ilfedo. They will remain here in the city until the task has been completed."

Ilfedo bowed to the megatrath and she lumbered toward her followers. With a series of harsh roars she called to her followers and the largest among them split out of the assemblage. Their forearms rippled with muscles that were as thick as large trees. There were nine tunnelers in total now, and they moved out into the city and toward the cliff face. Vectra grunted to Ilfedo, then lumbered off into the tunnel that would take her back into the adjacent caverns. The megatraths fell in behind her, a weaving mass of thick hides and limbs. Here and there a plume of yellow vapor glowed forth, as if reminding Ilfedo of the deadly might of that host.

As the last of the beasts disappeared down the

tunnel, Ilfedo turned to face the heart of the city. In the distance he heard the pounding of nails, the shouts of men as they labored in thick sweat, and the rumbling grunts of the megatrath tunnelers. The 'stairs' from the city to the exit tunnel had been begun.

Ilfedo frowned as he walked back through the city. The bustle of its citizens as they entered houses and carried out goods, the feel of warm damp air on his arms and neck, the gentle glow of the dewobins far above. He numbed himself to all of it. Captain Therman of the city guard, and his accusation of betrayal by Ardius troubled Ilfedo deeply. It seemed undeniable that no one else could have alerted Brunster Thadius Oldwell's minions to where they could find Oganna, thus making the kidnapping possible.

For Everett's sake Ilfedo hoped another explanation could be found. For his own peace of mind, however, he wanted to make an example of Oldwell's informant.

He arrived at the mayor's mansion to find Oldwell bound hands and feet, sitting upon the mossy ground. The megatrath guards had left the prisoner, yet a dozen warriors of light had formed a ring around him. Though their swords were sheathed they each kept a hand on the pommels of their weapons. They would draw if need be.

Oldwell laughed at Ilfedo as he passed. "Deeply troubled you seem, master of men," Oldwell scoffed.

Ilfedo hesitated. He did not give the man the satisfaction of looking at him, rather he kept his gaze casually before him. He spoke in a calm tone, "And you hide your uncertainty well, Oldwell, and yet you are master of none." As Ilfedo resumed his walk, striding up to the doors of the house, Oldwell fumed behind him.

With a measure of satisfaction Ilfedo closed the door behind him as he stood in the foyer.

"My Lord Ilfedo." Elhandra descended the stairs to stand before him. He noted the unassuming brown dress that she wore. No frills or lace, yet still of a graceful cut. She dipped a slight curtsy his way as she ushered him up the stairs. "The Lord Warrior is troubled, the Lord Warrior brings wrath, but the Lord Warrior must remember the balance of justice and mercy."

"I do bring wrath," Ilfedo grunted. "It is apparent to me that Captain Therman failed to keep Ardius's arrest a secret from you. I shall deal with him later. For now, I need to speak with Ardius."

Elhandra smiled in her gentle manner. Her gray eyes peered up into his as he hesitated on the stair. Something in her eyes reminded him of their first meeting, when she had spoken the prophecy he had already witnessed reach its fulfillment.

Ilfedo sighed, letting some of the stress out of his shoulders. "Forgive me, my lady. You have seen something of this moment in a vision, or something like that?" He gazed into her eyes.

"Something like that," she admitted, widening her smile.

"Is the conclusion the difficult decision that I fear it will be?" he asked.

She shook her head and he knew that she was not denying it, rather she expected him to discover the choice for himself.

"If Ardius has done this thing—" He furrowed his brow and slapped his fist against his forehead as he spoke for her to hear, "Dear Creator, why did this have to be my responsibility?"

"Speak with Ardius, my lord," Elhandra whispered. "Hear his words before you pass judgement. That is all that any of us expect of you. And please do not place blame on Captain Therman. It was I that alerted the others to this situation. Let your anger rest on me if I have stepped over your authority, for I deemed it wise that you not deal with this matter alone."

Ilfedo turned up the stair again. His heart felt as if a lead weight had been hung on it as he walked down the hallway to the room Elhandra guided him to. The bed in this room had been shoved aside in favor of a circle of five wooden chairs. Ardius sat in the farthest chair and he looked up as Ilfedo walked in. Everett, Ombre, and Oganna sat in the other seats. Neneila had coiled on the floor under Oganna's chair. Behind Ardius stood Captain Therman bedecked in his bronze armor, his hand resting on the pommel of his sheathed short sword. A pair of lanterns on the dark wood wall illuminated the contemplative group.

Ilfedo nodded to his daughter and the other men, then with a sweep of his arm settled Elhandra into the empty chair. He paced slowly, keeping himself behind the line of chairs, his gaze fixated on Ardius. "This meeting will be short, I hope, for I hope to hear that the suspicions brought to my attention are falsely founded." He stood still and looked down at the younger man. "Ardius, if you are innocent of any of the charges brought against you then I wish to hear so from your lips. If there is a reasonable case for your innocence then you have my promise that you will live among my people and be treated as a citizen of my realm."

With a nod of respect, Ardius replied, "Your

mercy and your wrath are apparent to me, my lord. I believe your judgment will be in accordance with your finding and that you will always do the right thing by me."

Resting his hands on the backs of Elhandra's and Oganna's chairs, Ilfedo leaned forward and relaxed his mouth. Ardius's words did not sound like those of a condemned man, but rather of one confident of his standing. "Do I understand then that you are denying the charge of treason?" Ilfedo asked.

"My lord, the charge is justified," Ardius said "I am guilty. I conspired with your enemy to allow the capture of your daughter——."

What other words Ardius spoke were lost to Ilfedo. The fog of doubt that he had envisioned around Ardius was driven away by a wind of vengeance. Ardius had betrayed him. Had betrayed Oganna. He had betrayed them all to that vile Brunster Thadius Oldwell. The spirit of that other Lord Warrior had reached from beyond the grave once again, raking its claws over Ilfedo's heart.

As Ilfedo's fingers teased the pommel of the sword of the dragon, the living fire raged up his arm. The armor of light clapped onto his shoulders, down his back, grew over his chest. Ilfedo let the sword absorb his focus, absorb his anger. It was the only thing that kept him from reaching out and grasping Ardius by the throat.

Another hand clasped his forearm and gave it a gentle squeeze. Ilfedo released his hold on the sword, letting the living fire return to its place as he looked down and found Oganna soberly regarding him. She let go of his arm and spoke to Ardius in a grave tone, such that the young man cringed as he looked back at her. "You have admitted guilt, Ardius, and I fear my father's wrath upon you for your part in my kidnapping. But for my part I would have you speak further of this and detail what you did, how, and why."

Ardius glanced away from her for a moment, but she spoke out vehemently, "Keep your attention here! On my eyes! And do not mistake my patience for weakness, for I am my father's daughter and I am bound to see that justice is done, whether it is pleasant or not. You have betrayed us in a gross manner. It appears that you deserve a traitor's death. Explain yourself and do so now!"

The room fell into a deathly silence. Ardius's countenance blanched as he acknowledged her demand. At last he spoke and what he said held everyone's attention such that Everett, Ombre, and Elhandra all leaned forward in their seats.

Among those that faced Ardius in that moment, one rose. Though short of stature, Everett seemed to tower over his companions. Ilfedo had been dreading this moment for Everett's sake. He could only imagine the level of betrayal Everett felt. He who had vouched for Ardius's character.

Everett pulled his pink robe tighter around his shoulders and took a stride toward where Ardius sat. The end of his long gray beard swept the floor as he approached the younger man. "Look at me," he commanded softly.

Ardius turned up his face.

"God is my judge, Ardius," he said, shaking his head. "Why? I must ask the why behind what you have done because I believed you to be a man of principle, and so did the parents of each of your students." His eyes were moist as he spread his arms wide. "I am listening. We are all listening." With effort he sat back in his chair. "Now, tell us what happened."

Ilfedo held up his fist, gaining Ardius's attention once again. "Direct your story to me, for whether you live or die is by my command."

"Yes, my lord." Ardius's chest rose with a deep breath, then he exhaled loud enough for all to hear. "You know that I hid the children in my home after Oldwell gained the upper hand in his battle with those loyal to you. What you do not know is that I saw him again after the dewobins mysteriously went dark. Nomand came to me. He and his men were checking house to house for any survivors. He said that the true Lord Warrior had a proposal for me and that if I did not take it he would take the children. More specifically, he promised that he would take their corpses." Ardius returned Ilfedo's hard gaze. "Yes, my lord, I did betray you. There is a bat which Oldwell would use to send messages to me, and by which I sent him the information to kidnap your daughter. It was a horrible choice, yet I saw it as an impossible one."

"You were a fool," Ilfedo said. "Had you come to me with this information I could have protected your children."

Ardius gave a firm shake of his head. "It is not so, my lord. Oldwell had command of the demons. And, besides that, he had command of the bat."

Ilfedo let out a grunt of frustration. "A bat is of no concern to me. I could fry it with a blast from the sword of the dragon."

The accused man chuckled. "Of that I have no

doubt. But the bat can fly high. It flies as a predator to the dewobins and it can drive them away, again, plunging this city into darkness."

Everett gasped and Ilfedo took a step back. Oganna glanced from face to face, for she did not understand.

Captain Therman shifted in the shadows. "That is why the city went dark? A bat."

"Not an ordinary bat," Ardius replied.

Ilfedo raised his hand to silence them all. "You betrayed me, Ardius. I cannot overlook this and so, on the morrow you will be brought to an executioner and a sword will sever your head from your body."

Ilfedo strode out of the room and made his way down the stairs. He hesitated, turning into the kitchen. He felt numb to everything around him. His fingers clasped a cloth on the counter and he clenched them around it. The door to the outside swung open easily and he breathed deeply of the cool air, half-closing his eyes.

The spirit of Brunster Thadius Oldwell caused Bromstead to rattle his chains, holding them up before him as Ilfedo approached. "What has thy traitorous friend revealed to you?"

Grasping the man's jaw, Ilfedo forced it open. "Your tongue runs rampant in the body of my friend, doing great damage," he said. "Fear not, I have a remedy for that." Thus saying he stuffed the cloth in Bromstead's mouth.

At that moment something thudded into Ilfedo's back. He rolled to the side, hearing his men cry out even as he saw the reason for their fear. A creature rose beside him on a pair of leathern wings. Dark fur covered its body and its eyes burned like candle flames. The bat stood as tall as a man, glaring down at him and snapping at the air with its needle-thin fangs.

FOREVER NIGHT

The creature before Ilfedo could have been taken from a nightmare written as myth. He grasped the sword of the dragon, igniting his body with the living fire. The giant bat beat the air with its wings, turning its head away from the brilliance of his sword. Its fangs glistened as thick venom dripped from them.

Ilfedo slid the sword out of its sheath, slashing at the creature. It squealed like a mouse and rose into the air. Kneeling on the ground beside Ilfedo, Oldwell grunted unintelligibly. Ilfedo could well imagine the curses the wicked spirt was trying to throw his way. Yet the gag Ilfedo had placed in the man's mouth forced his silence.

The bat flew in erratic circles, higher and higher toward the cavern ceiling. Then it latched its talons on the ceiling and, while it hung by its feet, it lashed out at the tiny birds that glowed so brightly all around it. The dewobins fled from the creature, gathering like an enormous pink snake that wove its way confusedly above the city. Releasing its hold the bat swooped among the birds.

With tiny whistles, the dewobins cried out as one. The whistles joined together a million strong, flooding the city with its cacophony of deafening sound. Some of the birds were seen to fall lifeless out of the flock as the giant bat flitted through, inflicting death in their midst.

Ilfedo was on his feet and he looked around at the line of startled Elite warriors who stood around him, their eyes glued to the strange battle above.

"My Lord Ilfedo!" Commander Veil barreled between the warriors, pointing at the scene above them. "Permission to call for an archer?"

Ilfedo did not answer with words. He only nodded his assent as he kept his eyes above, for dozens of the dewobins' corpses were now spiraling from the flock. Their glows dimmed as they fell, then went dark forever.

The archer must have been nearby for soon the first arrow zipped toward the bat. Alas the creature dodged the projectile, letting it ricochet off the stone ceiling.

Dewobins flittered closer to their companions, flocking away from the bat and toward the far end of the city where lay the caverns to Kraylan Abyss. The bat followed them, driving their glowing pink mass into the tunnel. Two more warriors ran after the creatures, drawing their bows. When the arrows flew one found its mark in the bat's head, but at the same moment the last dewobins fled down the tunnel, plunging the city of

Dresdyn into a deep darkness.

A few lanterns soon glowed out of the darkness, but other than that the only light was that of the glowing swords of the warriors of light.

"This is intolerable," Commander Veil said.

"That is especially true for those of our men that are working with the megatraths on making a stairs up to the exit tunnel." Ilfedo shook his head slightly. "We need more light if we are to make sure all of this city is safely evacuated."

Commander Veil, his face starkly illuminated by the light of his own sword, glanced at where the dewobins had last been seen. "Should we wait on the little birds to return?"

"That would be a waste of our time, commander," Ilfedo said. "Return to the stair and see what progress has been made. In the meantime the warriors of light must make sure that the last of the city's inhabitants are ready for the climb."

The door to the mayor's mansion opened and Elhandra stepped through, holding a burning lantern in her outstretched hand. She drew within a few paces of Ilfedo and dipped a deep bow. "Please, my lord, come with me."

"Now is not a good time," Ilfedo began to say, yet his words were cut off by the ferver in her eyes.

"You must finish what you began in this city, my lord. The prophecy must be completed." She held out her other hand. "It will be completed. Come with me. Trust me."

Ilfedo looked deep into her eyes. Yes, he did trust her. Beyond a hint of doubt he did trust this woman. He put his big hand into her softer one and let her lead him away from the crowd. They walked eastward in the city and as they progressed his memory was triggered, for this was the path to the old building the people had called the Observatory.

He had been there before. He could envision everything as if it had been that morning. The people of Dresdyn had declared to him that the observatory was haunted, as indeed it had at first seemed when he had entered it alone. He had discovered the megling, Arvidane, and the creature had spoken to him with what he had assumed were the voices of demons. Everything had descended into chaos from that moment. Bromstead had appeared and for the first time had spoken to him in the voice of Brunster Thadius Oldwell.

Yes, all had descended into chaos from that moment.

Elhandra's hand lightly squeezed his as she stood there. The round base of the strange building in front of which they were now standing was visible only at the outer edge of the light which radiated from the sword of the dragon. The building was nestled at the base of a cliff at the edge of this end of the cavern.

Beside him the prophetess let out a long breath. "I have waited a long time for this moment." She looked up at him and turned his face toward hers with a gentle touch of her other hand. "As we told you when you first visited our city, this building houses a device that long ago lit our city. It turned our underground night into day. It was built by the Lord Warrior and abandoned when he died.

"'Unbind the soul held within the prism. Break and scatter the pieces thereof, that the spirits shall release and be gone forever. Blessed is he that comes in the righteous indignation of his

Creator, for he sheds the light of truth from one Lord Warrior upon another.'"

Ilfedo flipped the sword in his hand, watching the flames that trailed behind it. He strode down the winding path to the building's tall open door. The door that had been left open since his first dual with Oldwell. The light of his sword revealed the giant gears that encircled the building like silent guardians, their bronze teeth glinting in the firelight. He entered the dark building and raised his sword high, flooding it with light as he advanced through the small outer room and through the inner door at its far end.

The room in which he now stood was circular and enormous. Its ceiling stretched to an immense height and crisscrossing beams ran from wall to wall some thirty feet above his head. As before, cobwebs overflowed the rafters, draping onto the machinery below.

Ah. The machinery. This is what he had come for.

Ilfedo walked through the room's midst, running his hand over the enormous gears that flanked the wide aisle. He followed the aisle to the room's far end where a faint glow emanated from a yellow floor panel. The wall behind the panel dangled with weights on chains, all at varying heights. An assortment of levers built into a hammered iron box arrayed the wall behind the panel.

He grasped one of the levers, tried to shove it forward, but it did not budge. He found himself gazing upward at the magnificent structure, wondering at the purpose of the gears.

At last he grabbed another lever and willed the living fire to strengthen his arm beyond that of any man. The flames roiled out of his white armor, lashing at his arm. His muscles trembled as the energy filled them, then he tightened his grip. "I am tired of this darkness," he said aloud. He pushed on the lever, which at first resisted, then he grunted with the effort and drove it forward. The lever screeched under the strain, at last slamming into position at arm's length.

Something clicked beneath Ilfedo's feet. The floor trembled, and with a groan the lines of heavy gears that stood beside the long aisle began to turn. The walls of the great building shook and continued to shake. The layers of dust that had accumulated over the past decades fell from them in clouds, then the vibrations ceased and the gears stilled.

Ilfedo grasped the next lever. It proved of equal difficulty as the last, but at the last it too surrendered to his arm. With a loud click the lever set off another turn of the gears.

A tile on the aisle floor began to rise. Ilfedo turned to watch as the tile slid away and a pedestal rose in its place. Rows of gears had been placed along its side and they dripped with oil. Being built from simple stone the pedestal itself was nothing to gawk at, yet upon it rested an amethyst the size his fist.

The gears alongside the aisle ground to a stop as Ilfedo walked up to it. He inclined his head to the side a bit, reaching toward it with his hand. As his fingers brushed the crystal, Ilfedo hesitated. The crystal thrummed beneath his touch and something ignited in its heart, yet only a spark that vanished.

"What are you?" he whispered.

A movement from the entry door caught his eye. He glanced up. There she stood, the prophetess, with a smile on her face. She had waited for this moment.

Perhaps she had not even thought to see it happen in her lifetime.

Ilfedo felt as if he were a third party to the moments that followed. He could hear Elhandra repeating the words of the prophecy, even as he fulfilled them.

"Unbind the soul held within the prism. Break and scatter the pieces thereof—"

He struck the amethyst with his sword and its sharp edge shattered it. The fragments rolled off of the pedestal, yet a small cloud of purple dust remained. He heard whispers as if from the dust, as of mutterings that were unintelligible.

"—that the spirits shall release—"

The voices gained clarity. "No, no. Oldwell, please torment us no longer!"

Ilfedo spoke in reassuring tones. "Oldwell is no longer a threat to you, for I have bound him."

There was a hesitation before the voice of a man spoke apart from the others. "Who are you?"

"An enemy of Brunster Thadius Oldwell and of all others who follow his wicked path," Ilfedo said. "A servant of the Creator and of his prophets." He waited but the voice said nothing so he continued. "Who are you?"

"I am the one they called caretaker, for I tended this observatory until our Lord Warrior betrayed us," the voice of a man said. "He somehow transformed my body to dust and inserted me into the prism. I know not how, yet the pain of those moments is as clear to me today as if he had burned my body just this morning."

Ilfedo took a step back and gazed around the room at its great gears. How could Oldwell transform a man into dust? Did the green blade possess powers beyond what Ilfedo had seen?

"There are others here with me," the voice said. "And our condition is intolerable. Victims of Oldwell. We are victims all. Death would be preferable to this worthless existence. Please! Show us a kindness by finding a way to destroy us."

The dust hovered as a small cloud, dropping within a foot of the floor, and Ilfedo knelt on one knee. He rested the point of his sword on the stone floor and ran his hand through the dust cloud. It felt warm as if charged with electricity.

Elhandra's skirt brushed the floor as she approached, each step of her bare feet was soft upon the stone. Ilfedo glanced up, his brow furrowed. "Prophetess?" His question was lost in the enormous room because she did not answer.

Her gaze fixed on the small cloud of dust. She held out her hands as if to cradle the cloud in them. "The caretaker? You are the one called Miles?" she said.

"I was the one," replied the cloud. "Yet now my essence is trapped without form, and that form is mixed with the remnants of the others Oldwell trapped along with me."

Ilfedo stroked his chin. "There must be a reason that he did this. Even in his evil deeds it seems he planned ahead."

The cloud expanded for an instant as the caretaker responded in an angry tone. "He did! Oh, he told me he had a use for me but that in the form of a man I could pose a threat to him. He spoke of keeping me here—in this state—so that he could call upon my knowledge when he had need of it." Bitterly, the caretaker added, "The Lord Warrior promised that I, and the others with me, would not be released from this life unless he deemed it necessary. Until then I am to remain in this form."

"I am sorry." Ilfedo stood back to his feet, shaking his head as he did so. "Be kind to me, and I will be kind to you, Caretaker."

"How?" replied the dust.

"I desire to use this observatory to once again light the City of Dresdyn, yet the workings of the mechanizations of this building elude me." He lowered his voice to convey the sincerity of his words. "Tell me how to use this device and in return I shall destroy you, thus releasing you from this life into the next."

"You would do this?" the caretaker said.

Elhandra opened her mouth in protest, then closed it again. She stood, bowing to Ilfedo as she backed away.

It was left for Ilfedo to finish a negotiation with a cloud of purple dust. The strangeness of the situation was not lost on him, yet as he listened to the Caretaker's instructions the manner in which the Observatory worked became clear. When the Caretaker had finished Ilfedo thanked him, then he lifted the sword of the dragon and blasted the little cloud with the living fire. The tornado of flames issuing from his blade scorched the floor. Cries of severe pain emanated from the cloud for an instant only, soon falling into utter silence. When the living fire calmed, retreating to the sword of the dragon's blade, nothing remained of the purple cloud.

Ilfedo closed his eyes and said a prayer, for his heart felt heavy at the loss of yet more lives. The people of Dresdyn had suffered for too long.

Turning his back to the charred floor, Ilfedo

moved back to the panel of levers. With the instructions of the Caretaker fresh in his thoughts he worked the mechanisms and the great Observatory obeyed his every touch as if he were its master engineer. Vertical segments of wall fell away from the structure, opening it to the dark outdoors. The mighty gears groaned, then turned with greater certainty. The observatory dome began to turn, brass gears screeching along its curvature until a long panel slid open skyward. Yet there was no sky, for only the darkness remained in the absence of dewobin light.

Ilfedo moved to the final pair of levers, grasping them with all his strength. He pulled one and simultaneously pushed the other. All at once the floor cracked open, eight screws as thick as oak trees twisted skyward around the room's perimeter. The prophetess stumbled back, though in the sword's glow Ilfedo detected a smile on her face. Something else rose from the floor's midst. It was of a long, tubular shape, and a piece of convex glass formed its head. Ilfedo stood back in stunned amazement as a thin line of green light erupted from the device. It pierced the blackness and struck the ceiling of the cavern.

The beam held steady as the green glow spread through the rock. The cavern ceiling collected the light. Ilfedo ran to Elhandra and grasped her hand. Willingly she followed him out of the observatory where together they observed the cavern's ceiling transform in an inexplicable way. For the stone became transparent so that they could see to the floor of the desert far above.

And the sun blazed in the sky with blinding brilliance.

People screamed at first. Then, as the sunlight

washed upon their city for the first time in their lifetime, the people began to laugh and cry for joy. Ilfedo could even hear his own soldiers from the Hemmed Land joining in with shouts of their own.

"Hurrah!"

A gentle pressure against Ilfedo's arm made him look down to find Elhandra leaning against him. She wrapped her arms around him and fixed her gaze skyward. She squinted her eyes and whispered, "Now shines the sun upon us as it did upon our ancestors. This is a miracle that will be long remembered in the history of our peoples."

Ilfedo squeezed her hand as he sheathed the sword of the dragon. As the armor of living fire receded from his body he led her back down the road to the heart of Dresdyn. "Come now, my lady. I fear there is still a serious matter to attend to."

One thing and one thing alone kept the spirit of joy from entering Ilfedo's soul, for he felt that his judgment on Ardius must be swift.

BETRAYAL JUSTIFIED

Rit-a-tat, rit-a-tat, thud! When he heard the sound, Ilfedo turned away from the crowds. Against the backdrop of the high cliff behind him, the carpenters of Dresyn had built a platform. It stood five feet high and thrice that in length.

The powerful tunnelers that Vectra had left with Ilfedo were tearing their way up the cliff, their sharp megatrath claws raining down fragments of stone that they chiseled from it. With relative ease they had cut a path some ten paces deep into the cliff's face, while behind them the woodsmen from the Hemmed Land hacked at the stone to smooth its surface for the future ease of passage for the women and children of Dresdyn. The path had already been carved in a long gentle arc a hundred feet up the face of the cliff. More than sixty women from the Hemmed Land and Dresdyn swept the path behind the men, clearing the fragments and other remaining debris.

The path would be safe. Twenty of the woodsmen laid the path with lumber torn from the now-abandoned homes of Dresdyn. The pounding of hammers on nails distinctly echoed through the cavern.

Lord Ilfedo grasped the makeshift railing and climbed the steps to the platform. The sword belted to his side slapped his leg a couple of times. He stood there, atop the platform and crossed to its midsection. With a heavy hand he ushered two of his Elite warriors up the steps behind him. The men each grasped one of the prisoner's arms as they guided Ardius up the stairs and onto the platform. The prisoner's peg leg again sounded with *Rit-a-tat* and his cane thudded into the step before him.

Ilfedo tried to keep his gaze fixed on the prisoner. Tried to reconcile this deed he must do with the victories he had at last achieved in this dark world.

Yimshi, his world's sun, shone down through the cavern's ceiling. For the first time in a long time the City of Dresdyn was filled with light. The warm sunlight had brought joy to the people of Dresdyn and had solidified their confidence in him.

The people were gathered now. Gathered before him. A couple thousand of them, of men, women, and children. Their numbers filled the drab and dilapidated structures at the city's edge and filled many of the streets beyond. They were his people now. His to lead with justice and strength. Between him and them stood a double line of the bronze-clad members of the city guard. Their swords remained sheathed, and their faces were grim.

Rit-a-tat, rit-a-tat, thud! Ardius stood beside Ilfedo, leaning heavily on his cane and breathing hard. The exertion on his single leg must have been painful.

Ilfedo looked out over the somber crowds. Only one man seemed happy with the scenario and he was not among the people. At the platform's other end knelt Bromstead, his cheeks grinning despite the gag Ilfedo had stuffed in his mouth. His eyes were still green, for he looked at Ilfedo with the eyes of Brunster Thadius Oldwell. That spirit retained possession of the body of Ilfedo's ally, the reminder of that fact caused Ilfedo to grit his teeth. Somehow Oldwell must be removed.

But that was a battle for another day. Oldwell could remain gagged for now until a permanent solution could be found. At least he could do Ilfedo and the people no more harm.

"It gives me no pleasure to bring before you a traitor," Ilfedo's voice boomed out over the assembly as he amplified its strength with the power of his sword. "Many, if not all of you, know of Ardius. Yet by his own admission this man conspired with Brunster Thadius Oldwell to give over my daughter, the princess of the Hemmed Land, as a prisoner and even a hostage. He delivered her whereabouts to our enemy and thereby nearly brought ruin upon you all."

Ilfedo swallowed hard as whispers floated among the crowd. He could well imagine the mix of feelings these people had about this situation. No doubt they had read the resolution in his eyes, and he knew that they did not doubt his intention to go through with the execution. It must be done.

"These are your jury," Ilfedo declared. As he spoke to the crowd, Everett Matthaliah trudged up the platform in his pink robe, and Elhandra followed close behind him. She cut a simple yet dignified figure in a simple brown dress and Ilfedo detected a calmness settling over the crowd upon her arrival.

Next came Ombre with Captain Therman. Immediately a man called out from the crowd in an angry tone, "You would have a traitor on the panel to judge a traitor?"

Ilfedo quickly found the individual in the numerous faces before him. The speaker was of average height, middle-aged, yet with eyes as dark as coal. Ilfedo lowered his tone, fully relying on the sword to convey his words with strength. "There is none better to judge a traitor than a traitor. He who has redeemed himself in the eyes of your Lord Warrior through his deeds."

The man to whom he had spoken lowered his gaze. Those around the man stepped away from him a bit, yet he bowed himself even to the ground and begged his Lord Warrior's forgiveness.

With a sweep of his long arm Ilfedo spoke again as he brought his gaze around the crowd. "No one escapes justice. No one escapes my wrath when they seek to harm those under my care. You are my own. You are my people." He pointed at Ardius. "The jurors will either confirm his guilt or declare his innocence." Ilfedo addressed the jury. "How do you find this man?"

Everett Matthaliah stood and his beard brushed the stand's wooden floorboards. There were tears in his eyes. He did not meet Ilfedo's gaze, and he did not look at Ardius. He stared at his feet. He folded his hands as if in prayer. "Beyond a doubt, Ardius is guilty of this thing. We heard him confess to it."

Ilfedo burned his gaze into Ardius. "How do you

plead?"

There was a long silence. The crowd held their breath, awaiting the young teacher's answer. Loud enough for many to hear him, Ardius said, "Truly I am guilty by my own admission. I will not deny it." Then he lowered his voice for only Ilfedo to hear. "You know what must be done, my lord. I only ask that you forgive me. But you should know that if I had to do it all over again, I would."

Ilfedo drew the sword of the dragon. How dare this man propose that he could betray Oganna again! Nothing on the world of Subterran must happen to her. Upon her rested the hopes of his people. In her lived the best of her mother and the strength of her dragon grandfather. Nothing must be allowed to happen to her.

Grasping Ardius's shoulder Ilfedo forced him to his knees, ordering him to bow his neck. Then Ilfedo stood behind him, holding the sword with both of his hands. Its point rested on the younger man's neck.

"You would betray your princess again if given the chance?" Ilfedo growled the words. "I am appalled by you."

"Think as you wish, my lord." Ardius spoke in a near whisper. "But the children under my tutelage are as dear to me as if they were my own. Just as you will do anything to protect your daughter, so I will do anything to protect my children. Even though it has cost me my life, I am grateful that they are now safe." As Ardius ended his words he let out a sob.

Ilfedo at first thought that Ardius was seeking an escape from his fate. Then he followed Ardius's gaze to the crowd before him. There stood his students, all in a huddle from the youngest to the oldest among them. Sobs rocked their little shoulders even as their eyes squeezed shut at the sight of their beloved mentor kneeling on the stage with the sword about to sever his head from his body.

"No. No," Ardius pleaded. "Turn them away from this. Do not let them see." He let out another sob as his own tears ran down his cheeks. He held himself up with one arm and waved his cane toward the children. "Find your parents and look away. Look away and remember only that I love you."

Ilfedo froze. Perhaps he should have driven the sword through the traitor's neck. But doubt filled his heart. Ardius's guilt had been established, yet perhaps Ilfedo would have reacted similarly if confronted by similar circumstances.

As the children wept all the louder, the crowd began to weep with them. Every eye fixated on the platform to see their Lord Warrior do the deed that they all knew must be done.

Ilfedo's arms resisted his urge to do the deed. He pushed through the resistance at first, the tip of the sword drawing a trickle of blood from the nape of Ardius's neck. As soon as the blood made contact with the blade, the living fire retreated from it. It twisted violently in his hands, redirecting itself.

Mouth agape, Ilfedo stumbled backward a step and pulled the sword away from the man's neck. Ilfedo had experienced this before. The sword would not take an innocent life. The dragon prophet had warned him that it would, of its own accord, turn on him if he tried to use it against an innocent.

But this man was not innocent! Ardius had unequivocally confessed to his crime.

Ilfedo looked away from the man and again over the crowd, resting his gaze on the children. He felt his shoulders relax as he lowered the sword's point to the floorboards. A grin spread across his face such as he had not felt in a long time. Turning his face upward to the bright rays of sunlight that now illuminated this cursed place he felt hope rise in his chest. In this moment the prophets were with him through the power of living fire.

He heard Ardius catch himself in surprise when the pressure from the sword was removed. Then he heard the crowd's sobs die and whispers of curiosity take their place. Ilfedo smiled down at the children in front of the platform as he sheathed his sword and strode toward them.

The people watched, mesmerized, as he knelt so that he could lift one little girl onto the platform. He dried her cheeks with the back of his hand and kissed her forehead. "Free your friend, little child, for I have spared his life."

She stared at him at first. Then her long curls danced as she wrapped her chubby arms around his neck and smothered his face with kisses.

Ilfedo laughed as he stood back. The child sprinted to Ardius and helped him stand with his cane.

At that moment the crowd burst into cheers so loud that Ilfedo felt certain they echoed deep into the underground and even to the tunnels of Vectra the megatrath. The cheers did not let up, only they were mingled with shouts of thanks to God and to the Lord Warrior.

"You are one of the people," Ilfedo said to Ardius as the man shifted on his peg leg. "I will never number you among my advisors, nor will you ever hold a position of preeminence among the people. But you will live. You will come with us to the Hemmed Land and continue your teaching profession."

Ardius dropped to his knees, spewing his gratitude and shouting thanksgiving.

Ilfedo turned to Everett, grasping the short man's shoulder as he looked over at Elhandra. She was smiling as he said, "God is pleased when mercy is given. Let us enter this new era of unity between our people with a song in our hearts."

Elhandra's face was lighted by a smile and she curtsied ever so slightly. Everett on the other hand wrapped his arms around Ilfedo's midriff and sobbed. Ilfedo waved to the guards that had been assigned to Ardius and they placed themselves strategically in front of the crowd to hide Everett's embarrassment.

When the little man had composed himself again, he spoke to Ilfedo, "You have spared me a very great sorrow on this day, cousin. Though we are related by blood it now gives me joy and relief to know that you know when to show mercy. Ardius is not only a good man. I consider him to be a friend. Therefore you have saved me the pain of losing another friend."

"Without demonstrating mercy our people are lost," Ilfedo said. "Ardius narrowly escaped my wrath on this day, but I give you my word that I have discarded all ill will toward him. He may live in peace among us and I believe he will do no harm, and perhaps much good."

"It gives me further joy to hear you say that," Everett said, and he bowed away and into the crowd where he and Ardius embraced.

Ilfedo separated himself from the throng and made his way toward the cliff face. Far above him the tunneling megatraths chipped and cut the pathway of stone, their belabored breathing echoed down to him. The camps of his Elite warriors backed to the cliff face, and the tents of the woodsmen stood in a cluster nearer to him.

A line of about a hundred of his Elite stood in front of their tents. They saluted as he approached, yet he focused on their commander. Veil barreled toward him, a tired expression on his face. But his eyes radiated exuberance when he stood before Ilfedo. The pathway to the top was almost completed, Veil told him. The megatraths had done their work masterfully. All that remained was to clear the remaining debris from the path, then work on makeshift steps to form a sort of stair that the people could climb to the top.

At last! Ilfedo turned to face the wooden city. "This city has all the lumber you will need, Commander Veil. Use as much of it as you need."

THE PHANTOM'S PROMISE

Two days had passed since Ilfedo pardoned Ardius. Bathed in the warm sunlight shining from the cavern's ceiling far above it, the City of Dresdyn waited. Many of its buildings had been stripped to their frames, the wood carried off and repurposed. Ilfedo had witnessed more than a few of the women looking at their former homes with tears slipping down their cheeks. And why not? They had known this underground world and nothing else.

Ilfedo strode down one deserted street. Flanking him were the remnants of houses. The woodsmen of the Hemmed Land along with the men of the city had found the best lumber the city could offer. Ilfedo could now see through the structures to the row of skeleton homes on the next street, and through those to a row of dismantled shops on the street beyond that. Thanks to the observatory, sunlight spilled all over the city and he could see to every corner of the enormous cavern.

The ground groaned as one of Vectra's tunnelers slammed his fists into the stone before him. "Human," the megatrath growled, "the work is done as my mistress commanded." It lowered its long narrow snout almost to the street. Yellow vapor exhumed from it nostrils before it rose to its full height again, looking down upon him.

Ilfedo nodded to the creature as the others of its kind lumbered off down the highway to form a half-circle behind it. These were the other tunnelers. Ilfedo looked up at them and expressed his great appreciation for what they had done. With a subtle action he touched the pommel of the sword of the dragon as it rested in its sheath at his side. He drew from it a burst of inhuman strength and stepped forward, striking his fist against the lead megatrath's chest.

The force of the blow made the creature wince, then its long snout formed a toothy grin. "Farewell, human. It was an honor to aid you in this endeavor." It rumbled deep in its throat and inclined its head to him again, then snapped its attention up to face the tunnel that exited the cavern. Both the lead megatrath and its companions lumbered off down the highway.

Turning about as they loomed all around him, Ilfedo watched them go. Their legs were as thick as some of the larger oak trees that had grown around his house in the Hemmed Land. Their scales glistened as if they had been polished by the waves of the sea. He watched until their forms melded into the dark tunnel which would lead them back to their underground realm, then he faced the far end of the cavern and made for the face of the cliff.

A mass of humanity could be seen from this distance. They formed a line that made a gradual ascent from the remains of the city and up a makeshift wooden ramp and stairs that curved along the cliff's face and ended at its highest point. From here he could not see it, yet he knew that the path to the exit tunnel began there. At last his people were heading to their new home.

When Ilfedo reached the base of the cliff a little while later, he found the encampments had been disassembled and, off to one side, two contingents of his elite warriors of light spread out in formation by the base of the enormous wooden stair. They stood expectantly, waiting for his command and his only. Their captains stood forefront a few paces from their ranks, every face staring straight ahead.

No doubt they were as eager as he was to be heading back home.

The people of Dresdyn had passed on, and the tail end of their multitude had reached the half-way point up the cliff's face. He knew that the greater part of the population was far above him and out of sight, following Veil and other members of the Elite up the long tunnel to the Hemmed Land. The glow of the swords of light would be needed to keep the women, the children, and the few that remained of their elders from tripping in the dark.

As Ilfedo approached the warriors another man stood apart from them and saluted. Ombre's grin seemed to reach his ears as he put his arm back to his side. "My lord," Ombre said.

Ilfedo smiled back. "This is a bright day after a

dark time, Ombre. I am glad that you could be here with me through all of this." He drew close to his friend, grasped his arm, and drew him in a quick embrace. "The Creator has smiled upon us."

"The last of the city has been emptied. We left only the dead, as you instructed." Ombre turned sober in that moment and he lowered his voice so that only Ilfedo could hear. "Some of the women wept over the homes they are leaving behind and among the young and the old there were many tears shed as they paid their respects for the last time at the graves of their loved ones." He hesitated for what seemed a long time, then said, "If this is a preview of what you intend to carry out in the Hemmed Land, I fear there will be a battle ahead of you."

Ilfedo, too, sobered as he grasped the man's shoulder and gazed into his eyes. "I fear you are right, yet I trust that those who stand with me will be many more than those who seek to oppose such a transition. For now I am grateful that the first part of my task is accomplished. The City of Dresdyn has been evacuated and its people will join us in the Hemmed Land. I will take these small victories where I find them so that we may be strengthened for the future."

At that moment Oganna walked toward him. A few younger heads among the Elite warriors' ranks did start to turn, then they corrected themselves by staring ahead. Oganna gave her father a gentle smile. She was wearing her trousers again, a fitting attire for the trek ahead of her. Neneila the viper hissed from around her neck. Belted at her side was the crimson bladed sword called Avenger. The sunlight from far above glinted subtly off the crystal boomerang attached to her other hip.

Often Ilfedo had forgotten that she carried the weapon. It blended so perfectly as to be almost invisible to the passing gaze.

Oganna's blue-gold eyes stared up at him with an irresistible energy. Her long blond hair had been brushed to a sheen. Just having her near lifted his spirits even higher.

"Father," she said, "with the aid of Elhandra the prophetess and Pastor Everett, as well as the other monks, I finished packing the last of the scrolls and books from the city library. The more fragile volumes were wrapped with the greatest of care and assigned to the monks. The woodsmen who came with us built crates for the majority of the manuscripts. We stuffed the crates with dewobin feathers so as to protect the manuscripts and the older volumes, and the woodsmen have already carried them into the tunnel above."

Throwing his arm around her shoulders Ilfedo took one last look over the city. Then he raised his arm and ordered the remaining warriors of light to ascend the stair. When the last of them had marched out of sight over the top of the cliff, Ilfedo followed with Ombre on one side and Oganna on his other.

They took care in the ascent because portions of the stair angled up rather steeply. The boards creaked beneath their feet as a cool blast of air ushered from the city.

They had only fifty paces or so remaining to the ascent. The end was in sight.

"Praise the Creator that this dark time is over for the people of this city," Oganna said in a hushed voice.

Then a familiar howl echoed into the cavern and all three of them froze. Ilfedo's gaze darted to the distant tunnel exit through which he had found the lost citizens of the city. A great hairy ape galloped out of the pitch blackness and into the sunlight. It shook its head in the sudden brightness and howled again.

"The beast," Ombre said in a hushed tone.

Ilfedo stared at the creature. It rolled its muscle-ridden shoulders, fists beating the stones under its feet. It cried out again, this time with a guttural roar that equaled the fierceness of a dragon's. The sunlight glinted off the twin horns twisting up from its head.

Ilfedo realized that he had grasped the pommel of his sword and the living fire had begun to rip through his veins.

"Father!" Oganna closed her smaller hand over his fist, cooling his rage.

"I will not allow such a monster to live, my daughter." He used his free hand to pull hers away, and began to draw the sword of the dragon from its sheath.

"All for revenge? Father, leave that beast. We have left the city! This is finished." She blocked his path as he faced down the great stair to the city below. "Will you vanquish every beast in this dark world before you allow yourself to leave it behind?"

"My child," he said, "you saw the men this thing slew."

Shaking her head, she gazed at the ground. "And they were good, noble men."

The viper raised its head to stare at Ilfedo, shaking its head, slicking out its tongue. "Ssstupidity. It will undo your speciesss."

Ombre drew his sword and grasped Ilfedo by the shoulder. "If you are going down there, we will go together. Let us make the kill swiftly. In memory of James, our brother-in-arms."

Seeing she had lost the argument, Oganna started to draw out her own sword.

Ilfedo returned her gaze and shook his head. "Put it away, my daughter. Stay up here until the deed is done."

Her mouth agape, Oganna tried to respond. Her eyes said it all. She felt betrayed. She glanced to Ombre for reassurance yet he, too, shook his head.

"Do not misunderstand," Ilfedo said. "You would be able to dispatch of that creature as well as I."

"Then I will go with you," she said.

Exchanging a solemn gaze with Ombre, Ilfedo drew the sword fully from its sheath. It blazed with fire as he strode past Oganna, advancing back down the ramp with Ombre at his side.

Ombre smiled at her. "This battle is personal. James was a friend."

Oganna released her hold on Avenger. "Now I understand. Very well, I will stay behind but if you get into trouble you can be certain that my crimson blade will join the fray."

The men chuckled and Ombre said, "My, my! What happened to my sweet little niece? The girl has been replaced by a woman." He winked back at her, then resolutely started to descend the ramp.

Then, in the distant tunnel behind the monkey beast, there appeared a glowing figure. Ilfedo and Ombre stopped dead on their feet. The figure hesitated only long enough for his eyes to adjust to the cavern's brilliant sunlight, then he yelled like a madman and ran after the ape. The sword in his hand was unmistakable, even from this distance. It glowed with the radiance of the

Elite Thousand.

"He is alive?" Ombre stood there with mouth agape, pointing at the distant figure.

Lowering his own sword, Ilfedo watched as the Elite warrior closed quarters with the ape. The beast lowered its horns, driving them toward his body, but James rolled to the side. The horns sparked along the cavern floor as the beast swung around. James grabbed hold of the beast's arm and swung himself over its neck. He held the sword's handle with both hands, with one stroke severing the tip of one of the beast's horns.

The beast squealed, spinning with deadly speed so that James was thrown off its neck. As the man rolled on the ground some distance off, the beast picked up the piece of severed horn and leaped onto the nearest house. It was a larger structure but much of it had been stripped to the frame. The building collapsed under the creature and something sparked in the foundation.

Perhaps a lighted oil lamp had been left behind. Whatever the cause, flames sprouted from all corners of the building. The ape took one glance at a spot of fire on its arm, then it howled and bounded to another building, beating its burning arm against the ground. The flames caught in the moss, and began spreading to the adjacent structures.

"Father!" Oganna cried out as they watched the blaze grow.

James was on his feet again. Somehow he managed to get atop the monkey's head. He struck it with the pommel of his sword, face-planting it in the dust. He was shouting something at the creature and, Ilfedo could hardly believe it, the beast lay still as if submitting to him. The beast's sides heaved heavily, revealing that it was still alive as James grabbed a discarded blanket from the street. Ilfedo could not understand what the Elite warrior was saying, yet he heard muffled shouts as if James were instructing or cursing the creature. James smothered the fire on the beast's arm with the blanket, then tossed it aside and clambered atop the back of its neck again.

The beast stood and started to shake James off, but the man cried out and battered its head with his sword. The creature took off at a maddened run toward the far corner of the cavern, swatting buildings on its way. It jumped onto a church belfry, then jumped a greater distance to the huge dome of the observatory. In the beast's wake the bell in the church belfry clanged as it fell from its supports and into the leaping rush of flames that had now spread through half the city.

"Come on, Ombre!" Ilfedo started to run down the ramp. "Let's get him out of there before he gets himself killed." Ombre started to follow, then he grabbed Ilfedo by the arm. "Look." He pointed into the distance at the observatory.

The monkey beast leaped into the thin line of green light that had brought light to this dark world. When the beast landed on the convex glass at the device's head, the beam dimmed and failed altogether. Ilfedo stared in stunned astonishment. The roar of the horned ape echoed through the cavern, and the cavern roof gradually reverted to its former state. In place of the transparent stone and sunlight, darkness filled the void. Dresdyn's streets flooded with shadows that were interrupted only by the raging fire that now consumed everything in its path.

The smell of smoke preceded the crackling of

burning wood as the fire spread to the great ramp. Ilfedo cried out his dismay as both he and Ombre turned to flee up the ramp, a wave of heat ushering from the abyss. When at last the three of them stood on the stone ledge far above the city, they looked back. In the fire's red glow the ramp groaned, its boards snapped, and it fell to the cavern floor. The fire greedily flooded in, devouring what remained of the wooden structure. A portion of the cliff's face collapsed after the ramp had, sliding down into the city in a cloud of dirt and smoke.

Far off, the ape's shadowed form broke through the walls of the observatory. James in his glowing armor was thrown from its shoulders. He struck the street and his sword flew from his hand, instantly hiding him in darkness.

"There is nothing either of you can do now," Ilfedo said to Ombre and Oganna. "But I can. Go on into the tunnel. I will get down there and help him."

"Uh, not going to let you do that." Ombre stepped between Ilfedo and the cliff's face. "You could easily get trapped down there. True, you could probably get down there without much trouble, yet there is now no return path."

Ilfedo shoved Ombre aside. "I cannot let this happen."

A gentle hand touched his arm and Oganna spoke softly in his ear. "Let him go, Father. He chose this reckless path when he pursued that beast into the caverns. Let him go."

Ilfedo's shoulders slumped. He dropped to his knees and stared down at the doomed city of Dresdyn. He knew they were right. A wise man would know to leave James to the fate he had chosen. Ilfedo squeezed his daughter's hand and nodded solemnly up at his friend. "Leave me here, for a short while. Both of you."

Perhaps it was the tone of his voice. It commanded obedience when he so required it. Perhaps they recognized that there was no longer any threat of him throwing his life in pursuit of a reckless cause. Ombre sheathed his sword as Oganna drew hers out. Avenger glowed as red as blood, its tip held mere inches above the stony ground, and the silver dress magically grew over her body, its light illuminating the path out of the underworld.

Ilfedo was left alone to watch the fire complete its work, consuming the city that he had come to both love and hate.

Beside him the stone crackled and, when he glanced over his shoulder, ice gathered over the surface. A woman walked barefoot upon it, her blue dress gently blowing as she approached the waves of heat that emanated from the city far below. The long end of a familiar sword dragged on the ground behind her from beneath a fold in her dress. He watched her approach without uttering a word. Her form was very beautiful and when she looked down at him her green eyes penetrated the pain in his heart.

"Meleese," he said.

The phantom smiled and leaned toward the edge of the precipice, peering down. "What destruction you have wrought!" She stepped back and circled to the other side of him, looking down at the city again. Ice formed everywhere she moved and melted in her wake. Her hair fell in thick waves to her waist and had taken on a reddish hue, mirroring the fire below. Her eyebrows were thinned and cut definitive lines that emphasized her cheeks in a not-so-subtle manner.

He tried to tear his gaze away to see how James fared, yet somehow he could not. When he had met Meleese her flesh had been awful to behold. When he and Oganna had healed her she had seemed no beauty. But all of that had changed.

"You like the transformation?" She was returning his gaze with her beautiful green eyes. Eyes that were as green as the vile sword she had taken from Brunster Thadius Oldwell. Pleasure filled her expression and she blushed.

Ilfedo at last spoke and he let his words convey sincerity. "Any man would be pleased to see you now, Meleese. Truly after our last encounter I feared what you would become."

She lifted her face and laughed, spreading her arms heavenward. "I have been reborn!"

Ilfedo smiled at last. "This pleases me."

Meleese heaved a sigh and dropped to one knee in front of him. She held up one finger, "I am going to touch my sword but I don't want you to be alarmed. I cannot interact with you without its power, and I do want to be able to touch you."

He remained on his knees, returning her gaze as she reached one hand under a fold of her skirt. Her eyes flashed as she connected with the sword's power, then she reached out and stroked the side of his face with her fingers. He half-closed his eyes. There was such affection in the touch. It soothed him.

"My dear Ilfedo," she whispered. "You seem to carry the weight of not only this world but of the next. I have watched you. You care for those around you like no other man that I have met. But pain weighs on your spirit and it is so deep that it carries to those around you." She sighed. "I recognize the pain you suffer. I have suffered the same for far too long. The one I loved was taken away from me when Oldwell began his corruption. My love was stolen from me, too."

Ilfedo felt tears forming in his eyes as he realized the depth of her revelation. "He is dead now. I killed the man you loved, didn't I?" He stared hard into her green eyes.

She seemed taken aback by his conclusion.

Ilfedo gently rested his hands on her shoulders. "Tell me if I am right, Meleese. Do not hide it from me."

"You—you did what had to be done," she said. "We—each— have lost."

Ilfedo let his hands fall to his sides. He stared off into the city as she wept. "We all make choices," he said. "Some choose right and some—" He pointed to the distant glowing form of James, just visible again. "Fools and men of loose conviction, they all die alike with the good."

The phantom followed his gaze. She said not a word as James again charged the hulking form of the monkey beast. As the beast's howl rose above the crackling of burning buildings, Meleese turned his face toward hers. She stared down at his lips and stroked the side of his face. "I will miss you, Ilfedo. I wish that I could have filled that void that your departed love left in your soul. But I can see that no one could." Then she did something that he could have stopped her from doing, but he did not. She closed her eyes and met his lips in a kiss.

When she withdrew her lips from his, she stood

to her feet. He stood beside her and stroked her hair for a brief moment. "I wish my heart could move on," he said, "but I know it will not. I only pray that I have not hurt you. If you could have known my wife you would know why I can never marry another."

She wiped a tear from her cheek and released her hold on the green sword. Ilfedo's hand passed through her hair as if she were a ghost. She had pulled her physical being out of his reach.

Touching the pommel of the sword of the dragon, Ilfedo let the living fire rush over his body. Meleese glanced up quickly, meeting his gaze as he put his arm around her shoulders. The power coursing through his being pulled her body back into physical form and he pulled her gently to his side. Meleese did not seem to need any more words. She sighed and rested her head against his shoulder.

For a long while they stood there together, watching Dresdyn burn to the ground. She did not move and neither did he. He told her then of his childhood. Of the bear that had killed his parents. Of Ombre and of Ombre's father, who'd raised him so that he would not grow up as an abandoned orphan. She smiled as he talked about the house he'd built, of his visions of Dantress. How at last he'd found her, married her, and had had a child by her. Then he related the misery of the years following her death, the joys of watching his daughter grow, the pain of leading his nation in war at Ar'lenon. How all through the years his love for his wife had never faded and how her image was still as clear in his mind, so that sometimes he'd had visions where she had helped him out of difficult circumstances.

When Ilfedo grew silent, Meleese told him of

the joys of her youth. How her parents had shown her wonderful places in the underworld, even places where plants and creatures produced light that made everything seem like magic. Then she told him of her love, a phantom named Thullen whose strength had been little but whose smile had warmed her every breath. She had loved him and he had loved her, or so she'd believed. But the misery of Brunster Thadius Oldwell corrupted many, and Thullen had fallen with most of her kind, following their queen to great evil. Meleese spoke of the years of lonely wandering when she had explored dark tunnels and caverns, avoiding those of her own kind that had been corrupted, all the while searching for any members of her race that had not fallen. Occasionally she had found a fairy willing to share her company, though the encounters had been brief.

The fires simmered in Dresdyn. Where homes and churches had once stood there now remained heaps of ash. The monkey beast howled again as the glowing form of James sprang atop its horned head, then it made a mad dash into the distant tunnel. The spire of light that was James was swallowed by the darkness. The city was left in dreadful silence.

Ilfedo sighed, shaking his head. "Farewell, my foolish warrior. Some men fall then rise again. Others fall into madness. May the sword of light protect you in this mad world." He took Meleese by her slim hands and they faced each other. "My offer still stands. Should you care to take it."

She laughed. "I am tempted to kiss you again for such kindness, but I will not try for fear of being disappointed should you reject it." She turned her face toward the city of glowing embers far below. "If you were asking me to come with you because you were declaring love for me, I would be inclined to go. Yet I know that it is not so, at least not for now. This underworld, troubled as it may be, is still my home. And I cannot abandon it. Nor can I let go of the hope that one day I may find others who hid from our queen's wicked vices."

Ilfedo bit his lower lip as she turned her lovely green eyes up to meet his gaze.

"For your sake," she whispered, "I will keep a watch over your crazed friend. If there is hope of restoring his sanity, I shall be there for him."

"Thank you, Meleese." Ilfedo released her and stood back with a bow. "When I think of you, I will do so with a tender heart."

Meleese lifted her voice in a loud laugh that filled his heart with bright hope. "You bow to me, lord of the Hemmed Land?"

"Yes," he said with a smile. "For I now believe in you, Meleese. When we first met I thought evil of you, and when you took Oldwell's sword I doubted more. But I believe that you hold the Creator's light in this dark realm. In my eyes you are a queen, and so I bow."

Her eyebrows lifted playfully. "Farewell, Ilfedo. I will mourn your departure as surely as I mourned Thullen." She lifted one hand and blew him a kiss, and as she did so her form wisped into smoke and vanished.

Ilfedo looked one last time upon the city of Dresdyn. Nothing remained except ashes. He felt troubled that he had allowed Meleese to kiss him. She had struck a part of him that he had thought died a long time ago. If he had let himself, he would have fallen in love again. "Would you forgive me if I had, Dantress?" he asked the darkness, then he turned his back on the cavern and strode into the tunnel that would take him home. The sword of the dragon blazed fervently in his hands as he held it before his face, its flames dancing on the walls of stone.

OLD FRIENDS BY THE FIRESIDE

The sidewalks filled with people flooding out of alleyways and buildings. Others stood on the balconies, looking down upon Ilfedo with awe on their faces as he rode his white stallion through the City of Gwensin. The creature's silvery mane flashed in the sunlight. The people cheered and some began to chant his name. Beside him on other silver-maned steeds rode Oganna, Ombre, and Commander Veil. Oganna smiled proudly up at him as the chant, "Ilfedo! Ilfedo! Ilfedo!" deafened his ears.

Ilfedo felt no need to return the gazes of the people of the city. As always Gwensin City glimmered with cleanliness, as well as the health of her people. But they paled in comparison to the armor of living fire now blazing on his body. Nearly one thousand warriors of light held their swords aloft as they marched in magnificent procession behind him. Yes, a few of them had lost their lives in the rescue of the people of Dresdyn, but he counted their lives worth the sacrifice. How few had fallen and how many had been rescued!

Behind the Elite Thousand marched the bronze-clad warriors he'd added to his ranks. In their wake followed the elders, the monks, the women, and the children of Dresdyn. Wonder filled their squinting eyes, for they still found it difficult to look fully on this sunlit world. They had lived for too long in the depths of Subterran. Their pink dewobin clothing made them appear strange in the Hemmed Land, and the carts that rolled along behind them carried the physical remnants of their cultural history. Theirs was a culture linked by lineage to the same ancestors as the people of the Hemmed Land. Many a citizen of the Hemmed Land turned a wonder-filled gaze upon their thick, gleaming armor, and the works of art and piles of books and scrolls that were visible in the carts. Ilfedo did not want these people welcomed as strangers, but as long-lost kinfolk.

As Ilfedo led the procession he bathed in the vindication the display of it all gave to the cause he had pushed so hard to accomplish. Let the naysayers be silenced. A victory had been attained and the path to finding a new homeland would be all the easier with the people's renewed spirit of loyalty to him.

His thoughts darkened for a long moment as he thought of Brunster Thadius Oldwell still inhabiting the body of Bromstead. Was there hope for him? Ilfedo shook the dreadful cloud out of his mind. He had left Bromstead in the care of twenty warriors of light. Bound and shackled, the man had still smiled his indifference when Ilfedo had ordered him to be marched to the safety of Fort Gabel. There he would be confined in a dungeon, awaiting Ilfedo's return.

The saddle creaked as Ilfedo shifted his weight, looking back upon those who walked behind him. Elhandra smiled up at him and Everett nodded solemnly, his pink monk's habit a stark reminder of his origin. Ilfedo turned his face ahead again, listening to the clip clopping of his stallion's hooves on the cobblestone street. He had a plan to bring the most trusted among his clerics to Fort Gabel, and there he would see if they could aid in dispelling the spirit of Oldwell from Bromstead's body.

As he brought the mighty column through the heart of the city and finally slowed to a halt at the mayor's mansion, he scanned the faces of the dignitaries who stood on the threshold. One of them limped toward him, a broad smile on his face, and reached out a hand in greeting. Ilfedo grasped it and pulled his friend close to embrace him. "Ganning, it is good to see you again."

"And what of me?" Honer stepped up beside Ganning, slapping Ilfedo's shoulder. "Welcome home, my lord. If you cannot already tell, the people are pleased to see both you and your daughter return."

Ilfedo put an arm around each man as Ombre dismounted and, laughing, joined them. "All of us together in one place at the same time?" Ombre said. "Bring out a scribe! This should be recorded for the history books."

"By all the stars," Honer said as he stepped apart from the group and helped Oganna to dismount. "When my wife watched you as a little baby . . . It all seems like only yesterday. Yet look at her now, Ilfedo.

Your daughter is a grown woman. Amazing isn't it? It makes me realize that we are no longer the young men we once were."

"Hey there." Ombre huffed. "You know how to cast a pallor on a good day."

Ilfedo turned to Elhandra and Everett, making short introductions, then he strode to the doors of the mansion. One of the remaining dignitaries in a monk's habit bowed particularly low and Ilfedo reached out, grasping the man's shoulder. "It is good to see you again, Brother Hersis."

"Praise God for your safe return, my lord." Brother Hersis stepped back as other men ushered Ilfedo into the mansion itself.

"How fares my lord Vortain?" Ilfedo said.

The assemblage grew somewhat quiet.

Brother Hersis took Ilfedo down a hallway, admonishing everyone else to remain behind. When they were alone, wending their way into the older portion of the structure, Hersis spoke. "I have spent much time with the mayor. Truly his condition is better than what I understand it was when you left, but things have grown strange in your absence."

"Strange how?" Ilfedo furrowed his brow deeply.

"The girl that you brought here, the former witch—" Brother Hersis licked his lips, mulling over how to say what he wanted to say as he shuffled along the corridor.

Ilfedo pulled the man to a stop. "Withhold nothing from me."

Hersis dropped his voice to a near whisper. "Through much conversing with her and with Vortain, it seems apparent to me that she has lost all of her memories that pre-exist the attack of her old master. She does not even recall how she came to the mayor's mansion, nor that it was Vortain himself that caused her horrific reconnection with the sorcerer. Much more than that she claims to have no recollection that she was a sorceress herself."

Ilfedo stared unseeing at the wall. "It is possible, I presume, that somehow her old master's attack damaged her memories. Perhaps even erased them?"

"But can she be trusted?" Brother Hersis bit his lower lip. "By my understanding there is no doubt that she reconnected with a sorcerer when Vortain pressed her. What is certain is that she once served the very enemy that may have been behind the destruction in Burloi." His voice gained strength. "I do not mean to cast more doubt into your mind, only to give you reason for caution. You will see a great change in the young woman, for she has attached herself to Vortain and dotes on him. My concern is that this budding relationship relies solely on the girl's word that she remembers nothing. I cannot help postulating that if Escentra has retained her memory, resentment toward Vortain may remain. Also, if her memory was not erased but rather was fragmented, what might that bode for you and your encounter with her in the Hidden Realm? So much is uncertain in this case."

Ilfedo followed Brother Hersis into the heart of the mansion, opening the door to Vortain's bedchamber.

The room that opened before him was lit on all sides by candlelight. Candles along the walls and a couple of lamps fixed on the wall above them. Ilfedo felt a sweat break on his brow as he stepped into the room, for it was quite warm and a bit damp. A large canopy bed filled a corner of the room. The blue and gold canopy had been tied to the bedposts so that its sides remained open, and there in the bed lay Vortain.

"Lord Ilfedo," Vortain said in a husky voice. He groaned as he sat up. Ilfedo nearly jumped as a dark womanly figure separated from the wall, stealing to Vortain's side. But Vortain waved the girl back a step. "I will rise of my own strength to greet my Lord Warrior," Vortain said to her. Escentra bowed her head and backed away.

As Ilfedo passed her and looked on her face, for her countenance was deep with concern yet warm with love, he said, "Child, do you remember me?"

She swallowed, biting her lower lip. "Yes. I think so. And master Vortain has told me more of you, of how you have done much good for your people and for me."

"Do you remember our first meeting?" he asked.

Escentra's eyes flicked to Vortain's bed. "I remember seeing you when master Vortain first took ill."

"My lord, please do not grill the young lady." Vortain laughed. "I would have thought Brother Hersis would have informed you by now that Escentra has no recollection of what happened prior to her master's attack. Please! Come sit on my bed so that you may share with me your adventure into Resgeria. Word quickly reached me that you succeeded under hostile conditions. Praise be to God!"

Ilfedo sat on the man's bed and began to converse with him. He studied the scars that now laced Vortain's face. Judging by the extent of the scars, the sorcerer had not been far from taking Vortain's life.

Through hours of conversation both with Escentra and with Vortain, Ilfedo came to the conclusion that all of the girl's memories pre-existing the sorcerer's attack had indeed been erased from her mind. She did not even recall her encounter with Ilfedo in the Hidden Realm, much less that she had once been a sorceress.

Somehow these facts changed the person that she became. In place of the deeply thoughtful, lost soul that had been Escentra, there now thrived a young woman hopeful of her future and eager to please those around her. She warmly welcomed Ilfedo's questions because she understood him to be the Lord of the Hemmed Land, but the persons she now felt closest to were Vortain and his wife.

One evening not long after returning to the City of Gwensin, Ilfedo sat again in Mayor Vortain's dining room as servants flitted in and out through side doors bringing food in and dirty dishes out. Vortain's wife sat on one side of the mayor and Escentra sat beside her. Vortain himself had grown considerably stronger, for Ilfedo had managed to give him a little healing strength from the sword of the dragon.

By strange circumstance Vortain's respect for Ilfedo seemed to have grown ever deeper after the sorcerer's attack. In his encounter with Escentra's evil master the mayor of Gwensin City had come to understand how dangerous the foes Ilfedo had often faced were. The man leaned forward to listen as Escentra whispered something to his wife, and as the two women giggled Vortain glanced sideways at Ilfedo and grinned. His cracked face was a horrible sight, yet his politician smile removed any aversion Ilfedo might have had.

"Is the steak to your liking, my lord?" Vortain gently stabbed a slice of red meat on his own plate as he asked the question.

Ilfedo nodded, his eyes once more distracted by Escentra.

Vortain lowered his voice. "She is so much different than I thought she would be. I cannot imagine what horrors she must have witnessed in her short life. Yet now she is an innocent young woman. It would seem that the Creator has given her a second chance at life."

Ilfedo turned to face him. "You have certainly formed a bond with her, and I am uncertain of the consequences. As your Lord Warrior, I must ask, what do you intend to do with that bond."

The mayor's answer was quick and his gaze held Ilfedo's without wavering. "She wishes to remain with us, and we wish to adopt her." He let Ilfedo soak in the revelation, then he stood. He rounded the table and stood behind the women. Patting Escentra's shoulders, Vortain said, "We want nothing less than her full acceptance as a member of our family."

Escentra and Vortain's wife smiled across the table at Ilfedo.

Doubts made Ilfedo hesitate for a long while. All three of these individuals appeared so content in each other's company that he did not want to disappoint them, but it was not a decision he could make lightly.

Somewhere in the heart of Vortain was a duplicitous individual, willing at times to betray Ilfedo's trust in matters of politics and even to side against him. Vortain had often enough been a thorn in Ilfedo's side, for he often persisted in dividing Ilfedo's counselors against the Lord Warrior's will. Though Ilfedo appreciated that Vortain spoke his mind without fear.

Then Ilfedo considered Escentra. She was young

and very beautiful. In the short time he had known her he had seen three versions of her personality. The rash, brainwashed witch whom he had fought in the Hidden Realm. The confused young woman he had brought back to the Hemmed Land, whose heart despaired of joy and whose face displayed great pain. And now, this latest version, a happy youth diligently caring for a man she hardly knew.

On the other hand, Ilfedo had no qualms with Vortain's wife. She had always extended hospitality to Ilfedo and his guests and had carried herself with humble confidence in the presence of affluent individuals. A long while ago Caritha had remarked that the only reason she could sleep soundly in Vortain's mansion was because his wife was as wise as she was kind.

The clock on the wall ticked away many minutes as Ilfedo weighed Vortain's request. When he looked up into Vortain's eyes the man was frowning back at him. "Escentra," Ilfedo said, ignoring the man's displeasure, "are you certain that this is your desire?"

The girl's countenance fell. "Of course, my lord. Vortain would not ask if it were not so. We all discussed the possibility three days ago, and seeing as I am an orphan—"

Ilfedo held up his hand and his words came out with great strength. "We do not know that you are an orphan."

"Well," the girl lowered her gaze, "I do not remember my parents, and somehow I have no desire to remember. I feel certain that my father is dead and what little I know of my past frightens me. I want a fresh start. A new beginning with people who care about me and can show me my place in this world."

Folding his hands, Ilfedo considered what she had said. The motivation was proper, but it concerned him that she could have so little regard to her birth family. But this was not a unique dilemma. He knew of a few younger children who had made similar decisions to abandon their blood heritage in favor of a new one granted by their adoptive families.

"I can say nothing against this," Ilfedo said at last. He sighed as he stood and waved his hand in blessing on their proposal. "Escentra, in accordance with the laws of this great land of ours, I bind you to Vortain as your father. You will conduct yourself in a manner that honors him until such time as, God willing, you give your heart to an honorable young man." Ilfedo gazed long and hard into Vortain's eyes. "To you, I give this charge: Instruct this young woman to live a godly life, protect her from bodily and spiritual harm, and instruct her to honor those in authority in this land."

Vortain's face relaxed. "It will be my greatest honor to do that, my lord."

As the man finished, Ilfedo added, "And I promise to hold you accountable to those terms, Vortain. Every man has his master. Do not forget yours." Ilfedo handed his dirty dish to a nearby maid, nodded when she curtsied to him, and then he walked out of the room and down the hallway.

At the base of the stairway Ilfedo drew to a stop. Ombre descended the last few steps and leaned his back against the baluster. "I do not like the look on your face, Ilfedo," his friend said. "What ill news do you have for me now?"

Ilfedo led Ombre out of the mayor's mansion and divulged what had transpired. Instead of condemning Ilfedo's decision, Ombre spoke in support of it. He reminded Ilfedo that his first obligation was to his own daughter, and not to the former witch. He felt that this would free Ilfedo for the tasks he most needed to tend to.

Together the men walked outside to the stables, remounted their magnificent stallions, and rode into the moonlit evening. Ilfedo gave instructions to a courier for how things should be run in his absence, then he and Ombre galloped down the city streets and out into the fields. It was time to go home to Oganna and his beloved nuvitors.

The two friends reveled in the fresh, cool air that dampened their cheeks. The sounds of frogs and crickets built a background chorus to the thudding of their horses' hooves on the woodland path. The trees rushed by and many a large clearing opened before them where the men of the Hemmed Land had devoured the forests, yet he had let his heart bring him back to the place he loved. Memories. Memories of forests thick and wild. Untamed. Memories of hunting with Honer, Ganning, and Ombre. And memories of the one love that had left his soul fractured in its departing. Dantress running through a field, laughing as he overtook her and tackled her to the green grass. Rolling on the ground with her then kissing passionately.

The horses raced onward, guided by Ilfedo and Ombre's honed responses to the path home. Silver manes flashed in the moonlight. Silver hooves dusted the path in glitter that seemed to glow for only a moment after they passed.

When the journey ended, heavy clouds slipped over the moon and thunder sounded in the distance as they led the horses into the stalls by Ilfedo's house. After brushing and patting down their mounts, the men wandered into the house. Oganna greeted them at the door. She had brewed hot cocoa and baked corn muffins. The house smelled of soap and flour, and a bit of mint that Oganna had gathered from their little-tended herb garden. Seivar and Hasselpatch were sound asleep in the nest they had built up in Ilfedo's room.

For a while Oganna chatted with them, then she excused herself to her room. Ombre stepped outside and Ilfedo followed, leaving the door cracked. Ombre began to speak of the Hemmed Land and of rumors he'd gathered from his short stay in Gwensin City. As Ombre began to speculate on things to come, Ilfedo stopped him.

"It will not be so." Ilfedo paced back and forth on the stones outside his front door. Beyond the shelter of his porch roof a torrential downpour soaked the grass and the trees at the edge of his clearing. A tiny field mouse darted out of the rain and stood on the front step, licking itself until Neneila lunged out of a shadow and swallowed the creature whole.

Ombre cringed, and turned his face away from the viper as it slithered back inside the house through the cracked door. Leaning against the wall, Ombre kept his arms crossed over his chest. His face furrowed. "Honer is adept at keeping relations with all manner of folk," he said. "I doubt he is wrong in this."

"I will not accept it until I hear it from Vortain's mouth," Ilfedo said, standing still. "I know that he has resented my declaration of exodus and I know that leaving the Hemmed Land goes against every fiber in his being, yet to accuse him of treason—"

Ombre waved a hand. "You give him much more faith than I ever have, brother. In fact, I suspect the rumor is true, exactly as it was told to Honer. Vortain is plotting against you, thus also against Oganna. Perhaps it is that witch you brought back with you. Though a young thing, maybe she is not as innocent as you'd like to believe. I think it good that your home is no longer shadowed by her presence."

Ilfedo turned a rebuking gaze on his friend. "Speculation is not going to serve any good end. We know nothing yet if anything of Escentra's involvement in the City of Gwensin. Do not attribute these dark rumors to her presence. I offered her sanctuary. I offered her a new life."

"She now has that, Ilfedo! By my estimation you left her in the hands of the least trustworthy of all your counselors. Yet I supported that decision because you needed distance from her." Ombre shook his head and sneered. "Do not take lightly my words. Of all those who have served you it is your close friends whose word you should trust foremost. Honer, Ganning, and myself, we have been with you from the beginning." He threw up his hands. "The beginning of all of this craziness. And we were there before, when life was simpler."

Ilfedo cooled his temper, focusing his attention on the falling rain instead and the dampness of the cool air. "I am sorry, Ombre. Do not doubt my reliance on your counsel, only realize please that what you are suggesting is the brewing of a civil war."

"Yes!" Ombre raised both fists and shook them. "Unthinkable as it seems that is exactly what Vortain has been leading up to all of these years. He bows to your face, yet behind your back he is always seeking preeminence. Even if he is not scheming such a thing, he is gathering supporters to oppose your command that we leave the Hemmed Land."

"Can we discuss this more in the morning?" Ilfedo opened the door to his home and sighed. "I cannot help but feel I have neither the energy nor the discernment to handle all of this information until I get some rest."

Ombre's face betrayed his realization. He reached out his hand to reassure Ilfedo. "Forgive me, brother, you are exhausted and rightfully so. Let's go inside and rest." He smiled broadly and followed Ilfedo into the living room where the flames flickered in the fireplace.

Oganna was sitting on the hearth, Hasselpatch lying on her lap. Neneila the viper had coiled as close to the fire as she possibly could without burning herself, yet the creature's gaze lingered on the nuvitor. With one hand Oganna stroked the white bird's back. In the other she held a steaming mug of cocoa. Ilfedo settled into a hammock hung from the ceiling rafters, Ombre laid in the other. Oganna did not look up, instead she stared at the nuvitor in her lap, her fingers gently stroking the creature's back. Hasselpatch cooed, keeping her beak tucked under one wing.

"Father," Oganna whispered, glancing up at him. Tears welled in her eyes. "Seivar wanted to come down to cuddle with you by the fire, but he said he did not have the strength." She started to choke on the last word.

Standing back to his tired feet, Ilfedo climbed the stairs to his bedroom. The nuvitors had built a nest in the rafters above his bed. Twigs and dry grass, bits of branches and chunks of clay. He could not see into it because of the height, yet the faithful old bird waddled to the edge of the nest and cooed down at him.

"Master!"

Ilfedo held up his hands and gently lifted the creature, holding it to his bosom. The bird breathed in labored wheezes. It rested its head against his chest as he carried it down the stairs. Struggling with the emotion of it all, Ilfedo choked back a sob of his own. "How are you, my friend?"

"Better now that you have returned, Master," the faithful creature said. "Though I fear my usefulness has reached an end. I tried to fly today." Seivar fluttered his folded wings without opening them. "No longer do I possess the strength I'm afraid."

Ilfedo clutched Seivar a bit tighter and carried him downstairs. He sat on the other side of the hearth, still holding Seivar.

The old nuvitor looked up at Oganna. "Mistress, thank you for caring so kindly for my mate."

"Oh, Seivar." Oganna began to cry in earnest as she reached out and stroked his feathered head. "I was hoping this time would never come. You have been such a dear companion to Father."

The bird gave her a nod. "You are so like your mother and so like your father. I think Master would have died a long time ago if you had not been born. When your mother passed she left a piece of herself behind, a part of her body and spirit that lives on through you. We are all part of a cycle of life and death, and it is part of the Creator's plan that we all die."

Hasselpatch raised her head and cooed at her mate. "And I think that time is almost upon us. You must tell Master before it is too late."

"Yes." Seivar looked up at Ilfedo. "We have been

with you for a long time, Master, and I hope that you have been pleased with our care both of you, of your wife, and of your little girl." Ilfedo clutched the bird to his chest. He spoke in a whisper. "Seivar, I cannot lose you. You are not my pet. You are my friend. If you die then a chunk of my heart—a piece that has remained intact even through my wife's passing—will be broken."

"No, Master," Hasselpatch chirped. "In our passing we leave to you a gift, just as dear Dantress left you a gift. For though we cannot be replaced in your heart it is certain that we can leave you a part of ourselves that will not only continue in our stead, but will multiply and grow to even be with Oganna to care for her as we have cared for you."

"I need no gift," Ilfedo said. "All that you have done in your lives is to care for and love me and my family. You are my friends. Irreplaceable. And I love the both of you." He took Hasselpatch from Oganna and set her beside Seivar in his lap.

Oganna put her hand over her mouth as she sobbed, her gaze fixed on the nuvitors as they nestled together. Ombre knelt beside her and wrapped her in his arms, his mouth set in a sorrowful line as he too watched.

It was Hasselpatch who expired first. Her eyes fluttered and her body trembled a bit. She wished Ilfedo a final farewell, then the corner of her face gently smiled as she nuzzled Seivar's neck. "We will fly together again on the other side," she whispered as a tear fell from Seivar's eye.

Ilfedo set both birds on the warm hearth and kissed Hasselpatch on the head. "I love you," he choked out, and she opened her eyes to reassure him one last time, then her eyes closed forever.

Seivar arched his neck under his mate's neck as she collapsed. Her head hung over his neck. The old bird set her head down on the hearth before pulling his from under her. Then he nuzzled her neck and a silvery tear dripped from the tip of his beak onto her feathers.

To Ilfedo's relief the nuvitor turned back to him and snuggled onto his lap. The two of them stayed there, silently soaking in the last moments of companionship.

Those moments stretched on for another hour or more. It seemed they were granted a reprieve from death. Then Seivar tilted back his head to gaze into Ilfedo's face. "Master, find joy in the life we leave behind. Love them as you have loved us and your heart will be healed, for they will love you in return."

Ilfedo's eyes widened. "To what are you referring, my friend? Who do you speak of?" He glanced at Oganna but she only shook her head. She had no clue what the bird was referring to.

Before Ilfedo could get an answer Seivar shuddered with his last breath.

Uncoiling from the fireside, Neneila slithered to Hasselpatch and licked the dead bird's head. Something dripped from the viper's eyes and Oganna reached out, dabbing at the tears the viper had shed for Ilfedo's companion. Neneila looked up at him then, blinking her round eyes. She hung her head with eyes closed and fresh tears forming.

Lifting Seivar's limp form in one arm and Hasselpatch's in the other, Ilfedo stood to his feet. His heavy heart seemed to drag on the floor and he kept his head down as he climbed the stairs to his bedchamber. He set them on the bed skins, then sat on the edge of the bed and wept for a while before Ombre's shadow fell over him.

Ombre put a hand on Ilfedo's shoulder, letting out a heavy sigh.

For a long while they stayed like that. Then Ilfedo, tears still soaking his cheeks, turned to the bedside table and pulled open the drawer. "It seems that doom has come to us all," he whispered as he looked at the envelope that lay within.

"Wh-what is that?" Ombre stood back, eyes widening and lips trembling. "Ilfedo, is that Caritha's handwriting?"

Ilfedo nodded and wiped the tears dripping off the end of his nose. He handed the envelope to Ombre, seeing him only as a blur. "Blame me, brother," he whispered hoarsely. He smacked his own chest. "Blame me! It was I that sent her to her doom. The Maiden Voyage—the ship—it should have returned by now. I do not want you to forgive me for what I have done, for I know that you loved her more than anything in this world. So blame me."

Leaning closer to the lamp's warm glow, Ombre read Caritha's handwriting on the envelope. His voice gained strength as he did so. *"For Ombre, my only love, in the event of my death."*

There was a long pause as Ombre pulled a handkerchief out of his pocket and handed it to Ilfedo, letting him dry his face. Ilfedo watched his friend pocket the envelope, and a smile brightened Ombre's countenance. "She loves me, Ilfedo. She loves me. Ah ha, I have her admission in indelible black and white. It matters not where you sent her. If she were dead, I would know it. I would feel it here!" He beat his breast. "Instead I feel hope, and nothing will dim that hope. If she does not return to me soon then I will move heaven and earth to find her." He stared intently into Ilfedo's eyes. "You think that she has died, don't you? Otherwise you would not have given me her letter."

Ilfedo grasped Ombre's arms. He could not have his friend living with such false hope. "She is not coming back."

Ombre stood free of his grasp and patted the pocket wherein he'd placed the envelope. A familiar intensity burned in his eyes. Ilfedo recognized it. The passion, the yearning, the faith that declared his devoted love through life and even death. "Hope has not failed me yet, Ilfedo, and it is not going to." Ombre grinned. "Even if it be years from now, I will find her. This envelope will remain unopened unless I feel in my heart that Caritha is truly dead."

Ilfedo remained on his bed, watching as his friend descended the stairs to the house's main floor. A spark dimly played in his heart, a spark that denied the eventuality of the Warrioresses' fates. Like Ombre he was ready to embrace hope instead of drowning in misery.

Oganna climbed the stairs after Ombre had left the room. She sat beside Ilfedo on the bed, and they wrapped their arms around each other and watched over the nuvitors' bodies.

They did not know how long they sat there, yet when soft chirps sounded from over their heads both of them glanced upward. Staring at them over the rim of the nuvitors' nest were three silver beaks and matching silvery eyes.

Slowly Ilfedo stood to his feet. His sorrow momentarily forgotten as he stared at the little birds' faces. He felt a warm shiver run up his spine as the birds chirped down at him. Oganna let out a gentle laugh. "So this is what Seivar and Hasselpatch meant to leave behind."

"Why would they not have told me?" Ilfedo reached up and stroked one of the little birds on its fluffy breast. The creature closed its eyes, cooing.

The other two cooed down at Oganna and she laughed as she reached out to let them peck playfully at her fingers. The young nuvitors were as white as freshly fallen snow. They chirped ceaselessly as Oganna touched their little heads.

Ilfedo sat back on the bed and smiled as he watched the three creatures play with his daughter. Seivar and Hasselpatch had indeed left behind a part of themselves to care for him and his daughter, just as Dantress had left behind Oganna when she had died. He turned to the bodies of his beloved birds and pulled a sheet over them.

He was about to leave the room when he noticed Oganna staring intently at the nuvitors' offspring. The little birds chirped in bursts, bobbing their heads as they did so. Oganna turned her beautiful blue-gold eyes to her father. "I can hear them, Father! I can understand them in my mind as if they were human babies that have just learned to speak. They are telling me about their parents."

Ilfedo smiled again as his daughter turned her attention back to the chattering creatures. As he walked down the stairs and then entered his living room he found Ombre swinging in one of the hammocks by the fireplace. Ilfedo strode to the hearth and threw another log on the fire. "We have seen a lot of death in our lives," he said to his friend. "Yet tonight I cannot help but feel that this only strengthens me for whatever battles lie ahead. Each death among those that I love makes me only that much stronger."

"Stronger how?" Ombre slanted his eyebrows in skepticism.

Ilfedo gazed into the fire. "Before when I marched into battle I used to hope that I would die. I knew that I would rejoin Dantress if that were to happen. Yet the thought of leaving Oganna behind kept me alive." He shook his head and chuckled. "Do you see it, Ombre? Do you see how the longer we live and the more loved ones we lose, the more ready we are for death, and the less we fear it? When I was a youth I knew that in death I would be reunited with my parents, but now it is much more than that. Death, when it comes for me, is a bridge across a chasm of sorrow, and on the other side of that chasm a crowd is waiting. My parents are there, your father is there, Dantress is there, and I have hope that the Creator himself will be standing behind them with my dear Seivar and Hasselpatch on his arm."

Retreating from the fireplace, Ilfedo sat on the other hammock and began to swing it back and forth. His hands were folded in his lap. He noticed that Ombre said nothing, instead he too was gazing into the fire.

The story continues in Book Five

IN SEARCH OF DRAGONS

Other books by Scott Appleton:

The Sword of the Dragon series

Swords of the Six

Dragon Offspring

Key of Living Fire

The Phantom's Blade

The Neverqueen Saga

Neverqueen

Neverqueen 2: The Suffering Chalice

Anthology

By Sword By Right

For more info visit: www.AuthorAppleton.com

About the Author

Scott Appleton is the author of the novels *The Sword of the Dragon series*, and *The Neverqueen Saga*, which are widely read by adult and young adult readers.

Besides these, Scott has also published a collection of short speculative fiction (*By Sword By Right*) which runs the gamut of science-fiction, fantasy, allegory, romance, poetry, and biblical.

Driven by a love of storytelling and an appreciation for the craft, Scott has spoken extensively at events across the United States. His specialization in fiction editing and writing has garnered praise from some prominent writers.

Scott was born in Connecticut and grew up there. He actively pursued astronomy through his teen years, built ships-in-bottles and, throughout his life, read and wrote extensively. Besides his writing he works in sales.

Currently Scott lives in Greenville, South Carolina with his wife, Kelley, and their five children. His activities of choice are reading with his kids, watching fantasy and science-fiction movies, reading, and playing the occasional Star Wars video game.

You can find him at **AuthorAppleton.com** and **facebook.com/scottappleton.fans**

Acknowledgements

It was with great satisfaction that I finished writing this novel, which had taken far longer to write and to publish than I had first anticipated. Many factors contributed to the delay but ultimately what was important to me was to get this story into eager readers' hands. In this special edition I have polished and edited, but little more than that.

I have loved the characters and they are a real part of me. The hardest part to write in this book was definitely the nuvitors' death scene. Seivar and Hasselpatch were such dear characters. They embodied the continuation of all that Ilfedo had known from his youth. They were a constant in his ever-challenged life. Their deaths were originally written over ten years ago in my original manuscript *The Lore of Etina*. I've known this was coming.

In addition to this I've been looking forward to introducing the hatchlings. Death is only part of the story. Life continues. The story evolves with the growth of characters and the changing world in which they live.

I want to extend a special thank you to my close friend James, for his crazy idea about a monkey in *The Sword of the Dragon*. James, I did it. You are here with a crazy monkey. Who would've guessed?

A special thank you to all the fans of *The Sword of the Dragon* series for your continued support and loyalty. In large part I write these stories for my own enjoyment but that is often eclipsed by the enthusiasm you have demonstrated when I have met you at book signings and school events, or even online.

The Phantom's Blade will be followed by *In Search of Dragons* and this storyworld has seen new growth in the expansion series *Neverqueen*.

Reading is a love. Writing is a passion. Creativity is a must!

To stay on this journey with me, sign up for the email newsletter on my website www.AuthorAppleton.com